"The world has changed

since the Sulcar ruled the waves about the oceans. They were fighters and fighting men get killed. The Kolder they fought, and they blew up Sulcarkeep in that fighting, taking the enemy—but also too many of their own—on into the Great Secret. Karsten they fought, and they were at the taking of Gorm, aye. Then they patrolled against the sea wolves of Alizon.

"Now if they take a ship out of the harbor they do it with others besides just their kin to raise sails and set the course.

"Now, let us to business between us, girl. I have learned much about you. You have some of the Talents of the Wise Women. You yourself said it— if any can treat with those devil females of Usturt, it must be one such as you. The whole land is hard pressed now for any who hold even a scrap of the Power. . . ."

LORE
OF
THE
WITCH
WORLD

Andre Norton

DAW BOOKS, INC.
DONALD A. WOLLHEIM, PUBLISHER

1633 Broadway, New York, N.Y. 10019

ACKNOWLEDGMENTS

Spider Silk, © 1976, by Lin Carter; *Sand Sister,* © 1979, by Page and Reinhardt; *Falcon Blood,* © 1979, by J.A. Salmonson; *Legacy from Sorn Fen,* © 1972, by Fantasy Pub. Co.; *Sword of Unbelief,* © 1977, by A.J. Offutt; *The Toads of Grimmerdale,* © 1973, by Dell Pub. Co.

FIRST PRINTING, SEPTEMBER 1980

1 2 3 4 5 6 7 8 9

DAW TRADEMARK REGISTERED
U.S. PAT. OFF. MARCA
REGISTRADA. HECHO EN U.S.A.

PRINTED IN U.S.A.

TABLE OF CONTENTS

Introduction

by C. J. Cherryh

Writing an introduction for one of Andre Norton's books is rather like applying gilt to a lily, superfluity to be sure. When I was offered the chance to do it, I first thought it was impossible and then sat down to try, and then began to think of thousands of readers who would *love* to get a line in . . . to say some things that want saying; things I don't think can be said too often, ever.

About the Witch World stories: For all of us who've ever created a world to dream about, for those of us who write and for those who keep theirs in their hearts . . . the Witch World stories hold a special place. It's a land, a world, a place of dark shadows and alien powers and human beings touched with strangeness, a place where men and women find extraordinary things within them, and match themselves against an environment at once marvelously detailed and full of mysteries. The Witch World is never explored. The smallest valley holds strange happenings and a past which reaches into things stranger still. The traveler finds the unexpected, the ancient, the bizarre at every turn. Nature is powerful here and those who open their hearts to it and to living things find themselves capable of marvels and involved in an old, old warfare. One meets old friends here, and hears of them; finds remnants of eldritch powers and visitants; finds . . . if one looks . . . ancient truths about courage and honesty and duty that involve the highborn and the ordinary, the young and the old, humans and the four-footed kind all in one fabric of magic and mystery.

The Witch World both lies within a tradition and generates a tradition of its own. It comes of that mythic tradition out of which comes Homer's wine-dark and fantastically mapped Mediterranean, peopled with gods and strange powers, which other heroes went on to sail in their turn, because it was a Place and a Time which had to exist; and which made heroes out of men and women of unlikely sort, because they met the unknown with *why?* and *what if?* and *why not?* The Witch World is one of those places a reader lives in, and some of those readers have become writers, and writers who never quite forget their journey in that ever-surprising and yet strangely familiar terrain. A lot of us who create worlds, whether we write them or dream them secretly, owe a great deal to this place, for its completeness, its way of underlaying daily life with the fantastical, its way of seeing vast forces implicit in the smallest and humblest things.

If the Witch World had never been written, so many other worlds would be the poorer.

And that brings me to Andre Norton herself.

There's been a great deal of fuss about women entering the science fiction field lately. Oh, no. Not lately. Andre Norton has been there, long before, doing things her way. I did some checking on publication dates and I was stunned to realize that Andre was publishing in this field the year this writer was a knobby-kneed kid in the third grade, struggling to get a bicycle home in what (to that third-grader) was the blizzard of the century . . . and I was too young to read the stories then, myself not one of the youngest of this crop who keeps getting asked about "women breaking into the field." . . . Andre's been there, writing her stories.

That skinned-knee kid with the pigtails didn't meet Andre Norton until 1977, although we'd corresponded a bit, because Andre out of the goodness of her heart did the introduction for my first book, which is one reason why I'd fight tigers to get the chance at this introduction. She asked me, *me*, the stranger from Oklahoma, to drop in on her to visit after Worldcon; and when that occasion turned into the chance for me to bring her the Gandalf Award she'd won from the World Convention for Life's Achievement in Fantasy—oh, I was delighted! For one thing, I figured that had to at least win me a welcome at the door. When I showed up at Andre's door and had a time to catch my breath I found myself with one of those people who do kindnesses as if it were nature's most logical process, who is on the side of good books and living things, who has the kind of definite ideas about what's right and what's just that might be expected of the creator of worlds where people stand by each other.

I *like* Andre Norton. I knew that from the start.

And when people sit down and start talking about how they got into this field in the first place, what writers were responsible for leading them deeper and deeper into that attitude we call sense of wonder, and which has to do with being really *alive* to this universe and all the possibilities of it—that most precious gift of learning how to see what we look at— Andre Norton's name is one that always comes to the front.

What has Andre Norton done for this field? She's written for all ages; she's been the gateway through which so, so many of us have come into this field in the first place. She created *women* who did things, such as Jaelithe, and she sparked imagination in a host of young minds who had rarely seen such a thing; she created heroes who were more than strong, and touched the hearts of countless young people who could never be quite the same afterward. There's a special look that comes into the eyes of these folk when they talk about Andre Norton, and you know full well that she has a very special place in their hearts, forever; that Andre's books are the ones they're going to put into the hands of their own sons and daughters and say with that special, waited-for hope: "I think you might like this. It's good." There's hardly a gift one can give another so precious as something that wakes us to what we call sense of wonder. That's what Andre's work has done for so very many of us. She's special. She's one of those talents without which this field would be inestimably the poorer. She reminds me curiously enough of John Wayne: a quiet person with strong convictions, who never much goes with fads but does things her way, whose style is her own, and who has shot straight and told the truth and given a lot of readers, young and old, a marvelous sense of heroism possible in their own lives, because it's right there pointed out to us what great possibilities there are, what great hearts in unlikely frames, what grand adventures likely for those who see their world with sense of wonder!

She writes. And the thing she does for this field has woven itself through so many lives that that influence keeps traveling. She's vexingly modest and deprecates such notions, but they're *true*, Andre! And I'm glad to have gotten the chance to say them. Thank you, Andre, for being there, for making worlds, for opening up so much of wonder to us. . . . *I* get to say it; but I say it for so many others. Thank you.

SPIDER SILK

1

The Big Storm in the Year of the Kobold came late, long past the month when such fury was to be expected. This was all part of that evil which the Guardians had drawn upon Estcarp when they summoned up their greatest power to blast and twist the mountain lands, seal off passes through which had come the invasion from Karsten.

Rannock lay open to that storm. Only the warning dream-sending to the Wise Woman, Ingvarna, drew a portion of the women and children to the higher lands, there to watch with fear and trembling the sea's fierce assault upon the coast. So high dashed those waves that water covered and boiled about the Serpent Teeth of the upper ledges. Only here, in pockets among the Tor rocks, could a fugitive crouch in almost mindless terror, awaiting the end.

Of the fishing fleet which had set out yesterday morn, who had any hopes now of its return save perhaps a scattering of wreckage, playthings of the storm waves?

There were left only a handful of old men and boys, and one or two such as Herdrek, the Twist-Leg, the village smith. For Rannock was as poor in men as it was in all else since the war years had ravaged Estcarp. To the north perched Alizon, a hawk ready to be unleashed upon its neighbor; from the south Karsten boiled and bubbled, if aught was still left alive beyond the wrecked mountain passes.

Men who had marched with the Borderers under Lord Simon Tregarth or served beneath the Banners of the Witch Women of Es—where were they? Long since, their kin had given up any hope of their return. There had been no true peace in this land since old Nabor (who could count his years at more than a hundred) had been in his green youth.

It was Nabor now who battled the strength of the wind to

11

the Tor, dragged himself up to stand, hunched shoulder to shoulder, with Ingvarna. As she, he looked to the sea uneasily. That she expected still their own fleet he could not believe, foresighted as all knew her to be.

Waves mounted, to pound giant fists against the rock. Nabor caught sight of a ship rising and falling near the Serpent's dread fangs. Then a huge swell whirled it over those sharp threats into the comparative calm beyond. Nabor sighed with the relief of a seaman who had witnessed a miracle, life won from the very teeth of rock death. Also, Rannock had the right of storm wrack. If that ship survived so far, its cargo was forfeit now to any who could bring it to shore. He half-turned to seek the shelter of the Tor hollows, rouse Herdrek and the others with this promise of fortune.

However, Ingvarna turned her head. Through the drifts of rain her eyes held his. There was a warning in her steady gaze. "One comes—" He saw her lips shape the words but did not hear her voice them above the roar of wind and wave.

At the same moment, there was such a crash as equaled the drum of thunder, the lash of lightning. The strange ship might have beaten the menace of the reef's fangs, but now had been driven halfway up the beach, where it was fast breaking up under the hammer blows of the surf.

Herdrek stumped out to join them. "It is a raider," he commented during a lull of the wind. "Perhaps one of the Sea Wolves of Alizon." He spat at the wreck below.

Ingvarna was already scrambling over the rocks toward the shore, as if what lay there were of vast importance. Herdrek shouted after her a warning, but she did not even turn her head. With a curse at the folly of females, which a second later he devoutly hoped the Wise Woman had not been able to pick out of the air, the smith followed her, two of the lads venturing in his wake.

At least when they reached the shore level, the worst of the storm was spent. Waves drew a torn seaweed veil around the broken vessel. Herdrek made fast a rope about his waist, gave dire warnings to his followers to keep a tight hold upon it. Then he ventured into the surf, using that cordage from wind-rent sails, hanging in loops down the shattered sides, to climb aboard.

There was a hatch well tamped down, roped shut. He drew belt knife to slash the fastening.

"Ho!" His voice rolled hollowly into the dark beneath him. "Anyone below?"

A thin cry answered, one which might issue from the throat of a seabird such as already coasted over the subsiding surface of the sea on hunt for the bounty of the storm. Yet he thought not. Gingerly, favoring his stiff leg, the smith lowered himself into the stinking hold. What he found there made him retch, and then heated in him dull anger against those who had mastered this vessel. She had been a slaver, such as Rannock's men had heard tell of—dealing in live cargo.

Of that cargo, only one survived. Her, Herdrek carried gently from the horror of that prison. A little maid, her small arms no more than skin slipped glovelike on bones, her eyes great, gray and blankly open. Ingvarna took the strange child from the smith as one who had the authority of clan and home hearth, wrapping the little one's thin, shivering body in her own warm cloak.

From whence Dairine came those of Rannock never learned. That slavers raided far was no secret. Also, the villagers soon discovered the child was blind. Ingvarna, though she was a Wise One, greatly learned in herbs and spells, the setting of bones, the curing of wounds, shook her head sadly over that discovery, saying that the child's blindness came from no hurt of body. Rather, she must have looked upon some things so horrible that thereafter her mind closed and refused all sight.

Though she might have been six or seven winters old, yet speech also seemed riven from her, and only fear was left to be her portion. The women of Rannock would have tried to comfort her, but secretly in their hearts they were willing that she bide with Ingvarna, who treated her oddly, they thought. For the Wise Woman did not strive to make life easier in any way for the child. Rather, from the first, Ingvarna treated the sea waif not as one maimed in body, and perhaps in mind, but rather as she might some daughter of the village whom she had chosen to be her apprentice in the harsh school of her own learning.

These years were bleak for Rannock. Full half the fleet did not return from out of the maw of that storm. Nor did any of the coastwise traders come. The following winter was a lean one. But in those dark days, Dairine showed first her skill. Her eyes might not see what her fingers wrought, yet she could mend fishing nets with such cleverness that even the experienced women marveled.

And in the following spring, when the villagers husked the

loquth balls to free their seeds for new plantings, Dairine
busied herself with the silken inner fibers, twisting and turning those. Ingvarna had Herdrek make a small spindle and
showed the child how this tool might be best put to work.

Good use did Dairine make of it, too. Her small, birdclaw
fingers drew out finer thread than any had achieved before,
freer from knotting than any the villagers had seen. Yet
never seemed she satisfied, but strove ever to make her spinning still finer, more smooth.

The Wise Woman continued her fosterling's education in
other ways, teaching her to use her fingers, her nose, in the
herb garden. Dairine learnt easily the spelling which was part
of a Wise Woman's knowledge. She absorbed that very
quickly, yet always there was about her an impatience. When
she made mistakes, then her anger against herself was great.
The greatest when she tried to explain some tool or need
which she seemed unable to describe but for which she
evinced a need.

Ingvarna spoke to Herdrek (who was now village elder),
saying that perhaps the craft of the Wise Woman might aid
in regaining a portion of Dairine's lost memory. When he demanded why she had not voiced such a matter before,
Ingvarna answered gravely: "This child is not blood of our
blood, and she was captive to the sea wolves. Have we the
right to recall to her past horrors? Perhaps Gunnore, who
watches over all womankind, has taken away her memory of
the past in pity. If so—"

He bit his thumb, watching Dairine as she paced back and
forth before the loom which he had caused to be set up for
her, now and then halting to slap her hand upon the frame in
frustration. It seemed as if she longed to force the heavy
wood into another pattern which would serve her better.

"I think that she grows more and more unhappy," he
agreed slowly. "At first she seemed content. Now there are
times when she acts as a snow cat encaged against her will. I
do not like to see her so."

The Wise Woman nodded. "Well enough. In my mind this
is a right choice."

Ingvarna went to the girl, taking both her hands, drawing
her around so that she might look driectly into those blind
eyes. At Ingvarna's touch, Dairine stood still. "Leave us!" the
Wise Woman commanded the smith.

Early that evening as Herdrek stood at his forge Dairine
walked into the light of his fire. She came to him unhesitat-

ingly. So acute was her hearing that she often startled the villagers by her recognition of another presence. Now she held out her hands to him as she might to a father she loved. And he knew all was well.

By midsummer, when the loquths had flowered and their blossoms dropped, Dairine went often into the fields, fingering the swelling bolls. Sometimes she sang, queer, foreign-tongued words, as if the plants were children (now knee height, and then shoulder height) who must be amused and cherished.

Herdrek had changed her loom as the girl suggested might be done. From Ingvarna she learned the mysteries of dyes, experimenting on her own. She had no real friend among the few children of the dying village. Firstly, because she did not range much afield, save with Ingvarna, of whom most were in awe. Secondly, because her actions were strange and she seemed serious and more adult than the years they believed to be hers.

In the sixth year after her coming, a Sulcar ship put in at Rannock, the first strange vessel sighted since the wreck of the slaver. Its captain brought news that the long war was at last over.

The defeat of the Karsten invaders, who so drained the powers of the rulers of Estcarp, had been complete. Koris of Gorm was now Commander of Estcarp, since so many of the Guardians had perished when they turned the full extent of their power upon the enemy. Yet the land was hardly at peace. The sea wolves of the coast had been augmented by ships of the broken and defeated navy of Karsten. As in times of chaos, other wolfheads, without any true lands or allegiance, now ravaged the land wherever they might. Though the forces under Captain General Koris sought to protect the boundaries, yet to defeat such hit-and-run raids was well beyond the ability of any defending force.

The Sulcar Captain was impressed by the latest length of Dairine's weaving, offering for it, when he bargained with Ingvarna, a much better price than he had thought to pay out in this forgotten village. He was much interested also in the girl, speaking to her slowly in several tongues. However, she answered him only in the language of Estcarp, saying she knew no other.

Still, he remarked privately to Ingvarna that somewhere in the past he had seen those like unto her, though where and when during his travels he could not bring to mind. Still, he thought that she was not of common stock.

It was a year later that the Wise Woman wrought the best she could for her sea-gift foundling.

No one knew how old Ingvarna was, for the Wise Woman showed no advance of age, as did those less learned in the many uses of herbs and medicants. But it was true that she walked more slowly, and that she no longer went alone when she sought out certain places of Power, taking Dairine ever with her. What the two did there no one knew, for who would spy on any woman with the Witch Talent?

On this day, the few fishing boats had taken to sea before dawn. At moonrise the night before the Wise Woman and her fosterling had gone inland to visit a certain very ancient place. There Ingvarna kindled a fire which burned not naturally red but rather blue. Into those flames she tossed small, tightly bound bundles of dried herbs so that the smoke which arose was heavily scented. But she watched not that fire. Rather, a slab of stone set behind its flowering. That stone had a surface like glass, the color of a fine sword blade.

Dairine stood a little behind the Wise Woman. Though Ingvarna had taught her over the years to make her other senses serve her in place of her missing sight, so that her fingers were ten eyes, her nostrils, her ears could catch scent and sound to an extent far outreaching the skill of ordinary mankind, yet at moments such as this the longing to be as others awoke in her a sense of loss so dire that to her eyes came tears, flowing silently down her cheeks. Much Ingvarna had given her. Still, she was not as the others of Rannock. And ofttimes loneliness settled upon her as a burdensome cloak. Now the girl sensed that Ingvarna planned for her some change. That it would make her see as others saw—that she could not hope for.

She heard clearly the chanting of the Wise Woman. The odor of the burning herbs filled her nose, now and then made her gasp for a less heavy lungful of air. Then came a command, not given in words, nor by some light touch against her arm and shoulder. But into her mind burst an order and Dairine walked ahead, her hands outstretched, until her ten fingers flattened against a throbbing surface. Warm it was, near to a point which would sear her flesh, while its throb was in twin beat to her own heart. Still, Dairine stood firm, while the chant of the Wise Woman came more faintly, as if the girl had been shifted farther away in space from her foster mother.

Then she felt an inward flow from the surface she touched, a warmth which spread along her hands, her wrists, up her arms. Fainter still came the voice of Ingvarna petitioning on her behalf, strange and half-forgotten powers.

Slowly the warmth receded. But how long Dairine had stood so wedded to that surface she could not see, the girl never knew. Except that there came a moment when her hands fell, as if too heavily burdened for her to raise.

"What is done, is done." Ingvarna's voice at the girl's left sounded as weighted as Dairine's hands felt. "All I have to give, this I have freely shared with you. Though being blind as men see blindness, yet you have sight such as few can own to. Use it well, my fosterling."

From that day it became known that Dairine did indeed have strange powers of "seeing" through her hands. She could take up a thing which had been made and tell of the maker, of how long since it had been wrought. A shred of fleece from one of the thin-flanked hill sheep put into her fingers would enable her to guide an anxious owner to where the lost flock member had strayed.

There was one foretelling which she would not do, after she came upon its secret by chance only. For she had taken the hand of little Hulde during the Harvest Homing dance. Straightway thereafter, Dairine dropped her grasp upon the child's small fingers, crying out and shrinking away from the villagers, to seek out Ingvarna's house and therein hide herself. Within the month, Hulde had died of a fever. Thereafter, the girl used her new sight sparingly, and always with a fear plain to be seen haunting her.

In the Year of the Weldworm, when Dairine passed into young womanhood, Ingvarna died swiftly. As if foreseeing another possible end, she summoned death as one summons a servant to do one's bidding.

Though Dairine was no true Wise Woman, thereafter she took on many of the duties of her foster mother. Within a month after the Wise Woman's burial, the Sulcar ship returned.

As the Captain told the forgotten village the news of the greater world his eyes turned ever to Dairine, her hands busy with thread she spun as she listened. Among those of the village she was indeed one apart, with her strange silver-fair hair, silver-light eyes.

Sibbald Ortis, Sibbald the Wrong-Handed—thus they had named him after a sea battle had lopped off his hand, and a smith in another land had made him one of metal—was that captain. He was new to command and young—though he had lived near all his life at sea after the manner of his people.

Peace, after a fashion, he told them, had encompassed the land at last. For Koris of Gorm now ruled Estcarp with a steady hand. Alizon had been defeated in some invasion that nation had attempted overseas. And Karsten was in chaos, one prince or lord always rising against another, while the sea wolves were being hunted down, one after another, to a merciless end.

Having made clear that he was in Rannock on lawful business, the captain now turned briskly to the subject of trade. What had they, if anything, which would be worth stowage in his own ship?

Herdrek was loathe to spread their poverty before these strangers. Also, he wanted, with a desire he could hardly conceal, some of the tools and weapons he had seen in casual use among them. Yet what had Rannock? Fish dried to take them through a lean winter, some woven lengths of wool.

The villagers would be hard put even to give these visitors guest-right, with the feast they were entitled to. To fail in that was to deny their own heritage.

Dairine, listening to the Captain, had wished she dared touch his hand to learn what manner of a man he was who had journeyed so far and seen so much. A longing was born in her to be free of the narrow, well-known ways of Rannock, to see what lay beyond in the world. Her fingers steadily twirled her thread, but her thoughts were elsewhere.

Then she lifted her head a little, for she knew someone was now standing at her side. There was the tang of sea-salted leather and other odors. This was a stranger, one of the Sulcar men.

"You work that thread with skill, maid."

She recognized the captain's voice. "It is my skill, Lord Captain."

"They tell me that fate has served you harshly." He spoke bluntly then, but she liked him the better for that bluntness.

"Not so, Lord Captain. These of Rannock have been ever kind. And I was fostering to their Wise Woman. Also, my hands serve well, if my eyes are closed upon this world. Come, you, and see!" She spoke with pride as she arose from her stool, thrusting her spindle into her girdle.

Thus Dairine brought him to her cottage, sweet within for all its scents of herbs. She gestured to where stood the loom Herdrek had made her.

"As you see, Lord Captain, I am not idle, even though I may be blind."

She knew that there, in the half-done web, there was no mistake.

Ortis was silent for a moment. Then she heard the hiss of his breath expelled in wonder.

"But this is weaving of the finest! There is no fault in color or pattern. . . . How can this be done?"

"With one's two hands, Lord Captain!" She laughed. "Here, give me a possession of yours that I may show you better how fingers can be eyes."

Within her there was a new excitement, for something told her that this was a moment of importance in her life. She heard then a faint swish as if some bit of woven stuff were being shaken free. A clinging length was pressed into the hand she held out.

"Tell me," he commanded, "from whence came this, and how was it wrought?"

Back and forth between her fingers the girl slipped the ribband of silken stuff.

Woven—yes. But her "seeing" hands built no mind picture of human fingers at the business. No, strangely ill-formed were those members engaged in the weaving. And so swift were they also that they seemed to blur. No woman, as Dairine knew women, had fashioned this. But female—strongly, almost fiercely female.

"Spider silk—" She was not aware that she had spoken aloud until she heard the sound of her own words. "Yet not quite spider. A woman weaving—still, not a woman. . . ."

She raised the ribband to her cheek. There was a wonder in such weaving which brought to life in her a fierce longing to know more and more.

"You are right." The captain's voice broke her preoccupation with that need to learn. "This comes from Usturt. Had a man but two full bolts of it within his cargo he could count triple profits from such a voyage alone."

"Where lies Usturt?" Dairine demanded. If she could go there—learn what could be learned. "And who are the weavers? I do not see them as beings like unto our own people."

She heard his breath hiss again. "To see the weavers," he said in a low voice, "is death. They hate all mankind—"

"Not so, Lord Captain!" Dairine answered him then. "It is not mankind that they hate—it is all males." From the strip between her fingers came that knowledge.

For a moment she was silent. Did he doubt her?

"At least no man sails willingly to Usturt," he replied. "I had that length from one who escaped with his bare life. He died upon our deck shortly after we fished him from a water-logged raft."

"Captain," she stroked the silk, "you have said that this weaving is a true treasure. My people are very poor and grow poorer. If one were to learn the secret of such weaving, might not good come of it?"

With a sharp jerk he took the ribband from her.

"There is no such way."

"But there is!" Her words came in an eager tumble, one upon the other. "Women—or female things—wove this. They might treat with a woman—one who was already a weaver."

Great, calloused hands closed upon her shoulders.

"Girl, not for all the gold in Karsten would I send any woman into Usturt! You know not of what you speak. It is true that you have gifts of the Talent. But you are no confirmed Guardian, and you are blind. What you suggest is such a folly— Aye, Vidruth, what is it now?"

Dairine had already sensed that someone had approached.

"The tide rises. For better mooring, captain, we need move beyond the rocks."

"Aye. Well, girl, may the Right Hand of Lraken be your shield. When a ship calls, no captain lingers."

Before she could even wish him well, he was gone. Retreating, she sat down on her hard bench by the loom. Her hands trembled, and from her eyes the tears seeped. She felt bereft, as if she had had for a space a treasure and it had been torn from her. She was certain that her instinct had been right, that if any could have learned the secret of Usturt, she was that one.

Now, when she put a hand out to finger her own weaving, the web on the loom seemed coarse, utterly ugly. In her mind, she held a queer vision of a deeply forested place in which great, sparkling webs ran in even strands from tree to tree.

Through the open door puffed a wind from the sea. Dairine lifted her face to it as it tugged at her hair.

"Maid!"

She was startled. Even with her keen ears she had not heard anyone approach, so loud was the wind song.

"Who are you?" she asked quickly.

"I am Vidruth, maid, mate to Captain Ortis."

She arose swiftly. "He has thought more upon my plan?" She could see no other reason for the seaman to seek her out in this fashion.

"That is so, maid. He awaits us now. Give me your hand—so. . . ."

Fingers grasped hers tightly. She strove to free her hand. This man—there was that in him which was wrong. Then out of nowhere came a great smothering cloak, folded about her so tightly she could not struggle. There were unclean smells to affront her nostrils, but the worst was that this Vidruth had swung her up across his shoulder so that she could have been no more than a bundle of trade goods.

2

So was she brought aboard what was certainly a ship, for in spite of the muffling of the cloak, Dairine used her ears, her nose. However, she could not sort out her thoughts. Why had Captain Ortis so vehemently, and truthfully (for she had read that truth in his touch), refused to bring her? Then this man of his had come to capture her as he might steal a woman during some shore raid?

The Sulcarmen were not slave traders, that was well known. Then why?

Hands pulled away the folds of the cloak at last. The air she drew thankfully into her lungs was not fresh, rather tainted with stinks which made her feel unclean even to sniff. She thought that her prison must lie deep within the belly of the ship.

"Why have you done this?" Dairine asked of the man she could hear breathing heavily near her.

"Captain's orders," he answered, leaning so close she not only smelt his unclean body but gathered with that a sensation of heat. "He has eyes in his head, has the captain. You be a smooth-skinned, likely wench—"

"Let her be, Wak!" That was Vidruth.

"Aye, captain," the other answered with a slur of sly contempt. "Here she be, safe and sound—"

"And here she stays, Wak, safe from your kind. Get out!"

There was a growl from Wak, as if he were close to questioning the other's right so to order him. Then Dairine's ears caught a sound which might have been that of a panel door sliding into place.

"You are not the captain," she spoke into the silence between them.

"There has been a change of command," he returned. "The captain, he has not brought us much luck in months agone. When we learned that he would not try to better his fortune—he was—"

"Killed!"

"Not so. Think you we want a blood feud with all his clan? The Sulcarmen take not lightly to those who let the red life out of some one of their stock."

"I do not understand. You are all Sulcar—"

"That we are not, girl. The world has changed since those ruled the waves about the oceans. They were fighters and fighting men get killed. The Kolder they fought, and they blew up Sulcarkeep in that fighting, taking the enemy—but also too many of their own—on into the Great Secret. Karsten they fought, and they were at the taking of Gorm, aye. Then they have patrolled against the sea wolves of Alizon. Men they have lost, many men. Now if they take a ship out of harbor they do it with others besides just their kin to raise sails and set the course. No, we do not kill Sibbald Ortis, we may need him later. But he is safe laid.

"Now let us to the business between us, girl. I heard the words you spoke with Ortis. Also did I learn much about you from those starvelings who live in Rannock. You have some of the Talents of the Wise Women, if you cannot call upon the full Power, blind as you are. You yourself said it—if any can treat with those devil females of Usturt, it must be one such as you.

"Think on that spider silk, girl. You held that rag that Ortis has. And you can do mighty things, unless all those at Rannock are crazed in their wits. Which I do not believe. This is a chance which a man may have offered to him but once in a lifetime."

She heard the greed in his voice. Perhaps that greed would be her protection. Vidruth would take good care to keep her safe. Just as he held somewhere Sibbald Ortis for a like reason.

"Why did you take me so, if your intentions are good? If you heard my words to the captain, you know I would have gone willingly."

He laughed. "Do you think those shore-side halflingmen would have let you go? With three quarters of the Guardians dead, their own Wise Woman laid also in her grave shaft, would they willingly have surrendered to us even your small Talent? The whole land is hard pressed now for any who hold even a scrap of the Power.

"No matter. They will welcome you back soon enough after you have learned the secret of Usturt. If it then still be in your mind to go to them."

"But how do you know that in Usturt I shall work for you?"

"Because you will not want the captain to be given over to them. They do not have a pleasant way with captives."

There was fear behind his words, a fear born of horror, which he fought to control.

"Also, if you do not do as we wish we can merely sail and leave you on Usturt for the rest of your life. No ship goes there willingly. A long life for you perhaps, girl, alone with none of your own kind—think of that."

He was silent for a moment before he added, "It is a bargain, girl, one we swear to keep. You deal with the weavers, we take you back to Rannock, or anywhere else you name. The captain, he can be set ashore with you even. No more harm done. And a portion of the silk for your own. Why, you can buy all of Rannock and make yourself a Keep lady!"

"There is one thing—" She was remembering Wak. "I am not such a one as any of your men can take at his will. Know you not what happens then to any Talent I may possess?"

When Vidruth answered her there was a deep note of menace in his voice, though it was not aimed at her.

"All men know well that the Talent departs from a woman who lies with a man. None shall trouble you."

"So be it," she returned, with an outward calm it was hard for her to assume. "Have you the bit of silk? Let me learn from it what I can."

She heard him move away the grate of whatever door kept snug her prison. As that sound ceased she put out her hands to explore. The cubby was small; there was a shelflike bunk against the wall, a stool which seemed bolted to the deck, nought else. Did they have Captain Ortis pent in such a hole also? And how had this Vidruth managed so well the take-over of the Captain's command? What she had read of Sib-bald Ortis during their brief meeting did not lead her to think he was one easily overcome by an enemy.

But she was sitting quietly on the stool when Vidruth returned to drop the length of ribband across her quiet hands.

"Learn all you can," he urged her. "We have two days of sail if this wind continues to favor us, then we shall raise Usturt. Food, water, what you wish, shall be brought to you, and there is a guard without so that you need not be troubled."

With the silk between her hands, Dairine concentrated upon what it could tell her. She had no illusions concerning Vidruth. To him and the others she was only a tool in their hands. Because she was sightless, he might undervalue her, for all his talk of Talent and Power. She had discovered many times in the past that such was so.

Deliberately, Dairine closed out the world about her, shut her ears to creak of timber, wash of wave, her nose to the many smells which offended it. Once more her "sight" turned inward. She could "see" the blue of those hands (which were not quite hands) engaged in weaving. Colors she had no words to describe were clear and bright. For the material she saw so was not one straight length of color, but shimmered from one shade to another.

Dairine tried now to probe beyond that shift of color to the loom from which it had come. She had an impression of tall, dark shafts. Those were not of well-planed and smooth wood; no, they had the crooked surface of—trees—standing trees!

The hands—concentrate now upon the moving hands of the weaver.

But the girl had only reached that point of recognition when there was a knock to distract her concentration. Exasperated, she turned her head to the door of the cubby.

"Come!"

Again the squeak of hinge, the sound of boots, the smell of sea-wet leather and man-skin. The newcomer cleared his throat as if ill at ease.

"Lady, here is food."

She swirled the ribband about her wrist, put out her hands, for suddenly she was hungry and athirst.

"By your leave, lady." He fitted the handle of a mug into her right hand, placed a bowl on the palm of the other. "There is a spoon. It is only ship's ale, lady, and stew."

"My thanks," she said in return. "And what name do you go by, ship's man?"

"Rothar, lady. I am a blank shield and no real seaman. But since I know no trade but war, one venture is nigh as good as another."

"Yet of this venture you have some doubts." She had set the mug on the deck, kept upright between her worn sandals. Now she seized his hand, held it to read. It seemed to Dairine that she must not let this opportunity of learning more of Vidruth's followers go, and she sensed that this Rothar was not of the same ilk as Wak.

"Lady"—his voice was very low and swift—"they say that you have knowledge of herb craft. Why then has Vidruth not taken you to the captain that you may learn what strange, swift illness struck him down?"

There was youth in the hand Dairine held and not, she believed, any desire to deceive.

"Where lies the captain?" she asked in as low a voice.

"In his cabin. He is fevered and raves. It is as if he has come under some ensorcelment and—"

"Rothar!" From the door, another voice sharp as an order. The hand she held jerked free from hers. But not before she had felt the spring of fear.

"I promised no man shall trouble you. Has this cub been at such tricks?" Vidruth demanded.

"Not so." Dairine was surprised her voice remained so steady. "He has been most kind in bringing me food and drink, both of which I needed."

"And having done so—out!" Vidruth commanded. "Now"—she heard the door close behind the other—"what have you learned, girl, from this piece of silk?"

"I have had but a little time, lord. Give me more. I must study it."

"See that you do" was his order as he also departed.

He did not come again, nor did Rothar ever once more bring her food. She thought, though, of what the young man had said concerning the captain. Vidruth's tale made her believe that the whole ship's company had been behind the mate's scheme to take command and sail to Usturt. There were herbs which, put in a man's food or drink, could plunge him into the depths of fever. If she could only reach the captain, she would know. But there was no faring forth from this cubby.

Now and again Vidruth would suddenly appear to demand what more she had learned from the ribband. There was such an avid greediness in his questions that sometimes rising uneasiness nearly broke through her control. At last she answered with what she believed to be the truth.

"Have you never heard, Captain, that the Talent cannot be forced? I have tried to read from this all which I might. But this scrap was not fashioned by a race such as ours. An alien nature cannot be so easily discovered. For all my attempts, I cannot build a mind picture of these people. What I see clearly is only the weaving."

When he made no answer, Dairine continued:

"This is a thing not of the body, but the mind. Along such a road one creeps as a babe, one does not race as one full grown."

"You have less than a day now. Before sundown, Usturt shall rise before us. I know only what I have heard tell of witch powers, and that may well be changed by the telling and retelling. Remember, girl, your life can well ride on your 'seeing'!"

She heard him go. The ribband no longer felt so light and soft. Rather, it had taken on the heaviness of a slave chain binding her to his will. She ate ship's biscuits from the plate he had brought her. It was true time was passing, and she had done nothing of importance.

Oh, she could now firmly visualize the loom and see the silk come into being beneath the flying fingers. But the body behind those hands, that she could not see. Nor did any of the personality of the weavers who had made that which she held come clear to her, for all her striving.

Captain Ortis—he came in the reading, for he had held this. And Vidruth also. There was a third who was more distant, lying hid under a black cloud of fear. Was this day or night? She had lost track of time. That the ship still ran before the wind, she sensed.

Then—she was not alone in the cubby! Yet she had not heard the warning creak of the door. Fear kept her tense, hunched upon the stool, listening with all her might.

"Lady?"

Rothar! But how had he come?

"Why are you here?" Dairine had to wet her lips with her tongue before she could shape those words.

"They move now to put you ashore on Usturt, lady! Captain Ortis, he came up leaning on Vidruth's arm, his body all atremble. He gives no orders, only Vidruth. Lady, there is some great wrong here—for we are at Usturt. And Vidruth commands. Such is not right."

"I knew that I must go to Usturt," she returned. "Rothar, if you have any allegiance to your captain, know he is a prisoner to Vidruth in some manner, even as I have been. And if I do not do as Vidruth says, there will be greater trouble—death—"

"You do not understand." His voice was very husky. "There are monsters on this land. To see them even, they say, makes a man go mad!"

"But I shall not see them," Dairine reminded him. "How long do I have?"

"Some moments yet."

"Where am I and how did you get here?"

"You are in the treasure hold, below the Captain's own cabin. I have used the secret opening to reach you as this is the first time Vidruth and the captain have been out of it. Now they must watch carefully for the entrance to the inner reef."

"Can you get me into the captain's cabin?" If in those moments she might discover what hold Vidruth had over Captain Ortis, she perhaps would be able to help a man she trusted.

"Give me your hands, then, lady. I fear we have very little time."

She reached out, and her wrists were instantly caught in a hold tight enough to be painful, but she made no sound of complaint. Then she found herself pulled upward with a vast heave as if Rothar must do this all in a single effort. When he set her on her feet once more, she sensed she was in a much larger space. And there was the fresh air from the sea blowing in as if through some open port.

But the air was not enough to hide from her that telltale scent—a scent of evil.

"Let me go, touch me not now," she told Rothar. "I seek that which must be found, and your slightest touch will confuse my course."

Slowly she turned away from the wind, facing to her right.

"What lies before me?"

"The captain's bed, lady."

Step by step she approached in that direction. The sniff of

evil was stronger. What it might be she had no idea, for
though Ingvarna had taught her to distinguish that which was
of the shadow, she knew little more. The fetid odor of some
black sorcery was rank.

"The bed," she ordered now, "do you strip off its coverings. If you find aught which is strange, be sure you do not
touch it with your hand. Rather, use something of iron, if
you can, to pluck it forth. And then throw it quickly into the
sea."

He asked no questions, but she could hear his hurried
movements. And then—

"There is a—a root, most misshapen. It lies under the pillow, lady."

"Wait!" Perhaps the whole of that bed place was now im-
pregnated by what evil had been introduced. To destroy its
source might not be enough. "Bundle all—pillow, coverings—give them to the sea!" she ordered. "Let me back then
into the treasure cubby, and if there be time, make the bed
anew. I do not know what manner of ensorcelment has been
wrought here. But it is of the Shadow, not of the Power.
Take care that you keep yourself also from contact with it."

"That will I do of a certainty, lady!" His answer was fer-
vent. "Stand well back, I will get rid of this."

She retreated, hearing the click of his sea boots on the
planking as he passed her toward the source of the sea wind.

"Now"—he was back at her side—"I shall see you safe,
lady. Or as safe as you can be until the captain comes to his
mind once more and Vidruth be removed from command."

His hands closed upon her, lowered her back down into
the cubby. She listened intently. But if he closed that trap
door, and she was sure that he had, it had fallen into place
without a sound.

3

She had not long to wait, for the opening on the floor level
of the cubby was opened and she recognized Vidruth's step.

"Listen well, girl," he commanded. "Usturt is an island,
one of a string of islands, reaching from the shore. At one
time, they may all have been a part of the coast. But now
some are only bare rock with such a wash of sea around
them as no man can pass. So think not that you have any
way of leaving save by our favor. We shall set you ashore
and keep down-sea thereafter. But when you have learned

what we wish, then return to the shore and there leave three stones piled one upon another. . . ."

To Dairine, his arrangements seemed to be not well thought out. But she questioned nothing. What small hopes she had she could only pin on Rothar and the Captain. Vidruth's hand tightened about her arm. He drew her to a ladder, set her hands upon its rungs.

"Climb, girl. And you had better play well your part. There are those among us who fear witchcraft and say there is only one certain way to disarm a witch. That, you have heard. . . ."

She shivered. Yes, there was a way to destroy a witch—by enjoying the woman. All men were well versed in that outrage.

"Rothar shall set you ashore," Vidruth continued. "And we shall watch your going. Think not to talk him out of his orders, for there is no place elsewhere. . . ."

Dairine was on the deck now, heard the murmur of voices. Where stood Captain Ortis? Vidruth gave her no time to try to sort out the sounds. Under his compelling, the girl came up against the rail. Then Vidruth caught her up as if she were a small child and lowered her until other hands steadied her, easing her down upon a plank seat.

Around her was the close murmur of the sea, and she could hear the grate of oars within their locks.

"Do you believe me witch, Rothar?" she asked.

"Lady, I do not know what you are. But that you are in danger with Vidruth, that I can swear to. If the captain comes into his own mind again—"

He broke off and then continued. "Through the war, I have come to hate any act which makes man or woman unwillingly serve another. There is no future before me, for I am wastage of war, having no trade save that of killing. Therefore, I will do what I may to help you and the captain."

"You are young to speak so, of being without a future."

"I am old in killing." he told her bleakly. "And of such men as Vidruth leads, I have seen many. Lady, we are near the shore. And those on the ship watch us well. When I set you on the beach, take forth carefully what you find in my belt. hide it from all. It is a knife made of the best star-steel, fashioned by the hand of Hamraker himself. Not mine in truth. but the Captain's."

Dairine did as he ordered when he carried her from the sand-smoothing waves to the drier reach beyond. Memory stirred in her. Once there had been such a knife and—fire-light had glinted on it—

"No!" she cried aloud to deny memory. Yet her fingers remained curled about that hilt.

"Yes!" He might not understand her inner turmoil, but his hold on her tightened. "You must keep it.

"Walk straight ahead," he told her. "Those on the ship have the great dart caster trained on you. There are trees ahead—within those, there the spiders are said to be. But, lady, though I dare not move openly in your aid now, for that would bring me quick death to no purpose, yet what I can do, that I shall."

Uncertainty held Dairine. She felt naked in this open which she did not know. Yet she must not appear concerned to those now watching her. She had the ribband of silk looped about her wrist. And within the folds of her skirt, she held also the knife. Turning her head slightly from one side to another, she listened with full concentration, walking slowly forward against the drag of the sand.

Coolness ahead—she must be entering the shade of the trees. She put out her hand, felt rough bark, slid around it, setting the trunk as a barrier between that dart thrower of which Rothar had warned, and her back.

Then she knew, as well as if her eyes could tell her, that it was not alone the ship's company who watched. She was moving under observation of someone—or something—else. Dairine used her sense of perception, groping as she did physically with her hands, seeking what that might be.

A moment later she gasped with shock. A strong mental force burst through the mind door she had opened. She felt as if she had been caught in a giant hand, raised to the level of huge eyes which surveyed her outwardly and inwardly.

Dairine swayed, shaken by that nonphysical touch, search. It was nonhuman. Yet she realized, as she fought to recover her calm, it was not inimical—yet.

"Why come you here, female?"

In Dairine's mind, the word shaped clearly. Still, she could build up no mental picture of her questioner. She faced a little to the right, held out the hand about which she had bound the ribband.

"I seek those able to weave such beauty," she replied aloud, wondering if they could hear, or understand, her words.

Again that sensation of being examined, weighed. But this time she stood quiet, unshaken under it.

"You think this thing beautiful?" Again the mind question.

"Yes."

"But you have not eyes to see it." Harshly that came, as if to deny her claim.

"I have not eyes, that is the truth. But my fingers have been taught to serve me in their place. I, too, weave, but only after the manner of my own people."

Silence, then a touch on the back of her hand, so light and fleeting Dairine was not even sure she had really felt it. The girl waited, for she understood this was a place with its own manner of barriers, and she might continue only if those here allowed it.

Again a touch on her hand, but this time it lingered. Dairine made no attempt to grasp, though she tried to read through that contact. And saw only bright whirls.

"Female, you may play with threads after the crude fashion of your kind. But call yourself not a weaver!" There was arrogance in that.

"Can one such as I learn the craft as your people know it?"

"With hands as clumsy as this?" There came a hard rap across her knuckles. "Not possible. Still, you may come, see with your fingers what you cannot hope to equal."

The touch slid across her hand, became a sinewy band about her wrist as tight as the cuff of a slave chain. Dairine knew now there was no escape. She was being drawn forward. Oddly, though she could not read the nature of the creature who guided her, there flowed from its contact a sharp mental picture of the way ahead.

This was a twisted path. Sometimes she brushed against the trunks of trees; again she sensed they crossed clear areas—until she was no longer sure in what direction the beach now lay.

At last they came into an open space where there was some protection other than branches and leaves overhead to ward off the sun. Her ears picked up small, scuttling sounds.

"Put out your hand!" commanded her guide. "Describe what you find before you."

Dairine obeyed, moving slowly and with caution. Her finges found a solid substance, not unlike the barked tree trunk. Only, looped about it, warp lines of thread were stretched taut. She transferred her touch to those lines, trac-

ing them to another bar. Then she knelt, fingering the length
of cloth. This was smooth as the ribband. A single thread led
away—that must be fastened to the shuttle of the weaver.

"So beautiful!"

For the first time since Ingvarna had trained her, Dairine
longed for actual sight. The need to *see* burned in her.
Color—somehow as she touched the woven strip, the fact of
color came to her. Yet all she could "read" of the weaver
was a blur of narrow, nonhuman hands.

"Can you do such, you who claim to be a weaver?"

"Not this fine." Dairine answered with the truth. "This is
beyond anything I have ever touched."

"Hold out your hands!" This time Dairine sensed that the
order had not come from her guide, but another.

The girl spread out her fingers, palms up. There followed a
feather-light tracing on her skin along each finger, gliding
across her palm.

"It is true. You are a weaver—after a fashion. Why do you
come to us, female?"

"Because I would learn." Dairine drew a deep breath.
What did Vidruth's idea of trade matter now? This was of
greater importance. "I would learn from those who can do
this."

She continued to kneel, waiting. There was communication
going on about her, but none she could catch and hold with
either eye or mind. If these weavers would shelter her, what
need had she to return to Vidruth? Rothar's plans? Those
were too uncertain. If she won the good will of these, she had
shelter against the evil of her own kind.

"Your hands are clumsy, you have no eyes." That was like
a whiplash. "Let us see what you *can* do, female."

A shuttle was thrust into her hand. She examined it carefully by touch. Its shape was slightly different from those she
had always known, but she could use it. Then she surveyed,
the same way, the web on the loom. The threads of both
warp and woof were very fine, but she concentrated until she
could indeed "see" what hung there. Slowly she began to
weave, but it took a long time and what she produced in her
half inch of fabric was noticeably unlike that of the beginning.

Her hands shaking, the girl sat back on her heels, frus-
trated. All her pride in her past work was wiped out. Before
these, she was a child beginning a first halting attempt to
create cloth.

Yet when she had relaxed from concentrating on her task and was aware once more of those about her, she did not meet the contempt she had expected. Rather, a sensation of surprise.

"You are one perhaps who can be taught, female," came that mind voice of authority. "If you wish."

Dairine turned her face eagerly in the direction from which she believed that message had come. "I do wish, Great One!"

"So be it. But you will begin even as our hatchlings, for you are not yet a weaver."

"That I agree." The girl ran her fingers ruefully across the fabric before her.

If Vidruth expected her return into his power now—she shrugged. And let Rothar concentrate upon the captain and his own plight. What seemed of greatest importance to her was that she must be able to satisfy these weavers.

They seemed to have no real dwelling except this area about their looms. Nor were there any furnishings save the looms themselves. And those stood in no regular pattern. Dairine moved cautiously about, memorizing her surroundings by touch.

Though she sensed a number of beings around her, none touched her, mind or body. And she made no advances in turn, somehow knowing such would be useless.

Food they did bring her, fresh fruit. And there were some finger lengths of what she deemed dried meat. Perhaps it was better she did not know the origin of that.

She slept when she tired on a pile of woven stuff, not quite as silky as that on the looms, yet so tightly fashioned she thought it might pass the legendary test of carrying water within its folds. Her sleep was dreamless. When she awoke, she found it harder to remember the men or the ship, even Rothar or the captain. Rather, they were like some persons she had known once in distant childhood, for the place of the weavers was more and more hers. And she *must* learn. To do that was a fever burning in her.

There was a scuttling sound and then a single order: "Eat!"

Dairine groped before her, found more of the fruit. Even before she was quite finished, there came a twitch on her skirt.

"This ugly thing covering your body, you cannot wear it for thread gathering."

Thread gathering? She did not know the meaning of that. But it was true that her skirt, if she moved out of the open space about the looms, caught on branches. She arose and unfastened her girdle, the lacing of her bodice, allowed the dress to slip away into a puddle about her feet. Wearing only her brief chemise, Dairine felt oddly free. But she sought out her girdle again, wrapped it around her slim waist, putting there within the knife.

There came one of those light touches, and she faced about.

"Thread hangs between the trees"—her guide gave a small tug—"touch it with care. Shaken, it will become a trap. Prove that you have the lightness of fingers to be able to learn from us."

No more instructions came. Dairine realized they must be again testing her. She must prove she was able to gather this thread. Gather it how? Just as she questioned that, something was pushed into her hand. She discovered she held a smooth rod, the length of her lower arm. This must be a winder for the thread.

Now there was a grasp again on her wrist, drawing her away from the looms, on under the trees. Even as her left hand brushed a tree trunk came the order: "Thread!"

There would be no profit in blind rushing. She must concentrate her well-trained perceptive sense to aid her to find thread here.

Into her mind slid a very dim picture. Perhaps that came from the very far past which she never tried to remember. A green field lay open under the morning sun and on it were webs pearled with dew. Was what she sought allied to the material of such webs?

Who could possibly harvest the fine threads of such webs? A dark depression weighed upon Dairine. She wanted to hurl the collecting rod from her, to cry aloud that no one could do such a thing.

Then she had a vision of Ingvarna standing there. That lack of self-pity, that belief in herself which the Wise Woman had fostered, revived. To say that one could not do a thing before one ever tried was folly.

In the past her sense of perception had only located for her things more solid than a tree-hung thread. But now it must serve her better.

Under her bare feet, for she had left her sandals with her

dress, lay a soft mass of long-fallen leaves. Around here there appeared to be no ground growth—only the trees.

Dairine paused, advancing her hand until her fingertips rested on bark. With caution, she slid that touch up and around the trunk. A faint impression was growing in her. Here was what she sought.

Then—she found the end of a thread. The rest of it was stretched out and away from the tree. With infinite care, Dairine broke the thread, putting the freed end to the rod. To her vast relief, it adhered there as truly as it had to the tree trunk. Now. . . . She did not try to touch the thread, but she wound slowly, with great care, moving to keep the strand taut before her, evenly spread on the rod.

Round and round—then her hand scraped another tree trunk. Dairine gave a sigh of relief, hardly daring to believe she had been successful in harvesting her first thread. But one was little enough, and she must not grow overconfident. Think only of the thread! She found another end and, with the same slow care, began once more to wind.

To those without sight, day is as night, night is as day. Dairine no longer lived within the time measure of her own kind. She went forth between intervals of sleep and food to search for the tree-looped thread, wondering if she so collected something manufactured by the weavers themselves or a product of some other species.

Twice she made the error she had been warned against, had moved too hastily, with overconfidence, shaken the thread. Thus she found herself entrapped in a sticky liquid which flowed along the line, remaining fast caught until freed by a weaver.

Though she was never scolded, each time her rescuer projected an aura of such disdain for this clumsiness that Dairine cringed inwardly.

The girl had early learned that the weavers were all females. What they did with the cloth they loomed she had not yet discovered. They certainly did not use it all, nor had she any hint that they traded it elsewhere. Perhaps the very fact of creation satisfied some need in them.

Those who, like her, hunted threads were the youngest of this nonhuman community. Yet she was able to establish no closer communication with them than she did with the senior weavers.

Once or twice there was an uneasy hint of entrapment about her life in the loom place. Why did everything which had happened before she arrived now seem so distant and of such negligible account?

If the weavers did not speak to her save through mind speech—and that rarely—they were not devoid of voices, for those at the looms hummed. Though the weird melody they so evoked bore little resemblance to human song, it became a part of one. Even Dairine's hand moved to its measure and by it her thoughts were lulled. In all the world, there were only the looms, the thread to be sought for them—only this was of any importance.

There came a day when they gave her an empty loom and left her to thread it. Even in the days of her life in the village, this had been a matter which required her greatest dexterity and concentration. Now, as she worked with unfamiliar bars, it was even worse. She threaded until her fingertips were sore, her head aching from such single-minded using of perception, while all about her the humming of the weavers urged her on and on.

When fatigue closed in upon her, she slept. And she paused to eat only because she knew that her body must have fuel. At last she knew that she had finished, for good or ill.

Now her fingers, as she rubbed her aching head, were stiff. It was difficult to flex them. Still, the hum set her body swaying in answer to its odd rhythm.

To Dairine's surprise, no weaver came to inspect her work, to say whether it was adequately or poorly done. When she had rested so that she could once more control her fingers, she began to weave. As she did so, she discovered that she too hummed, echoing the soft sound about her.

As she worked, there was a renewal of energy within her. Maybe her hands did not move as swiftly as the blur of elongated fingers she had seen in her mind, but they followed the rhythm of the hum and they seemed sure and knowing, not as if her own will but some other force controlled them. She was weaving—well or ill she did not know or care. It was enough that she kept to the beat of the quiet song.

Only when she reached the end of her thread supply, and sat with an empty shuttle in her hand, did Dairine rouse, as one from a dream. Her whole body ached, her hand fell limply on her knee. In her was the sharpness of hunger. There was no longer to be heard the hum of the others.

The girl arose stiffly, stumbled to her sleeping place. There was food which she ate before she lay down on the cloth, her face turned up to whatever roof was between her and the sky, feeling drained, exhausted—all energy gone from her body, as was logical thought from her mind.

4

Dairine awoke into fear, her hands were clenched, long shivers shook her body. The dream which had driven her into consciousness abruptly faded, leaving only a sense of terror behind. However, it had broken the spell of the weavers, her memory was once more sharp and clear.

How long had she been here? What had happened when she had not returned to the shore? Had the ship under Vidruth's control left, thinking her lost? And Rothar? the Captain?

Slowly she turned her head from side to side, aware of something else. Though she could not see them, she knew that the looms ringing her in were vacant, the weavers were gone!

Now Dairine believed she must have been caught in some invisible web, and had only this moment broken free. Why had she chosen to come here? Why had she remained? The ribband of stuff was gone from her wrist—had that set some ensorcelment upon her?

Fool! She could not see as the rest of the world saw. Now it appeared that even her carefully fostered sense of perception had, in some manner, deceived her. As Dairine arose, her hand brushed the loom where she had labored for so long. Curiosity made her stoop to finger the width her efforts had created. Not quite as smooth as the ribband, but far, far better than her first attempt.

Only—where were the weavers? The shadow of terror lingering from her dream sent her moving purposefully about the clearing. Each loom was empty, the woven cloth gone. She kicked against something—groped to find it. A collecting rod for thread.

"Where—where are you?" she dared to call aloud. The quiet seemed so menacing she longed to set her back to some tree, to raise a defense. Against whom—or what?

Dairine did not believe that Vidruth and his men would dare to penetrate the wood. But did the weavers have other enemies, and had fled those, not taking the trouble to warn her?

Breathing faster, she set hand on the hilt of the knife at her girdle. Where *were* they? Her call had echoed so oddly that she dared not try again. Only her fear grew as she tried to listen.

There was the rustle of tree leaves. Nothing else. Nor could she pick up by mind touch any suggestion of another life form nearby. Should she believe that the cloth missing from each loom meant her co-workers had left for an ordered purpose, not in flight? Would she be able to track them?

Never before had she put to such a use that sense Ingvarna had trained in her. Also, that the weavers had their own guards Dairine was well aware. She was not sure that she herself mattered enough in their eyes for them to set any defense against her seeking their company. Suppose, with a collecting rod in her hand, she were to leave the loom place as if on the regular mission of hunting thread?

First she must have food. That she located, by scent, in two bins. The fruit was too soft, overripe, and there were none of the dried sticks left. But she ate all she could.

Then, rod conspicuously in hand, the girl ventured into the woods. All the nearby threads must have been harvested, her questing fingers could find none as she played out her game for any who might watch.

And there *were* watchers! Not the weavers, for the impression these gave her was totally different—more feeble sparks as compared to a well-set fire. As she moved, so did they, hovering near, yet making no attempt to come in contact with her.

She discovered a thread on a tree. Skillfully, she wound it on her rod, took a second and third. However, at the next, she flinched away. Any thread anchored here must have been disturbed, for she smelled the acrid odor of the sticky coating.

The next two trees supported similarly gummed threads. Did that mean these had been prepared to keep her prisoner? Dairine turned a little. Already, she was out of familiar territory. Thus she expected to meet at any moment opposition, either from the threads or those watchers.

Next was a tree free of thread. Trusting to her sense of smell, she sought another opening, hoping that the un-threaded trees would mark a trail. Though she moved a little faster, she kept to her pretense of seeking threads from each tree she encountered. The watchers had not left her, though she picked up no betraying sound, only knew they were there.

Another free tree—this path was a zigzag puzzle. And she

had to go so slowly. One more free tree, and then, from her left, a sound at last—a faint moaning.

It was human, that sound, enough to feed her fear. This— somehow this all seemed a shadow out of her now-forgotten dream. In her dream she had known the sufferer—

Dairine halted. The watchers were drawing in. She could tell they had amassed between her and the direction from which the moan came. Thus she had a choice—to ignore the sound or to try to circle around.

No sign, make no sign that she heard. Keep on hunting for threads, strive to deceive the watchers. All her nature rebelled against abandoning one who might be in trouble, even if he were one of Vidruth's men.

She put out her hand as if searching for thread, more than half expecting to touch a sticky web. From those watchers she believed she picked up an answering sensation of uncertainty. This might be her only chance.

Her fingers closed about a thick band of woven stuff. That led in turn downward to a bag, the flap of the top turned over and stuck to the fabric so tightly she could not open it. The bag was very large, pulling down the branch from which it was suspended. And within it—something had been imprisoned!

Dairine jerked back. She did not know if she had cried out. What was sealed within that bag, her perception told her, had been alive, was now only newly dead. She forced herself to run fingers once more along the surface of the dangling thing. Too small—surely too small to be a man!

Now that the girl knew no human was so encased, she wanted no greater knowledge of the contents. As she stepped away, her shoulder grazed a second bag. She realized that she moved among a collection of them, and all they held was death.

Only, she could still hear that moaning. And it was human. Also, at last the watchers had dropped behind. As if this place were one they dared not enter.

Those bags—Dairine hated to brush against them. Some seemed far lighter than others and twirled about dizzily as she inadvertently touched them. Others dipped heavily with their burdens.

The moans—

The girl made herself seek what hung before her now. Her collecting rod was in her girdle. In its place, she held the knife. When she touched this last bag feeble movement answered. There was a muffled cry which Dairine was sure was a cry for help.

She ripped at the silk with knife point. The tightly woven fabric gave reluctantly, this was no easily torn material. She hacked and pulled until she heard a half-stifled cry!

"For Sul's sake—"

Dairine dragged away the slashed silk. There was indeed a man ensnared. However, about him now was sticky web, for its acrid scent was heavy on the air. Against that, her knife was of no avail. To touch such would only make her prisoner, too.

She gathered up the folds of the torn bag and, using pieces to shield her fingers, tore and worried at the web. To her relief, she was succeeding. She could feel that his own struggles to throw off his bonds were more successful.

Also, she knew whom she fought to free—Rothar! It was as if he had been a part of that dream she could not remember.

Dairine spoke his name, asking him if he were near free.

"Yes. Though I still hang. But that now is a small matter—"

Dairine heard a threshing movement, then the sound of his weight touching the ground. His breath hissed heavily in and out.

"Lady, in nowise could you have come at a better time." His hand closed about her arm. She felt him sway and then recover balance.

"You are hurt?"

"Not so. Hungry and needful of a drink. I do not know how long I have hung in that larder. The captain—he will think us both dead."

"Larder!" That one grim word struck her like a blow.

"Did you not know? Yes this is the spider females' larder, where they preserve their males—"

Dairine fought rising nausea. Those bags of silk, the beautifully woven silk! And to be used so.

"There is someone—something—out there," he said.

The watchers, her protective sense, alerted her. They were now moving in again.

"Can you see them?" Dairine asked.

"Not clearly." Then he changed that to "Yes!"

"They have throwing cords of web, such as they used on me before. No blade can cut those—"

"The bag!"

"What do you mean?"

Covered with the bag's rent material, she had been able to pull loose his bindings. Those sticky cords could not find purchase against the woven silk. As she explained that, her knife was wrenched from her hold and she heard sounds of ripping.

The watchers—as Rothar worked to empty other bags, Dairine strove to perceive them by mind. They had neared, but once more had halted, as if this were a place which they feared to enter even if ordered to do so to hold the humans captive.

"They spin their lines now," Rothar told her. "They plan to wall us in."

"Let them believe us helpless," she commanded.

"But you think we are not?"

"With the bags, perhaps not."

If she could only *see!* Dairine could have cried aloud in her frustration. Who were the watchers? She was sure they were not the weavers themselves. Perhaps these were the ones who supplied the thread she had harvested so carefully in the past.

Rothar once more was back at her side, a bundle of silk from plundered bags. The girl dared not let herself remember *what* had been in those bags.

"Tell me," she said, "what is the nature of those spinning out there?"

She could sense his deep aversion, revulsion. "Spiders. Giant spiders. They are furred and the size of hounds."

"What are they doing?"

"They are enwebbing an opening. Beyond that on either side are already nets. Now they are disappearing. Only one is left, hanging in the center of the fresh web."

Through her grasp on his wrist, Dairine could read his thoughts, his mind picture, even more clearly, to add to the scene his words had built for her.

"Those others may have gone to summon the weavers"— she made an alarming guess. "So for the present, we have only that one guard to deal with."

"And the web—"

She loosed her hold upon him, clutched a length of the raggedly cut silk. "This we must bind about our bodies. Do not touch the web save with this between your flesh and it."

"I understand."

Dairine moved forward. "I must loose the web," she told

him. "The guard will be your matter. Lead me to a tree where the web is anchored."

His hand was on her shoulders. Under his gentle urging, she was guided to the left, was moved forward step by cautious step.

"The tree is directly before you now, lady. Have no fear of the guard." His promise was grim.

"Remember, let nothing of the web touch your flesh."

"Be sure I am well shielded," he said.

She fingered rough bark, around her hand and arm the silk was well and tightly anchored. There—she had discovered the end of an anchoring thread far stronger and thicker than any she had harvested before.

"Ha!" Rothar gave a cry—was no longer beside her.

Dairine found a second thread, felt vibrations along it. The guard must be making ready to defend its web. However, she must concentrate on the finding of each thread, of breaking them loose from the tree.

There was no way for her to know how many threads she must snap so. From her right came the sound of scuffling, heavy breathing.

"Ah!" Rothar's voice fiercely triumphant. "The thing is safely dead, lady. You are right, the cords it threw at me were well warded by the cloth."

"Keep watch. Those which were with it may still return," she warned.

"That I know!" he agreed.

The girl moved as swiftly as she could, discovering thread ends, snapping them. Not only might the spiders return, but the weavers, and them she feared even more.

"The web is down," he told her.

However, she felt little relief at what might be a small victory.

"Lady, now it would be well to wrap our feet and legs with this silk, they could well lay ground webs for our undoing."

"Yes!" She had not thought of that, only of the threading cords from tree to tree.

"Let me get more silk."

Dairine stood waiting, her whole body tense as she strained to use ears and inner senses to assess what might lie in wait beyond. Then he was back and, with no by-your-leave, busied himself wrapping her feet and legs with lengths of silk, tying the strips tightly in places.

She, who had once so loved the ribband Captain Ortis had

shown her, wanted to shrink from any touch of that stuff. Save now it might be their salvation.

"That is the best I can do." He released her foot after tying a last knot about her ankle. "Do you hear aught, lady?"

"Not yet. But they will come."

"Who—what are the weavers?" he asked.

"I know not. But they do not hold our kind high in esteem."

He laughed shortly. "How well do I know that! Yet they did you no harm."

"Because, I think, I am without sight, and also a female who knows a little of their own trade. They are proud of their skill and wished to impress me."

"Shall we go then?"

"We must watch for trees bare of threads."

"Those I can see, lady. Perhaps trusting in my kind of sight, we can go the quicker. There has been much happened. The captain, though he is still weak, again commands his ship. Vidruth is dead. But the captain could not get that scum which his mate has signed to come ashore. And only he can hold them in control."

"Thus you alone are here?"

He did not answer her directly. "Set your hand to my belt, and I shall take heed in my going, I promise," was all he said.

Such a journey was humiliating for Dairine. So long had it been since she must turn to one of her kind as a guide. But she knew that he was right.

So Captain Ortis, released from the evil spell, had taken command. She wondered briefly how Vidruth had died, there had been a queer little hesitancy in Rothar's telling of that. For now she must put her mind on what lay immediately before them. That the weavers would allow them to escape easily she did not believe.

A moment later she knew she was right. They were once more under observation, she sensed. This new, stronger contact was not that of the watchers.

"They come!" she warned.

"We must reach the shore! It is among the trees that they set their traps. I have a signal fire built there, ready to be lighted, which will bring in the *Sea Raven.*"

"Can you see any such traps?"

She could feel his impatience and doubt in the slight contact of her fingers against his body where they were hooked about his belt.

"No. But there are no straight trails among the tress. Webs hang here and there; one can only dodge back and forth between them."

Dairine was given no warning, had no time to loose her hold. Rothar suddenly fell forward and down, bearing her with him. Her side scraped painfully against a broken end of branch. It was as if the very earth under them had opened.

5

The smell of freshly turned soil was thick in her nostrils. She lay against Rothar, and he was moving. In spite of her bruises, the jarring shock of that fall, Dairine sat up. Where they had landed she did not know, but she guessed they were now under the surface of the ground.

"Are you hurt?" asked her companion.

"No. And you?"

"My arm caught under me when I landed. I hope it is only a bad bruising and no break. We are in one of their traps. They had it coated over." There was a note of self-disgust bleak in his voice.

Dairine was glad he had told her the bald truth. Rising to her feet, the girl put out her hands to explore the pit. Freshly dug, the earth of its sides was moist and sticky. Here and there a bit of root projected. Could they use such to pull themselves out? Before she could ask that of Rothar, words shot harshly into her mind.

"Female, why have you stolen this meat from us?"

Dairine turned her head toward the opening which must be above. So close that voice, she could believe that a head bobbed there, eyes watched them gloatingly.

"I know not your meaning," she returned with all the spirit she could summon. "*This* is a man of my people, one who came seeking me because he felt concern."

"That with you is our meat!"

Cold menace in that message brought not fear, but a growing anger to Dairine. She would not accept that any man was—*meat*. These weavers—she had considered them creatures greater than herself because of the beauty they created, because of their skill. She had accepted their arrogance because she also accepted that she was inferior in that skill.

Yet to what purpose did they put their fine creations? Degrading and loathsome usage, by her own belief. With a flash of true understanding, she was now certain that she had not been free here, never so until she had awakened in the deserted loom place. They had woven about her thoughts a web of ensorcelment which had bound her to them and their ways, just as at this moment they had entrapped her body.

"No man is your meat," she returned.

What answered her then was no mind words, rather a blast of uncontrolled fury. She swayed under that mental blow, but she did not fall. Rothar called out her name, his arm was about her, holding her steady.

"Do not fear for me," she said and tried to loosen her grip. This was her battle. Her foot slipped in the soft earth of the pit and she stumbled. She flung out her arms to keep herself off the wall. There was a sharp pain just above her eyes, and then only blackness in which she was totally lost.

Heat—heat of blazing fire. And through it screaming—terrible screaming—which tortured her ears. There was no safety left in the world. She had curled herself into a small space of blessed dark, hiding. But she could still see—see with her *eyes!* No, she would not look, she dared not look— at the swords in the firelight—at the thing streaming with blood which hung whimpering from two knives driven like hooks into the wall to hold it upright. She willed herself fiercely *not* to see.

"Dairine! Lady!"

"No—" She screamed her denial. "I will not look!"

"Lady!"

"I will not—"

There were flashes of color about her. No mind pictures these—the fire, the blood, the swords—

"Dairine!"

A face, wavery, as if she saw it mirrored in troubled water, a man's face. His sword—he would lift the sword and then—

"No!" she screamed again.

A sharp blow rocked her head from side to side. Oddly enough, that steadied her sight. A man's face near hers, yes, but no fire, no sword dripping blood, no wall against which a thing hung whimpering.

He held her gently, his eyes searching hers.

They—they were not—not in the Keep of Trin. Dairine shuddered; memory clung about her as a foul cloak. Trin was long, long ago. There had been the sea, and then Ingvarna and Rannock. And now—now they were on Usturt. She was not sure what had happened.

But she *saw*.

Had Ingvarna believed that some day this sight would return to her? Not sight totally destroyed, but sight denied by a child who had been forced to look upon such horrors that she would not let herself face the true world openly again.

Her sight had returned. But that was not what the weavers had intended. No, their burst of mind fury had been sent to cut her down. Not death had they given her, but new life.

Then *she*, who had sent that thrust of mind power, looked over and down upon the prey.

Dairine battled her fear. No retreat this time. She must make herself face this new horror. Ingvarna's teachings went deep, had strengthened her for this very moment of her life, as if the Wise Woman had been enabled to trace the years ahead and know what would aid her fosterling.

The girl did not raise her hand but she struck back, her newfound sight centering upon that horror of a countenance. Human it was in dreadful part, arachnoid in another, such as to send one witless with terror. And the thought strength of the weaver was gathering to blast Dairine.

Those large, many-faceted eyes blinked. Dairine's did not.

"Be ready," the girl said to Rothar, "they are preparing to take us."

Down into the pit whirled sticky web lines hurled by the weavers' spider servants. Those caught and clung to root ends and then fell upon the two.

"Let them think for this moment," Dairine said, "that we are helpless."

He did not question her as more and more of the lines dropped upon them, lying over their arms, legs. Dull gray was the cloth which they had wound about them. That had none of the shimmering quality her mind had given to it. Perhaps the evil use to which this had been put had killed that opalescence.

While the cords fell, the girl did not shift her gaze, but met straight the huge, alien eyes, those cold and deadly eyes, of the weaver. In and in; Dairine aimed her power, that power Ingvarna had fostered in her, boring deep to reach the brain behind the eyes. Untrained in most of the Wise Woman's skills, she intuitively knew that this was her only form of attack, an attack which must also serve as defense.

Were those giant eyes dulling a little? The girl could not be sure, she could not depend upon her newly restored sight.

About them, the web lengths had ceased to fall. But there was new movement around the lip of the pit above.

Now! Gathering all her strength, pulling on every reserve she believed she might have, Dairine launched a direct thought blow at the weaver. That weird figure writhed, uttered a cry which held no note of human in it. For a moment, it hunched so. Then that misshapen, nightmare body fell back, out of Dairine's range of sight. She was aware of no more mental pressure. No, instead came a weak panic, a fear which wiped away all the weaver's strength.

"They—they are going!" Rothar cried out.

"For a while, perhaps." Dairine still held the creatures of the loom in wary respect. They had not thought her a worthy foe, so perhaps they had not unleashed against her all that they might. But while the weavers were still bewildered, shaken, at least she and Rothar had gained time.

The young man beside her was already shaking off the cords. Those curled limply away from his fabric-covered body, just as they fell from hers as he jerked at them. She blinked. Now that the necessity for focusing her eyes on the weaver was past, Dairine found it hard to see. It was a distinct effort for her to fasten on any one object, bring that into clear shape. This was something she must learn, even as she had learned to make her fingers see for her.

Though he winced as he tried to use his left arm, Rothar won out of the pit by drawing on the root ends embedded in the soil. Then he unbuckled his belt and lowered it for her aid.

Out of the earth prison, Dairine stood still for a long moment, turning her head right and left. She could not see them in the dusky shadows among the trees, yet they were there, weavers, spinners, both. But she sensed also that they were still shaken, as if all their strength of purpose had lain only in the will of the one she had temporarily bested.

All were that weaver's own brood—the arachnoid-human, the arachnoid complete. They were subject to the Great One's will, her thoughts controlled them, and they were her tools, the projections of herself. Until the Great Weaver regained her own balance, these would be no menace. But how long could such a respite last for those she would make her prey?

Dairine saw mistily a brighter patch ahead, sunlight fighting the dusk of this now-sinister wood.

"Come!" Rothar reached for her hand, clasped it tight. "The shore must lie there!"

The girl allowed him to draw her forward, away from the leaderless ones.

"The signal fire," he was saying. "But let me give light to that and the captain will bring in the ship."

"Why did you come—alone from that ship?" Dairine asked suddenly, as they broke out of the shade of the forest into a hard brilliance of the sun upon the sand. So hurting was that light that she needs must shade her eyes with her hand.

Peering between her fingers, Dairine saw him shrug. "What does it matter how a man who is already dead dies? There was a chance to reach you. The captain could not take it, for that rogue's spell left him too weak, though he raged against it. None other could he trust—"

"Except you. You speak of yourself as a man already dead, yet you are not. I was blind—now I see. I think Usturt has given us both that which we dare not throw lightly away."

His somber face, in which his eyes were far too old and shadowed, became a little lighter as he smiled.

"Lady, well do they speak of your powers. You are of the breed who may make a man believe in anything, even perhaps himself. And there lies our signal waiting."

He gestured to a tall heap of driftwood. In spite of the slippage of the sand under his enwrapped feet, he left her side and ran toward it.

Dairine followed at a slower pace. There was the captain and there was this Rothar who risked his life, even though he professed to find that of little matter. Perhaps now there would be others to touch upon her life, mayhap even her heart in years to come. She had these years to weave, and she must do so with care, matching each strand to another in brightness, as all had heretofore been wrought in darkness. The past was behind her. There was no need to glance back over her shoulder unto the dusk of the woods. Rather must she search seaward whence would come the next strand to add to her pattern of weaving.

SAND SISTER

1

The moment of birth came in the early dawning when the mists of Tormarsh night still curled thick and rank about the walls of Kelva's hall. This in itself was an ill thing, for, as all well knew, a child who is to have the foresight and the forereach must come into the world at that time: the last moment of one day and the first of the next; while under a full moon of the Shining One is indeed the best time to welcome a new Voice among the People.

Also this was no lusty child who entered the world crying a demand for life and the fullness thereof. Rather the wrinkled skin on its undersized body was dusky, and it lay across the two hands of the healer limply. Nor did it seek to draw a breath. But because all children were necessary for the Torfolk and each new life was a barrier against the twilight of their kind, they labored to save this one.

The healer set lips upon the cold flaccid ones of the baby and strove to breathe air into its lungs. They warmed it and nursed it, until at last it cried feebly—not to welcome life but to protest that it must receive it. At the sound of that cry Mafra's head inclined to one side as she listened to that plaint which was more like the cry of a luckless bird trapped in a net than that of any true child of Tor.

Though her eyes were long since blind to what the Folk could see, being covered with a film which no light could hope now to pierce, Mafra had the other sight. When they brought the child to her for the blessing of the Clan and House Mother, she did not hold out her hands to receive the small body. Rather she shook her head and spoke:

"Not of the kindred is this one. The spirit who was chosen to fill this body came not. What you have drawn to life in it is—"

She fell silent then. While the women who had brought the child drew away from the Healer, now staring at the baby

49

she held as if the wrap cloth of the clan birthing enfolded some slimy thing out of the encroaching bog land.

Mafra turned her head slowly so that her blind eyes faced each for the space of a breath.

"Let no one think of the Dark Death for this one." She spoke sharply. "The body is blood of our blood, bone of our bone. This much I also say to you: what now dwells within that body we must bind to us, for there is a strength indwelling in it which the child must learn to use for herself. Then when she uses it for those she favors it will be both a mighty tool and a weapon."

"But you have not named her, Clan Mother. How can she dwell in the clan house if she bears not our name freely given?" ventured then the boldest of those who had faced Mafra.

"It is not in my gift to name her," Mafra said slowly. "Ask that of the Shining One."

It was now morning and the mist was curtain heavy, blanking out the sky. However, as if her very words had summoned the creature out of the air, there swooped across the women there gathered one of the large silver-gray moths that were dancers in the night air. This settled for an instant on the wrapping of the child, fanning gently its palm-wide wings. Thus the healer spoke:

"Tursla—" Which was a name of the Moth-maid in the very ancient song-tale of Tursla and the Toad Devil. Thus it was that the child who-was-not-of-the-clan spirit was given a name which was in itself uncanny and even a little tinged with ill-fortune.

Tursla lived among the Torpeople. After the fashion of their ways she who had borne the child was never known to her as "mother" for that was not the custom. Rather all the children of one clan were held in love by the elders of their House and all were equal. Since Mafra had spoken for her, and the Tormarsh itself had sent her a name, there was no difference made between Tursla and the other children—who were very few now.

For the Torfolk were very old indeed. They spoke in their Remember Chants of a day when they had been near unthinking beasts (even less than some of the beasts of this old land) and how Volt, The Old One (he who was not human at all but the last of a much older and greater race than man dared to aspire to equal) had come to be their guide and

leader. For he was lonely and found in them some spark of
near thought which intrigued him so he would see what he
might make of them.

Volt's half-avian face still was one they carved on the
guard totems set about the fields of loquths and in their
dwelling places. To his memory they offered the first fruits of
their fields, the claws and teeth of the dire wak-lizard, if they
were lucky enough to slay such. By Volt's name they swore
such oaths as they must say for weighty reasons.

Thus Tursla grew in body, and in knowledge of Tormarsh.
What lay across its borders was of no consequence to the
Torfolk, though there was land and sea and many strange
peoples beyond. Not as old naturally as Torfolk, nor with the
same powers, for they had not been blessed by Volt and his
learning in the days their clans were first shaped.

But Tursla was different in that she dreamed. Even before
she knew the words with which she might tell those dreams
they caught her up and gave her another life. So that many
times the worlds which encased her periods of sleep were far
more vivid and real than Tormarsh itself.

She discovered as she grew older that the telling of her
dreams to those of her own age made them uncomfortable
and they left her much to herself. She was hurt, and then an-
gered. Later, perhaps out of the dreams, there came to her a
newer thought that these were for her alone and could not be
shared. This brought a measure of loneliness until she discovered that Tormarsh itself (though it might not be the worlds
through which her dreams led her) was a place of mystery
and delight.

Such opinion, however, could only be that of one who
wore a Tor body and was reared in a Tor Clan; for Tormarsh
was a murky land in which there were great stretches of
noisome bog from which reared the twisted skeletons of
long-dead trees—and those were oftentimes leprous seeming
with growths of slimy substances.

There were the remnants of very ancient roads, which tied
together in a network the islands raised from these marshy
lands, and age-old stone walls enclosed the fields of the Torfolk, rearing also to form the clan halls. Always the mists
gathered at night and early morning and wreathed around the
crumbling stones.

But to Tursla the mists were silver veiling, and in the many
sounds of the hidden boglands she could single out and name

the cries of birds, the toads, frogs, and lizards, though even those were not like their distant kin to be found other places.

Best of all she loved the moths which had given her her own name. She discovered they were drawn to the scent of certain pale flowers which bloomed only at night. This scent she came to love also and would place the blossoms in the silvery fluff of her shoulder-length hair, weave garlands of them to wear about her neck. Also she learned to dance, swaying as did the marsh reeds under the winds, and as she danced the moths gathered about her, brushing against her body, flying back and forth in their own measures about her upheld, outstretched arms.

But this was not the way of the other Tormaidens, and when Tursla danced she did so apart and for her own pleasure.

The years are all the same in Tormarsh and they pass with a slow and measured beat. Nor do the Torfolk reckon them in any listing. For when Volt left his people they no longer cared to reckon time. They knew that there was war and much trouble in the outer world. Tursla had heard that before she had been born a war leader of that other land had been brought into Tormarsh by treachery and had been taken away again by his enemies with whom the Torfolk had made an uneasy and quickly broken pact.

Also there was still an older story—but that was whispered and could only be learned if one plucked a hint there, added a word here. Even further back in time there had been a man from outside whose ship had floundered on the strip of shore where Tormarsh actually came down in a point to the sea. And there he had been found by one who was a clan mother.

She had taken pity on the man, who had been sore hurt, and had, against all custom, brought him to the healers. But the end to that had been sadness, for he had laid a spell of caring on the First Maiden of that clan and she had chosen, against all custom, to go forth with him when he was healed.

There had come a time when she returned—alone. Though to her clan she had said the name of a child. Later she had died. Yet the name of the child remained in the chant of the Rememberer. Now it was said that he, too, was a great warrior and a ruler in a land no Torfolk would ever see.

Tursla often wondered about that story. To her it had more meaning (though why she could not have said) than any of the other legends of her people. She wondered about the ruler who was half Tor. Did he ever feel the pull of his part blood? Did the moon at night and perhaps one of the lesser mists which might lay in his land awake in him some dream as real as the strange ones which haunted her? Sometimes she said his name as she danced.

"Koris! Koris!" She wondered if his mate among the stranger people held his heart in truth and if so, what was she like? Did he feel divided in his heart as Tursla did? She was by all the rights of blood fully of Tor and yet had this ache in her spirit which would never be stilled and which waxed stronger with every year of her life.

She grew out of childhood and she set herself obediently to the learning which she should have. Her fingers were clever at the loom and her weaving was smooth, with delicate pale patterns quite new among the Torfolk. Yet no one remarked upon any strangeness in those designs and she had long since ceased to mention her dreams. Lately she had indeed come to feel that there was a certain danger in allowing herself to become too deeply immersed in such. For sometimes they filled her with an odd feeling that if she were not careful she would lose herself in that other world, unable to return.

There was an urgency in those dreams, which plucked at her, wishing her to do this or that. The Torfolk themselves had strange powers. Among them such talent was not accounted in any way alien. Not all of them could use these—but that, too, was natural. Was it not true that all had each his or her own gift? That one could work in wood, another weave, a third prove a hunter or huntress skilled in tracking the quarry. Just so could Mafra, or Elkin, or Unnanna, transport a thing here or there by will alone. The range of such talents was limited, and the use of them drew upon the inner strength of the user to a high degree so that they were not for common employment.

In her dreams lately Tursla had not roamed afar in those strange landscapes. Rather she had come always to stand beside a pool of water, not murky or half overgrown with reed and plant as were the pools of Tormarsh, but rather a clear green blue.

More important, what she had felt in each of those recurring dreams was that the reddish sand which rimmed it around, as the old soft gold the Torfolk used would rim a gem, had great meaning. It was the sand which drew her—always the sand.

Twice with the coming of the Shining One in full sighting, she had awakened suddenly, not in Kelva's House but in the open, awakened and was afraid for she knew not how she had come there. So mused that she might have wandered into one of the sucking bogs and been trapped forever. She came to be afraid of the night and sleep, although she did not share with any the burden she bore. It was as if one of the geas set by Volt himself bound her thoughts, laid a silencing finger across her lips. She grew unhappy and restless. The isle of the clan houses began to feel like a prison.

It was on the night of the highest and brightest coming of the Shining One that the women of the Torfolk must gather and bathe in the radiance of the One's lamp (for so was the body quickened and made ready that children might come forth) and there were too few children. But Tursla had never come to the Shining One's place of blessing, nor had this been urged upon her. This night when the others arose to go she stirred, meaning to follow. But out of the darkness there came a quiet voice: "Tursla—"

She turned and saw now that some of the light insects had crawled from their crevices to form a circle on the wall, giving the light of their bodies to illuminate the woman sitting on the bed place there. Tursla bowed her head even though that woman could not see her.

"Clan Mother—I am here."

"It is not for you—"

Tursla did not need Mafra to tell her what was not for her. But in her was the heat of shame, and also a little anger. For she had not chosen to be what she was; that fate had instead been thrust upon her from the hour of her birthing.

"What then is for me, Clan Mother? Am I to go unfulfilled and give no new life to this House?"

"You must seek your own fulfillment, moth-child. It lies not among us. Yet there is a purpose in what you are and a greater purpose in what awaits you—out there." Mafra's hand pointed to the open door of the House.

"Where do I find it, Clan Mother?"

"Seek and it will find you, moth-child. Part of it already lies within you. When that awakes you will learn and learning—know."

"That is all you will tell me then, Clan Mother?"

"It is all I can tell you. I can foresee for the rest. But between your spirit and mine rolls a mist thicker and darker than any Tormarsh gives birth to in the night. There is this—" She hesitated a long time before she spoke again.

"Darkness lies before us all, moth-child. We who foresee

can see, in truth, only one of many paths. From every action there issue at least two ways, one in which one decision is followed, one in opposition to that. I can see that such a decision now lies before the folk. Ill, great ill may come from it. There is one among us who chooses even now to ask for the Greater Power."

Tursla gasped. "Clan Mother, how can this thing be? The Greater Power comes not by a single asking. It is called only when there is danger to all whom Volt taught."

"True enough in the past, moth-child. But time changes all things and even a geas may fade to a dried reed easily snapped between the fingers. Such a calling needs blood to feed it. This I say to you now, moth-child. Go you out this night—not to seek the place of the Shining One—there are those there who tend strange thoughts within. Rather go where your dreams point you and do what you have learned within those dreams."

"My dreams!" Tursla wondered. "Are they of use, Clan Mother?"

"Dreams are born of thought—ours—or another's. All thought is of some use. That which entered into you at your birthing cannot be denied, moth-daughter. You are now ripe to seek it out and deal with it. Go. Now!"

Her last word had the force of an order. Tursla still hesitated however. "Clan Mother, have I your blessing, the good will of this House?"

When Mafra did not reply at once Tursla shivered. This was like being before the House and seeing the door barred, shutting one out of all touch with kin and heart-ties.

But Mafra was raising her hand.

"Moth-daughter, for what it may be worth to you as you go to fulfill the future laid before you, you have the good-willing of this House. In return you must open your mind to patience and to understanding. No, I will not tell this foreseeing, for you must be guided not by any words of mine but by what comes from your own heart and mind when you are put to the test. Now, go. Trust to what the dreams have laid in your mind and go!"

Tursla went into the moonlight, into a world which was the black of bog-buried wood, the silver of mist and the pallid moonlight. But where was she to go? She flung out her arms. This night no moths came to dance with her.

Trust to what the dreams had laid in her mind. Would such point her in the direction she must take? Following the discipline of those who used the talent, she strove to clear her mind of all conscious thought.

Tursla began to walk, steadily, as one who has a purpose and a definite goal. She did not turn to the east, but faced westward, her feet on the blocks of one of the lesser roads. Though her eyes were open, she was not aware of what she saw, or even of her moving body. Somewhere before her lay the pool of her dreams and about it the all important sand.

The mist clung about her like a veiling, now concealing what lay ahead, what she had left behind. She crossed one of the islands and another. The road failed at last but unerringly her feet found tussocks and hillocks of solid land to support her. At last the mist itself was tattered by a wind, strong, carrying in it a scent which was not that of the Tormarsh.

That wind awoke Tursla from her trance. She slowed to a halt at the highest point of a hillock covered with grass, shaped like the finger of a giant, pointing due west. The girl used both hands to keep the silk soft strands of her hair out of her eyes. Now the moon was bright enough to show her that this ridge of land ran on to farther rises beyond.

Then, she began to run—lightly. In her some barrier had broken and she was swallowed up by this great need to find what lay ahead; that which had waited for her so long—so very long!

Nor was she surprised to come at last into that very place of her dreams. Here was the clear pool, and the sand. Though in the moonlight the colors of her dream had been leached away, the sand was dark and so was the pool.

She tore off her robe, letting the length of cloth, spattered with the mud and slime of her marsh journey, fall from her. But she did not allow it to drop onto the sand. It was as if nothing must sully or mark that sand.

Nor did Tursla step upon its smooth surface. Rather she climbed a small rock just beyond its edge and from that sprang out, to dive into the waiting water. That closed about her body, neither cold nor hot, but rather silken smooth, caressing. It held her as might a giant hand cupped about her, soothing, gentle. She surrendered to the water, floating on the surface of the pool.

Did she sleep then, or was she entranced by some magic beyond the knowledge of those who had bred her? Tursla was never quite sure. But she was aware that there came a change within her. Doors opened and would never close again. What lay behind those doors she was not yet sure, but she was free to explore, to use. Only the first thing—

As she lay floating on the soft cushion of the water Tursla began to hum, and then to sing. There were no words in her song, rather she trilled as might a bird, first gently, quietly, then with a rising—call? Yes, a call!

Though she lay with her face turned up to the sky, the moon, the stars, those far-off night jewels, she was aware that about her was a stirring; not in the water which cradled her, but in the sand. It was arising, partly to her will, or rather her call, partly to the need of—of—someone.

Still Tursla sang. Now she dared to turn her head a little. There was a pillar of sand from which came a tinkling, a faint chiming, caused as one grain of its substance rubbed against the other in a whirl so fast it would seem that there was no sand but only a solid column of the dark grit. Louder grew Tursla's song, more and more the pillar thickened. It no longer reached skyward, rather kept to a height no greater than her own.

The contours of the pillar began to alter, to thin here, thicken there. It took on the appearance of a statue—crude at first, a head which was a ball, a body with no grace or shape to it. But still the sand changed, the figure it formed became more and more human-like.

At last the sense of movement was gone. A figure stood there on rock from which her birth had drawn all the sleeping sand. Tursla trod water, drew into the shore and climbed out to front this being for whom her song had opened the door and wrought a shaping.

Into her mind there came the name she must now speak— the name which would anchor this other, make sure and safe the bridge between her world and another one that she could not even imagine, so alien was its existence.

"Xactol!"

The sand woman's eyelids quivered, raised. Eyes which were like small red-gold coals of fire regarded Tursla. The girl saw the rise and fall of the stranger's breasts, the moonlight was reflected from a dark skin as smooth seeming as her own.

"Sister—"

The word from the other was hardly more than a whisper. It held in it still some of the sound of sand slipping over sand. But neither woman nor voice wrought any fear in Tursla. Her open hands went out, offering kinship to the sand woman. Hands as firm to the touch as her own caught and held, in a clasp which welcomed her in return.

"I have hungered—" Tursla said, realizing in this moment that she spoke the truth. Until those hands closed about hers there had been this deep lack, this hunger in her which she had not even truly known she carried until it was so assuaged.

"You have hungered," Xactol repeated. "Hunger no more, sister. You have come—you will have what you seek. You shall do thereafter what must be done."

"So be it."

Tursla took another step forward. Their hands fell apart, but their arms were wide. They embraced as indeed close kin welcomed one another after some long time apart. Tursla found tears on her cheeks.

2

"What is asked of me?" The girl drew back from that embrace, studied the face so close to her own. It was calm and still as the sand had been before her power had troubled it.

"Only what you yourself choose," came the murmured reply. "Open your mind, and your heart, sister-one, and it shall be shown to you in the appointed time. Now—" The right hand of the sand woman arose, and the slightly rough fingertips touched Tursla's forehead, held so for the space of several heartbeats. Then they slid down, over the eyelids the girl instinctively closed and again held so, before going on to her lips. The touch withdrew, came again to her breast over the faster beating of her heart.

From each of those touches there issued an inflowing of strength so that Tursla's breathing quickened; she felt a kind of impatience, of a need to be busy, though with what task she could not have said. This inflow of energy made her flesh tinkle, alive in a way she had never experienced.

"Yes—" her voice was swift, her words a little slurred. "Yes, yes! But how—and when? Oh, how and when, sand sister?"

"The how you shall know. The when is shortly."

"Then—then I shall find the door? I shall be free in the place of my dreaming?"

"Not so. For each her own place, sister-one. Seek not any gate until the time. There is that for you to do here and now. The future is the threaded loom upon which there is not yet

any weaving. Sit before it, sister-kin, and fix the pattern you
desire in your mind, then take up the shuttle and begin your
task. In one sense we, in turn, are shuttles in the service of a
greater purpose and we are moved to form a pattern we cannot see, for to its weaving we are too close. We can know the
knotting and the breakage and perhaps even mend and
reweave a little—but we are not that Great One who views it
all. The time has come for you to set your portion of the pattern into the unseen design."

"But with you—"

"Younger sister, my bridging of the space between us cannot be held for long. We must hasten to the task set upon us
both. Your mind is open, your eyes can now see, your lips
are ready for the words, and your heart is prepared for what
must come. Listen!"

So there by the dream pool Tursla listened. It was as if her
mind was as porous and empty as one of those leaves of the
draw-well, a sponge ready to be filled when one dipped it into
water. She drew in strange words, and heard stranger sounds
which she must shape her lips to form. Though that was a
difficult thing, for it would seem that some of those sounds
were never meant for her to utter. Her hands moved to pattern designs in the air. While following the movements of her
fingers there remained for an instant thereafter a faint tracing
of color—that which was red-brown like the sand which had
formed the body of her teacher, or else green-blue as the pool
beside which they sat.

Again she got to her feet and moved her body in the
measures of a dance—to no music save that which seemed to
be locked into her own mind. All this had a meaning, though
she was not sure what that might be, save that what she
learned now was her true birthright and also both a weapon
and a tool.

At last her companion was silent and Tursla, now slumped
upon the sand, felt as if that energy which had filled her had
seeped away little by little, driven out of her again by the
learning which she had so eagerly grasped.

"Sand-sister, you have given me much. To what purpose? I
cannot set aside Volt's ways and be ruler here."

"That was never intended. In what manner you can serve
these people—that you will see from time to time. Give them
what is best for their needs, but not openly, not claiming for
yourself any powers. Give it only when such giving shall not
be marked. There will be a time when your giving will set an-

other part of the design to work—then, oh, younger sister, give with all your heart!"

She who answered to the name Xactol and whose true form and kind Tursla only dimly could perceive (and then only in her mind) arose. She began to turn, and that turning became faster and faster, a blur of movement. Just as she had put on the substance of the sand so now she lost it. Tursla covered her face with her hands, protecting her eyes against the trails of grit which spun out and away from what was becoming once more only a pillar.

The girl sank forward, feeling the drift of the sand over her. She was so tired, so very tired. Let her sleep now dreamlessly, she asked something beyond, the nature of which she recognized no more than she did the real form of Xactol. As the sand arose about her body, covered her lightly as might a soft cloth of spider silk, she indeed slept without dreams, even as she had petitioned to do.

It was the warmth of the midday sun beaming down upon her which roused her at last. She sat up, sand cascading from her. The colors of her dream were here, bright—green of pool, red of sand. But last night had not been a dream. It could not be. Tursla gathered up a palmful of the sand and allowed it to sift between her fingers. It was very fine, more like powder ash than the grit she expected.

She brushed it from her body and then she knelt by the pool, troubling its mirror-smooth surface to wash the sand from her hand, her arms, her face, splashing the water over her body. The wind blew steadily and, after she had retrieved the robe she had discarded, she went on, past the rocks which rimmed the pool site.

So she came to the sea and for the first time looked out onto that part of the outside world which she had heard spoken of but had never seen. The play of the waves as they crashed in shore and broke, leaving that which had formed them to drain away, enchanted her. She ventured out upon the water-smoothed sand. The wind, so much stronger here, whipped her robe and tugged at her hair. She flung her arms wide to welcome the wind which had none of the marsh scent.

It was good to be in the open. Tursla settled down on the sand to watch the breaking waves, singing softly to herself in wordless sounds which were not meant to evoke any answer but which were an attempt to match the music of wind and wave.

She saw shells in the sand and picked them up in wonder and delight. Like and yet unlike they were for, seeing them closely, she could perceive that each had some small difference to set it apart from its kind. Not unlike those of her own species—each with some part of him or her which was only his or hers.

At last she reluctantly turned her face from the sea to the Tormarsh. The sun was already westering. For the first time Tursla wondered if any had sought her and what she must say when she returned which might cloak this thing which had happened to her.

Slowly she dropped her harvest of shells. There was no need to advertise her visit to a place which custom forbade any to see. But that was no reason why she might not come this way again. No rule of Volt said definitely that the sea was forbidden to those who followed his ancient rules of living.

Tursla found the marsh oddly confining as she passed swiftly along the trail toward the House island. So as she went she plucked certain leaves which were for dyeing, glad that fortune favored her in that several plants were of the Corfil—a rarity much prized as it produced a scarlet dye which was mainly used for the curtains of Volt's own shrine, thus was always eagerly sought.

As Tursla came along the westward road she had her skirt upheld into a bag, a goodly harvest in that. But one moved out to intercept her before she gained Kelva's House.

"So, moth-sister—you have thought to return to us? Did the winged ones tire of you so soon, night walker?"

Tursla tensed. Of all those she wished the least to meet Affric was the one. He leaned now on his spear, his eyes regarding her mockingly. There was a belt with a fringe of wak-lizard teeth about his middle, attesting to both his courage and skill. For only a man with both nearly supernormal reflex and cunning dared hunt those great lizards.

"Fair day to you, Affric." She did not warm her words. He flouted custom in his familiar greeting. The very fact he did so was disturbing.

"Fair day—" he repeated. "And what of the night, moth-sister? Others danced with the moon."

She was more than startled. For any Torman to speak of the Calling, and to such as her who had not named any man before Volt for a choosing!

He laughed. "Send me no spears from your eyes, moth-sister. Only daughters of Volt—true daughters—need make a man watch his tongue by custom." He took a step nearer. "No, you did not seek the moon last night, so then whom *did* you seek, moth-sister?" There was an ugly set to his mouth.

She did not make any answer. To do so would be indeed lessening herself in the eyes of all. For there were those who listened, if from a distance. What Affric said and did was a raw affront.

Tursla looked away and walked forward. He would not dare, she was sure, attempt to stop her. And he did not. But the fact that he could publicly address her in that manner was frightening. Also, not one of those listening had spoken up in rebuke. It was almost as if this had been deliberately arranged to insult her. Her hands tightened on her improvised bag of leaves. Why—?

None stood before the door of Kelva's House and she walked head high, back straight, from the day into the dusk.

"Back at last, are you, then?" Parua, who tended the store cupboards and served as eyes for Mafra, regarded her sourly. "What have you there which needed to be cropped by night? A night when your duty lay elsewhere?"

Tursla shook out the leaves to fall upon a mat.

"Parua—do you really think that such as I should dance for the Shining One's favor?" she asked in a voice from which she was able to keep all emotion.

"What do you mean? You are woman grown. It is your duty to bring forth children—if you can!"

"If I can—you yourself say that, Mother-one. Have I not heard otherwise all my life? That I am one who is not true Tor born, and therefore I must not give life to a child because of the strangeness which is a part of me?"

"We grow too few—" Parua began.

"So thus the clan will welcome even the flawed? But that is not custom, Parua. And when custom is broke it must be done openly before Volt's shrine, with all his People assenting."

"If we grow few enough," Parua countered, "Volt will have none here to raise his name. There are to be changes, even in custom. There will be a Calling, a Great Calling. So it has been decided."

Tursla was astounded. Great Callings she had heard talked of; the last had been years ago when the Torfolk had allowed their stronghold to be invaded for a short time by strangers. It was then that the war leader of the outside lands had been prisoner here—together with her who, it was whispered, had been Koris' chosen lady. There had come no great ill from that, save that it had reached them later that, even as they had closed the marsh, so was now the outer world closed to them in turn. But even then there had been two minds about the right and the wrong of what they did.

It was true that births grew fewer each year. She had heard that Mafra and one or two of the other Clan Mothers speculated as to the reason for that. Perhaps even that their race was too old, had taken mates only among themselves too long so that their blood thinned, their creative powers were dimming. Thus it might be a fact that they would try to force her to their purposes. For it would only be by force that she would come to a Choosing—there was no Torman she had ever looked upon with favor. And now, she was not conscious she was pressing her hands against her breast; even less was she a daughter of Volt!

"So, moth-one," Parua continued, looking at her, Tursla thought, slyly and near maliciously, "your body being Torborn, that might well serve Volt's purposes. Consider that."

Tursla turned quickly toward that wall alcove which was Mafra's. The Clan Mother seldom left her private niche nowadays. She had hands whose skill had outrun her vanished sight, and, by touch alone, she made those useful to her people, shaping small pots to be fired, or spinning fibers more smoothly than any of her house descendants could.

Now Tursla saw that those hands lay strangely still, loosely clasped in the old woman's lap. Her head was held up, just slightly a-tip as if she listened. As the girl stood hesitantly before her, uncertain if she dared break into that trance-like state, Mafra spoke: "Fair day, moth-child. Fair be your going, fair be your coming, firm your steps upon the crossing places, full your hands with good labor, your heart with warmth, your mind with thoughts which will serve you."

Tursla sank to her knees. That was no common greeting! It was—it was that given to any clan daughter who knew she was at last with child! But—why—

Mafra raised one hand, stretched it forth. Tursla quickly bent her head to kiss those long, age-thinned fingers.

"Clan Mother—I am not—not as you have welcomed me," she said hurriedly.

"You are filled," Mafra said. "Not all filling is with a life which will separate itself in time from yours and become all in all to itself. There is life within you now and, in due time, it will come forth. If it does so in a different fashion, then that is the will of Volt, or of what power stood behind him when he came to lead our people up out of savagery. It shall be with you as with the Filled. So shall it be said in this House and Clan. And if it is said so among those who are your own, then it will be the same elsewhere among the Folk."

"But, Clan Mother, if my body does not contain a life they will understand, and the time passes when I should bear the fruit which House and Clan need, then will there not be a reckoning? What can be said then for one who had misled House and Clan?"

"There will be no misleading. There is set before you a task that you shall do by virtue of the life you hold. What will follow from that will lead to the two roads of which I told you—one this way—" Her hand swept to the right. "One that way." She indicated the left. "I cannot foresee past that choice which shall be yours. But I think what you will choose shall be of wisdom. Parua—" she raised her voice and the other woman came near, going to her knees as did Tursla.

"Parua, this Tursla, moth-daughter, is Filled and so let House and Clan be guarded according to custom."

"But she—there was no Choosing, no moon dance," Parua protested.

"She was sent out by my wisdom, Parua. Do you question that?" Mafra's tone was chill. "Into the night she went with my blessing. What she sought—and found—was by the will of Volt as revealed to me in foresight. She has returned, filled. I recognize it so, and, by my Volt-given gift, I proclaim that now."

Parua's mouth opened again as if she would protest and then it closed. Clan Mother had spoken, she had said that Tursla was Filled. And, if she who had the farsight for her own said this, then no one dared question the truth of it. Parua bowed her head submissively and kissed the hand held out to her. She backed away, her gaze still on Tursla, and the girl sensed that she might have to admit openly Mafra's judgment was right, but her own reservations were still stubbornly alive.

"Clan Mother," the girl said quickly, as soon as she was sure Parua must be beyond hearing the murmur of a voice she held to the edge of a whisper, "I do not know what is expected of me."

"This much I can tell you, moth-child. There will soon

come one whom Unnanna will summon—not with voice or message—but by the Calling itself. He has such blood ties that this calling can catch and hold him as one snared in a net. But the purpose for which they would bring him—" There was a new note in Mafra's voice. "That is, in the end, death. If his blood is spilt upon the ground before Volt's shrine, that blood shall call aloud. And *its* calling will bring the forces of the outer world upon us with fire and steel. Volt's people will die and Tormarsh shall be a barren and cursed place.

"We count our children as the fruit of all of us together. No one claims any child as his or hers alone. But this is not the way of the Outside. There they hold not to House Clans, but are split into smaller gatherings. There a child has but two on which to call in trouble—she who gave him birth and he who filled her at some time of choosing. This seems strange and wrong to us, a breaking up of the bonds which are our strength. But it is their way of life.

"However, this different way also gives other bonds which we do not understand. Strange indeed are these bonds. Let anyone there raise hand against a child—and the mother-one and he who filled her will take up the hunt with the fury of a wak-lizard who sights man. The one whom Unnanna would summon for her purposes is son to a man who is perhaps the greatest threat the Outside can raise against us. I fear for our people, moth-child.

"It is true that we grow fewer, that only a hand-finger count of children may be born after any choosing. But that is our sorrow and perhaps the will of life itself. To bring in blood-giving—no."

"And my part in this, Clan Mother?" Tursla asked. "Do you wish me to stand against Unnanna then? But even though you have named me Filled, who would listen to my words? She is a Clan Mother, and, since you go no more to the moon dance, it is she who leads."

"That is so. No, I lay no task on you, moth-daughter. When the time comes for you to do as you must, you yourself will know it, for that knowledge will be inside you. Give me now your hands."

Mafra held out both of her own palms up, and Tursla placed hers thereupon, palms down. Again, just as it had been when she and Xactol had communed with one another, there was a feeling of quickening within her, a stirring of energy she longed to use but did not yet know how to put to any testing.

"So—" Mafra's voice was but a whisper, as if this were a very secret thing. "I knew that you were from elsewhere at your birthing, but this is indeed a strange thing."

"Why did this happen to me, Clan Mother?" Tursla voiced her old protest.

"Why do many things happen—those for which we can see no meaning or root? Somewhere there is a master pattern of which we must all be a part."

"So did *she* say also—"

"She? Ah, think of her, picture her in your mind, moth-child!" There was an eagerness in Mafra now. "See her for me!" she ordered.

Obediently Tursla pictured the spinning pillar of sand, and she who had been formed by that.

"Indeed you have been Filled, moth-child," sighed Mafra after a long moment. "Filled with such knowledge that perhaps you alone in this world can begin to comprehend. I wish we might talk of this and of your learning, but that cannot be. For it was not meant for me to gain any other than I have. Do not share it, moth-daughter, even if you are so moved. A basket woven to hold loquth seeds, no matter how skillfully made, cannot carry water which is intended to fill a fired clay jar. Go you now and rest. And live after the manner of the Filled until the time comes and you know it."

So dismissed, Tursla went to her own portion of the clan house—that small section given to her when she was judged more girl than child. She pulled close the woven reed mats which made it into a private place and sat upon her double cushion to think.

Mafra's pronouncement would not only excuse her from any Moon dancing, but would speedily put to punishment any speeches such as Affric had made to her, any gesture even from any man of any House. She would be excused also from certain kinds of work. The only difficulty she might face at first would be that she could not leave the settlement island alone from now on. The Filled were ever under guard for their own protection.

She ran her hands down her own slender body. How long before the fact that her belly did not swell would be noted? The women were sharp-eyed about such matters, since birth was their great mystery and they were jealous of the keeping of it. Perhaps she could devise some sort of padding within her robe. Also the Filled often had unusual desires for different food, altered their habits of living. Maybe she could turn such fancies to her account.

But eventually the time would come when she would be found out. Then what? To her knowledge no one among the Folk had ever made a false statement concerning such a thing. It would strike at the very root of all of their long held beliefs. What punishment could be harsh enough for that? Why had Mafra done this?

No one of the Torfolk, Tursla was sure, would accept the idea of a Filling with knowledge. And Mafra—she, Tursla, had not made the claim—it had been the Clan Mother. Such a deliberate flouting of custom, just so that she would be left to hold herself ready for this other action of which Mafra had only given her hints.

A Calling for the purpose of blood. Tursla drew a deep breath. If Mafra meant by that what Tursla could guess, then that was a great breaking of custom also. Sacrifice—of a—*man*? But there were no such sacrifices ever made to Volt; a man whose killing might bring down a doom of ending on Tormarsh and Torfolk. What part would she have?

She could—no, something within Tursla forbade that for now. This was no time to open that door in her mind which guarded what she had learned from Xactol.

Patience must be hers and this role must be played well. The girl drew aside her private curtain and arose. What she wanted most was food and drink. Suddenly she was very hungry and thirst made her mouth dry. She started for the supply jars, intent only on tending her body, sternly closing down the whirl of thoughts in her mind.

3

Three days went by; Tursla spent the time quietly at work with her spindle in her hands, but, more to her own desires, also with her thoughts. Mafra's word had been accepted by the House clan—how could it not be? She was given the deference accorded the Filled, served first with the choicest of foods, left to her own thoughts since she seemed to wish it so.

But on the third day the girl aroused from the half trance in which she had allowed herself to drift as she attempted to sort out and store what she had learned. Most of what she discovered lay only in hints. Yet she was sure that such hints were only way markers to deeper knowledge that she must have and that she still could not now remember. The struggle to do so only made her tense and restless, her head ache, and sleep hard to come by.

Nor could she summon up any of her dreams. When she slept now it was fitfully, more like a light doze from which she could be awakened by such a small thing as a sleeper in the next mat place turning over.

Knowledge was of no help if one could not tap it, Tursla believed with an ever growing distress. What lay before her?

Wishing to be alone with that spark of fear which was fast growing into a flame, she arose from her stool before the loom and went from the Kelva's House. She neared the group of women before she noted them, so entangled was she in her thoughts.

Unnanna stood there, the others facing her as if she were laying upon them some duty. Now her gaze rested on Tursla, and a small smile—a smile which held no kindness in it—lifted the corners of her thin-lipped mouth.

"Fair be the day—" She raised her voice a little, plainly to address the girl. "Fair be your going. Fair be the end of the waiting for you."

"I give thanks for your good wishing, Clan Mother," Tursla replied.

"You have not spoken before Volt the name of your Choosing—" Unnanna's smile grew wider. "Are you not proud enough for that, Filled One?"

"If I choose to spread Volt's cloak about me and am challenged for so doing," Tursla returned, hoping to hold her pretense of serenity, "then there must be a changing of custom."

Unnanna nodded. Her outer pose was one of good will. It was not unheard of that some maid at her first Filling chose not to announce the name of her partner in the moon ritual. Though generally it was a matter of common knowledge as soon as her Clan Mother proclaimed the fact to the satisfaction of the clan.

"Wear Volt's cloak then, moth-daughter. In days to come you will have sisters in aplenty." There was an assenting murmur from the women about her, an eager assenting.

But Unnanna was not yet through with Tursla.

"Do not go a-roaming, moth-daughter. You are precious to us all now."

"I go only to the fields, Clan Mother. To Volt's shrine that I may give thanks."

That was a worthy enough reason for leaving the place of

Houses and no one could deny her such a small journey. She passed Unnanna and started down the moss-greened pavement of the ancient road. Nor did any follow her there, for again custom decreed that one who so sought Volt's shrine should be granted privacy for any petition or thanks the worshipper desired to raise.

Volt's shrine—time had not dealt well with it. Walls had sunk into the ever hungry softer ground of the marsh, or else tumbled the stone of their making across pavement, because no man could put hand to any rebuilding here.

For these were the very stones which Volt himself had laid hands upon in the very long ago, set up to make his shelter. It had been a large hall, Tursla guessed, as she traced the lines of those crumbling walls. But by all legend Volt himself was larger in body than any of the Torfolk.

Now she wove a way between those crumbling walls. Under her feet the earth and stone were beaten hard into a path during the countless years Torfolk had sought comfort here. Thus she came into the inner room. Though the roof was gone, and the light of sun shone down upon what was the very heart of Volt's domain—a massive chair seemingly carved of wood (but such a wood—strange to Tormarsh—which no damp could rot). On either side of the chair stood tall vases wrought of stone and set in them, ready for any call to Volt, the quick firing pith of those trees waterlogged in the marsh whose spongy outer bark could be flaked away, leaving an inner hardness which burned so brightly. Here were no light insects, but fire which destroyed and yet was so brilliant in its death.

For a long moment Tursla hesitated. What she would do now was allowed by custom, yes, but only if one were greatly moved by some happening which could not be understood and from which there seemed to be no answer in any human mind. Was that her case now? She believed she could claim it was.

Tursla put out her hand, setting her palm flat on the petrified wood of the chair's wide arm. Then she drew herself up the one shallow step which raised the seat about the flooring of that near destroyed hall, and seated herself upon the chair of Volt.

It was as if she were a small child settling herself into the chair of some large-boned adult. Tall as she was among the Torfolk, here her feet did not meet the pavement as she wriggled back until her shoulders touched the wood behind her. To lay her hands out upon the arms was a strain but this she did before she closed her eyes.

Did Volt indeed listen from wherever he had gone when he withdrew from Tormarsh? Did that essence of Volt which might just still exist somewhere in the world care now what happened to those he had once protected and cherished? She had no answer to those questions, nor could any within the bounds of Tor give her more than such guesses as she herself might make.

"Volt—" her thought shaped words as she did not speak aloud—"we give you honor and call upon your good will in times of need. If you still look upon us— No, I do not cry now for help as a helpless child calls upon those of the clan house. I wish only to know who or what I am, and how I must or may use what has Filled me as Mafra swears I have been Filled. It is no child that I carry in truth; perhaps it is more—or less. But I would know!"

She had closed her eyes, and her head rested now upon the back of the chair. There was the faint scent of the tree candles from either hand, less than they would give off at their igniting. She had seen the Clan Mothers hold such before them and the smoke had wreathed them around while they chanted.

She—

Where was she? Green grass grew out before her, a fan which stretched to the feet of rises of gray rock. Scattered in the grass, as if someone had carelessly flung wide a handful of bright and shining stones, were flowers, their petals wide, their shapes and colors differing as the shells on the shore had differed. Above the flowers fluttered moths—or winged things which resembled moths. Those were also brightly colored, sometimes bearing more than one shade or hue on their wings.

There was nothing of Tormarsh in this place. Nor was it, she was sure, another sighting of her dream land. She willed to move forward and her will gave birth to action for she passed, not on her feet step by step, but rather drifted in the air, as might those flying things.

So Tursla was wafted by her will to those rocks which rose above the grass. Again her desire lifted her higher, to the topmost pinnacle of the rocks. Now she gazed down into a greater valley wherein there ran a river. Across that wide ribbon of water spanned a bridge of stone, and the bridge served a road which ran across the green of the land.

While on the road, approaching the bridge, there was—

Horse—that was a horse. Though Tursla had never seen such an animal, she knew it. And on the horse—a man.

Her will to see drew him to her sight in a strange way, though in truth she had not moved from her place on the hill, nor had he yet come upon the bridge. Still she saw him as clearly as if he and his mount were within such distance that she could put forth a hand and lay it on the horse's shoulder.

He wore metal like a silken shirt, for it had been fashioned of small rings linked one upon the other. Above that a cloak dropped down his shoulders, fastened at his throat with a large brooch set with dull green and gray stones. There was a belt with like stones about his waist and from that hung a sheathed sword.

His head was covered with a cap also of metal, but this was a solid piece, not chained rings. It had a ridge beginning above the wearer's forehead and running back to a little below the crown of his head. This ridge possessed sockets into which were fastened upstanding feathers of a green color.

But Tursla's attention only marked that in passing, for it was the man himself she would see. So she studied the face beneath the shadow of the cap.

He was young, his skin was fair, hardly darker than a Torman's. There was strength in his face, as well as comeliness. He would make a good friend or clan brother, she decided, and a worse enemy.

As he rode he had been looking ahead, not truly as if he saw the road, but rather as if he were busied with his thoughts, and those not pleasant ones. Now, suddenly, his head jerked up a fraction and his eyes were aware—and they looked upon her! While a quick frown marked a sharp line between his brows.

Tursla saw his lips move, but she heard nothing, if he had spoken. Then one hand lifted, was held out toward her. At that same moment all was gone. She whirled away in a dizzy, giddy retreat. When she opened her eyes she sat once more in Volt's chair, and she saw nothing save the time-breached walls of his shine. But now—now she knew! Volt had indeed answered her wish! She was linked with the horseman and in no easy way. Their meeting lay before her and from it would come danger and such a trial of strength as she could not now measure.

Slowly the girl arose, drawing a deep breath, as one preparing for a struggle, though she knew that the time for that was not yet. He had been aware of her, that horseman, nor did he in the mind's eye grow blurred with the passing of moments. No, somewhere he rode and was real!

In the later afternoon she sought out Mafra again. Perhaps the Clan Mother could or would give her no answers, yet she must share Volt's vision with someone. And in all this place only Mafra did she trust without reservation.

"Moth-child—" Though Mafra turned sightless eyes in her direction never was she mistaken concerning the identity of those who came to her. "You are a seeker—"

"True, Clan Mother. I have sought in other places and other ways, and I do not understand. But this I have seen; from Volt's own chair did I venture out in a stange way beyond explaining." Swiftly she told Mafra of the rider.

For a long moment the Clan Mother sat silent. Then she gave a quick nod as if she affirmed some thought of her own.

"So it begins. How will it then end? The foreseeing reaches not to that. He whom you saw, moth-child, is one tied to us by part blood—"

"Koris!"

Mafra's hand, where it rested upon her knee, tightened, her head jerked a fraction as if she strove to avoid a blow.

"So that old tale still holds meaning," she said. "But Koris was not your rider. This is he whom I told you about—the child of those who would move mountains with spells, slay men with steel, that naught comes to harm him. He is Koris's son, and his name is Simond, which in part was given by that outlander who fought so valiantly beside his father to free Estcarp of the Kolder."

Mafra paused and then continued. "If you wonder how these things are known: when I was younger, strong in my powers, I sometimes visited in thought beyond the edge of Tormarsh, even as this day you have done. It was Koris's friend Simon Tregarth who was brought hither through strangers' magic and delivered to his enemies. Also with him was she who was Koris's choice of mate after the manner of the outlanders. Then we chose ill, so that in turn the outlands set their own barriers against us. We cannot go, even if we wish, outside the Marsh, nor can anyone come to us."

"Is the seashore also barred, Clan Mother?"

"Most of the shore, yes. One may look at it, but the mist which rises between is a wall as firm as the stone ones about us now."

"But, Clan Mother. I have trod the sand beside the sea, found shells within it—"

"Be silent!" Mafra's voice was a whisper. "If this much was given you let no other know it. The time may come when it will be of worth to you."

Tursla allowed her voice to drop also. "Is that a foreseeing, Clan Mother?"

"Not a clear one, I only know that you will have need for all your strength and wit. This I can tell you, Unnanna calls tonight and, if she is answered, then—" Mafra lifted her hands and let them fall again to her lap. "Then I leave it to your wit, moth-daughter. To your wit and that which is in you from that other place."

She gave the sign of dismissal and Tursla went to her own place and took up her spindle, but if any watched her for long they would know that she had little profit from her labors.

Night came and around her the women of the clan stirred and spoke to one another in whispers. None addressed her; being Filled she was carefully set apart that nothing might threaten that which she was supposed now to carry. Nor did they approach Mafra either, rather ranged themselves with Parua and slipped quietly away.

There were no guards set about the House isle, save on the two approaches by which a wak-lizard might come. No one would watch those bound for the Shrine in any case, so that Tursla, pulling a drab cloak about her, even over the soft silver of her hair, thought she could follow behind without note.

Once more she crept along the same path she had taken earlier that day. Those ahead carried no lighted torches; there was no gleam save the moonlight, but she saw that every house must be represented. This could not be a complete Calling after all for there were no men. Or so she had thought until she caught sight of moon gleam on a spear head and noted those cloaked men, ten of them, standing in a line facing the Chair. While in that seat huddled a figure who raised her face to the light even as Tursla found a hiding place back behind a pile of fallen rock.

Unnanna sat in the place of Seeking. Her eyes were closed, her head turned slowly from side to side. Those standing below began to croon, first so softly that it was hardly to be heard over the lap of water, the wing rustle of some flying thing. Then that hum grew stronger—no words, but rather a sound which made Tursla's skin tingle, her hair move against

her neck. She found that her head was swinging also in the
same way as Unnanna's and, at that moment, realized the
danger which lay in being trapped into becoming a part of
what they would do here.

She raised her hands and covered her eyes so that she
might not see that swaying, while she thought, as one catches
a line of safety thrown wide, of the sand sister, or the racing
sea waves. Though a pulse now beat within her, Tursla also
fought her own body; and, without being fully conscious of
what she did, she rose to her full height and began to move
her feet, not in the pattern Unnanna's head had set, but in
another fashion, to break for herself the spell the Clan
Mother was rising.

There was power building here; her body answered to it.
Force pressed in upon her like a burden, trying to crush her.
Still Tursla countered that, her lips moving in words which
sprang from behind those doors in her mind which she had
earlier tried to open and could not. Only such danger as this
would free them for her.

She opened her eyes. All was as before—save that Unnanna had moved forward on the chair of Volt. One after
another those waiting men came to her. She touched them on
the forehead, on the eyes. Then each made way for his fellow. From the tips of those fingers which she used to touch
them came small cones of light, and those who stepped back
from her anointing carried now a mark on the forehead of
the same eerie radiance.

When all had been so marked they turned and made their
way from the hall, the women giving back to open their path.
As they passed by Tursla she saw that their eyes were set and
they stared as men entranced. Their leader was Affric; and
those who followed him were all young, the most skilled of
the hunters.

When they had gone from her sight, Tursla looked back to
the hall. Once more Unnanna sat with closed eyes. Power
surged; it came from each of them there. Unnanna, in some
manner, drew that unseen energy from them, consolidated it,
shaped from it a weapon, aimed that weapon, and sent out
on course.

Tursla was not one of them. Now she stood tense, seeking
within herself something she sensed must be ready to answer
her call. She used her thought to mold it, thinking of what
she would hurl—not as the spear Unnanna's wish had fostered—no, what then? A shield? She did not hold strength

enough in herself to interpose any lasting barrier. But perhaps there was something else she could mind-fashion. She thought of the likenesses of all the weapons known to the Torfolk, and fastened in the space of a breath upon—a net!

Clenching her hands until her nails cut into her own flesh, the girl centered all of her unknown energies, untested to their full extent since that night by the pool, and thought of a net—a net to entangle feet, to impede those who marched by night, those who would set a trap. They themselves would be now entrapped.

As blood draining from a grievous mortal wound, the energy Tursla summoned seeped from her. If she could only call upon that greater well of strength which Unnanna could tap for herself! But a net—surely a net! Let it catch about the feet of Affric; let it ensnare him where he would go. Let it *be!*

The girl stumbled back against the wall, weakness in her legs, her arms hanging heavily by her sides, as she had neither the will nor strength now to raise them. With her back against the rough stone she slipped downward, the ruins rising around her like a protective shield. Her head fell forward on her breast as she made her last attempt to send what remained in her to reinforce the net her vivid mind picture had set about Affric's stumbling feet.

It was cold and she was shivering. Dark lay about her, and she no longer heard that sound which had built up the energy for Unnanna's mind dart. Rather what came was the whisper of wings. Lifting her head, Tursla looked upward to the night sky above the pocket in the ruins where she rested.

There were two moths a-dance, their beautiful shadowy wings outlined with the faint night shine which was theirs when they flew in the deep dark. Back and forth they wove their meetings and partings. Then the large spiraled down, and for just a moment it clung to the dew-wet robe on her breast, fanning its wings, tiny eyes which were alight looking into hers . . . or so it seemed to the bemused girl.

"Sister," Tursla whispered. "I give you greeting. Fair flying for your night. May the blessing of Volt himself be with you!"

The moth clung for another instant and then flew away. Stiffly Tursla pulled herself up. Her body ached as if she had done a full day's stooping at the loom, or at harvest in the fields. She felt stupid, also, when she tried to think clearly.

She tottered along, one hand against the wall to support

her. There was no one here—Volt's chair was empty. For a
moment she wavered as she gazed upon that seat. Should she
try again? There was a longing in her, a strange longing. She
wanted to see how the rider fared. What had Mafra named
him? Simond, an odd name. Tursla repeated it in a whisper
as if a name could be tasted, said to be either sweet or sour.

"Simond!"

But there was no answer. And she knew that, even if she
mounted Volt's chair again, this time there would be no answer. What she had done or tried to do here this night had
exhausted for a time her power. She had nothing to aid her
to reach out.

Walking slowly, catching now and then on some half-bro-
ken wall or pile of stones, she won out of Volt's hall. But she
needed to sit and rest several times before she got back to the
clan house.

Then it took all the skill she had to be able to make her
way through Mafra's house to her own corner. Should she tell
the Clan Mother what had been done this night? Perhaps—
but not in this hour. To rouse any of the nearby sleepers
would be the last thing she wished.

She lowered herself onto the sleeping mat. In her mind
then there was only one picture, already becoming fuzzed
with sleep—the image of Affric fighting a web about his feet,
his sneering mouth open as if he shouted aloud in fear.
Though she was not conscious of it, Tursla smiled as she fell
asleep.

4

Mist was heavy about the island where the ancient clan
houses stood, hanging curtains between house and house,
turning those who went outside into barely seen shadows
moving in and around through the fog. The moisture in it
pearled on every surface in large drops which gathered substance and then trickled downward. That same damp clung to
skin, matted hair, made clammy all garments.

Such fen mists had been known to Tursla all her life. Still
this one was far thicker than any she could remember; and it
would seem her uneasiness was matched within the clan
house for no hunters went forth, while those within stirred
higher the fires, drawing in closer for the light and heat. Perhaps they did this not for any warmth to send their garments

steaming but because the very brightness of the flames themselves had a kind of cheer.

Tursla had sought out Mafra again. But the Clan Mother appeared unwilling to talk. Rather she sat very still, her blind eyes staring unwinking at the fire and those about it, though she made no move to add herself to the circle of company there. At length Tursla's foreboding of a shadow to come made her greatly daring and she touched timidly one of Mafra's hands where it lay palm up on the woman's lap.

"Clan Mother—?"

Mafra's head did not turn, yet Tursla was sure she knew that the girl was beside her. Then she spoke, in so low a voice Tursla was sure it could not carry beyond her own ears.

"Moth-child, it comes close now—"

What—the fog? Or that other thing which Tursla felt, though she had no part of Mafra's powers.

"What may be done, Clan Mother?" The girl shifted her body restlessly.

"Nothing to stop these witless ones. Not now." There was a bitter note in that. "You cannot trust in anything or anyone save yourself, moth-child. The ill act has been begun."

At that moment there sounded, through the doorway of the clan house (like the bellow of some great beast), a call which brought Tursla and all the rest sheltering within to their feet. Never before had the girl heard such a sound.

Then the cries of those by the fire, who were now all turning to the mist-hidden doorway, running toward that, made her understand. That had been the Great Alarm, which had never been sounded in her lifetime, perhaps even in the lifetimes of all now here. Only some action of overpowering peril could have brought the sentries on the outer road to give that alert.

"Girl!" Mafra was also standing. Her hand tightened about Tursla's arm. "Give me your strength, daughter. Ill, thrice ill, has been this thing! Dark the ending thereof!"

Then she, who so seldom left her own alcove nowadays, tottered beside Tursla. At first her slight body bore heavily upon the girl's support. Then she straightened, and it appeared that strength returned to her limbs as she took one step and then another.

They came into the open but there the mist was very thick. Figures could only be half seen and that just when close by. Mafra's pressure on her arm drew Tursla in a way which it would seem the blind woman knew well.

"Where—?"

"To Volt's Hall," Mafra answered her. "They would carry this through to the end—profane the very place which is the heart of all we are, have ever been. They will slay, in the name of Volt. And, if such a slaying comes, why, then their own deaths must follow! They have decided upon their road—and evil is the end of it!"

"To stop—" Tursla got out no more than those two words when her companion interrupted her.

"Stop—yes. Girl, open now your inner thoughts, give yourself freely to what may lie within you. That is the only way! But it must be quick."

She had never believed that Mafra's strength might still be such as to send the Clan Mother at so fast a pace. There were others around them, all were heading in the same direction. The stones of the ancient road under their feet were slimed with water, yet Mafra, for all her lack of sight, made no missteps.

About them loomed the broken walls of Volt's Hall. Still on they pressed, until they were in the place of the chair. Here through some trick perhaps of emanations from the ancient stones themselves, the mist thinned, raised, to lie above their heads like a ceiling, yet allow them full sight of all which was below.

Those torches set upright in the vases to either side of the chair were ablaze. Other brands were in the hands of those standing along the walls. In Volt's chair sat Unnanna once again. Braced with a hand on either arm of the giant seat she leaned forward, an eager, avid expression on her face.

Those she so eyed were gathered immediately below. Affric stood there; but he had not the arrogant pride which he had worn so confidently when he had strode forth from this place at the Clan Mother's bidding. He was pale of countenance, and his clothing was smeared with swamp slime, while one arm was bound to his side with vine fiber, as if bones had been broken that must be straightened and protected for healing.

Seeing him so brought a picture into Tursla's mind: that of Affric unsure of foot as if he had been caught in some snare, stumbling and falling, falling against one of the upright pillars which bore Volt's own face deep carven. Her wish—dream! Had that indeed left Affric like this?

If so, she had not done all that she had wished. For between two of Affric's followers was the stranger she had seen mounted on the road, the one Mafra had named Simond.

His helm was gone, so his fair hair, near as bleached as her own, shown in the torch light. But his head rolled limply forward on his breast. It was plain his legs would not support him and he had to be kept on his feet by the help of his guards. There was a matting of blood in his hair.

"Done!" Unnanna's voice rang out, silencing the murmurs of those gathered there, producing a quiet through which the sounds of the marsh life without could be heard. "Done, well done! Here is that which shall give us new life! Did I not say it? Into our hands has Volt brought this one that we may drink of his strength and—"

Tursla did not know if she had made some signal but the guards suddenly released their hold upon Simond and he fell forward. There must have remained some spark of awareness in him, for he put out his hands, though he was on his knees, to catch at the edge of the step on which the chair stood. Now he raised his head by visible effort and lurched forward and up, for he grasped at the chair itself, and dragged himself to his feet.

The girl could not see his face. Without knowing she had done so, she broke from Mafra's side and edged along, pushing by others, seeing none of them, coming closer to where the captive stood.

"What do you want of me?" he asked as he edged around, so that he half faced the Torfolk.

Affric took a step forward and spat. His mouth was a vicious slit.

"Half-blood! We want from you what you have no right to—that part which is of Tormarsh!"

There was a sound like the far-off squall of a wak-lizard. Unnanna laughed.

"They are right, half-blood. You are part of Tor. Let that part now give us what we need." Her tongue curled over her lower lip, swept from side to side as if she licked moss-honey and savored the sweetness of that delicacy.

"We need life," she leaned closer to the arm of the chair where Simond still had his hand, using that hold to support him. "Blood is life, half-breed. By Volt's word we dare not take it from our own kind, and we cannot take from one who is full outlander, for between the twain of us there is no common heritage. You are neither one nor the other; therefore you are ripe for our purpose."

"You know of what House I am." Simond held his head high and now his eyes caught the Clan Mother's in a compelling stare. "I am the son of him who took Volt's axe—by Volt's own wishing. Do you think then that Volt will look with approval on the fate you would give me?"

"Where is the axe now?" Unnanna demanded. "Yes, Koris of Gorm took it; but is it not now gone from him? Volt's favor follows the axe. With it destroyed, he has lost interest in you."

The murmur which had begun at Simond's words died away. Tursla pushed closer. She had done as Mafra had urged, laid her mind open to whatever power lay in her. But she felt no swelling of force, no new warmth within. How then could she stop this thing which was of dark evil and which would indeed bring an end to the Torfolk?

"Take him—" Unnanna was on her feet, her arms spread wide. In her pale face there was exultation.

Tursla moved. Those about her were so intent upon the scene before them that they were not aware of her until she was through their line and had shoved past one of Affric's followers to reach Simond. Once there she stationed herself before him, facing the man moving in to obey Unnanna's order.

"Touch me if you dare," she said. "I am one Filled. And this one I take under my protection."

The nearest man had raised his hands to sweep her aside. Now he stood as rooted as one of the dead trees, while those behind him retreated a step or two. Unnanna leaned closer from her perch upon the chair.

"Take him!" She lifted her hand as if to strike Tursla in the face, so drive her away. The girl did not flinch.

"I am one Filled," she repeated.

The Clan Mother's face twisted with stark rage. "Stand aside," she hissed as might one of the pallid vipers of the deep muck. "In Volt's name, I order, stand aside! And if you are truly Filled—"

"Ask it of Mafra!" challenged the girl. "She has said it—"

"Shall it be needful then—" Mafra's voice rang out from the gathering of the Torfolk, "for a Clan Mother to state this again? Do you aver that on such a thing there can be a false swearing, Unnanna?"

The crowd stirred, fell away to form a lane. Along that Mafra advanced. She did not totter now, but walked as firmly as if she could indeed see what lay before her, bumping into no one, but keeping straight course down that open way until she, too, came to stand before the chair of Volt.

"You take much upon you, Unnanna, very much."

"You take more!" Unnanna shrilled. "Yes, once you sat here and spoke for Volt, but that day is past. Rule your own clan house as you may until the messenger of Volt comes to call you. But do not try to speak for all in this time."

"I say no more than is my right, Unnanna. If I say this house daughter is Filled, then do you deny it?"

Unnanna's mouth worked. "It is your word before Volt, then? You take on you much in that, Mafra. This one came not to the moon dancing—who then filled her?"

"Unnanna—" Mafra raised her right hand. Her fingers moved in the air as if gathering threads of mist and rolling them into a ball. In the silence which now fell between them, she made a tossing motion, as if what she had pulled out of invisibility had indeed substance. Unnanna shrank back until her shoulders touched the high back of the chair.

Suddenly she flung both hands up before her face. From behind that slight defense she sputtered words which had no meaning as far as Tursla was concerned. But that Unnanna was, for the moment, at bay, the girl understood. Turning a little she caught at Simond's arm which was closest to her.

"Come!" she ordered.

Whether they could win from Volt's Hall, and if so what she might do then, Tursla had no idea. For the moment all she could think of was to get away from this place where only the slender thread spun by custom had so far protected her.

She did not even look to Simond. But he apparently yielded to her urging, for when she stepped away from Volt's chair he did in truth come with her. Hoping that he would continue to be able to stay on his feet, Tursla led him forward.

Affric moved into their path. His good arm raised, he balanced a short stabbing spear. Tursla met his gaze squarely and moved closer to Simond. She said no word but her intention was plain. Any attack upon the stranger would be met by her. To raise a weapon against a Filled One—Affric snarled, but he gave way when she did not, just as those others made a path for her, even as they had for Mafra.

Somehow they reached the outer wards of the Hall. Tursla was breathing as fast as if she had run all the way. Where now—? They could not return to the clan houses. Not even

Mafra could hold back the weight of outraged custom long enough for Simond to escape. And the trails out from here would be speedily covered.

The trail to the pool, the sea! That flashed into her mind even as if some voice out of the mist had reminded her. For the first time she spoke to her companion:

"We dare not stay here. I do not think even Mafra can long hold Unnanna. We must go on. Can you do it?"

She had noted that he staggered though he kept his feet. Now she could only hope.

"Lady—by the Death of the Kolder—I shall try!"

So they went into the boiling of that strange, heavy mist. She could not even see beyond the length of an out-held hand before her. This was the strongest folly. If they missed the road, the step-tussocks farther on, the marsh itself might claim them and no one would ever know how they passed.

Still she walked, and brought him with her. After a space they went side by side, as she drew his arm about her shoulders, took a measure of his weight. He muttered now and then—broken words without any meaning.

They were well away from the clan-house isle when once again the deep-throated alarm trumpet of the Torfolk aroused echoes across the marsh. Now they could expect pursuit. Would this mist which enclosed them work as well to delay the hunters? She feared because such as Affric knew the outer ways of the Tormarsh far better than she.

On and on, Tursla fought a desire to hurry. For he whom she now half supported could never step up the pace. The surface of the road was still under them. She was, she realized, trusting in an inner guide which was an instinct and something she had never called upon before. Unless it was that same feeling of rightness which had led her this way when she had met Xactol under the moon. Always she listened, after the echoes of the alarm died away, for any sounds which might mean they were closely followed.

There were ploppings from swamp sloughs where small creatures, disturbed by their passing, leapt into hiding; and the hoarse cries and calls of other life. They did not move out of the mist, nor did that grow any thinner.

Time lost any measurement. From one moment to the next Tursla could only hope that they were still well ahead of any pursuers. That she had been proclaimed Filled would save her, for a space, until her false claims would be proven. But she could not hope to protect Simond.

Why did she risk all for this stranger? Tursla could not have answered that. But when she had seen him in that vision which had visited her in Volt's Hall she had known that, in some way, they were linked. It was as if some geas of power had been laid upon her; there was no avoiding what must be done.

They were nearly to the end of the pavement now. Though she could see nothing, the girl could sense that in an odd way as if the knowledge came to her by a talent which had nothing to do with sight, hearing or touch. She halted and spoke sharply to her companion, striving to bring him, by the very force of her will, out of the daze of mind in which he walked.

"Simond!" Names had power; the use of his might well awaken him to reality. "Simond!"

His head raised, turned a little so he could eye her. Like the Tormarsh men he was of a height such that they could see each other on a level. His mouth hung a little open; there was a runnel of blood from one temple clotting on his cheek. But in his eyes there was also the look of intelligence.

"We must take to the swamp itself here." She spoke slowly, pausing between words as one might do with a small child or a person gravely ill. "I cannot hold you—"

He closed his mouth and his jaw line firmed. Then he tried to nod, winced and his eyes blinked in pain.

"What I can do—that I shall," he promised.

She looked on into the mist. Folly to venture so blindly. But this mist might lie for hours. With the Torfolk aroused they had no hours; they might not even have more than the space of a dozen breaths. She had as yet heard no sounds of pursuit, for Torfolk were wily and had learned long since to move with practiced silence through their territory.

"You must come directly behind me," Tursla bit her lip. That they could do this at all she was dubious. But there was no other choice.

He drew himself straight. "Go—I'll follow," he told her quietly.

With a last glance at him the girl stepped out into the mist. That inner guide had led her aright; her foot came down on the firmness of the hassocks he could not see. She went slowly, lingering before she took each step to make sure that he saw her, though for him this blind journey must be much worse, for he did not have the same certainty which was hers.

Step by step she wove a way, trying hard to remember how

long this most perilous part of their flight must last. Still he did not call to her, and each time she turned her head she could see him well upright, safely balanced on a foothold.

Then she stumbled out on firm ground, the tenseness of her body leading to pain in her back and shoulders, a warning tremble in her legs. This was, at last, that island like a finger which marked the last part of the way to the pool. With her feet fimly planted she waited once more for him to draw close to her. When he gained that solid stretch of land he fell to his knees and his body swayed from side to side. Swiftly she knelt beside him, steadied him.

There was the sheen of sweat across his face and the clotting blood melted under that. He breathed heavily through his mouth, and his eyes, when he looked at her, were dull. He frowned as if she were difficult to see and he must expend much effort to hold her within his range of vision.

"I—am—near—done—Lady—" he gasped, word by painful word.

"There is no more. From here the footing is good. It is only a little way."

His mouth stretched in a stark shadow of a smile. "I can—crawl—if—it—not—be—too far—"

"You can walk!" she said firmly. Rising, she stooped and locked both her hands under his nearer armpit. Exerting the full of her remaining strength, Tursla indeed brought him to his feet. Then, pulling his arm once more about her shoulders, she led him on, until they were on the rocks above the silent pool encircled in sand.

Her hands fumbled first with the fastenings of her robe. She moved now in answer to her knowledge of what must be done. The answer slipped into her mind as the maker of dye might measure and add a handful of this, a counter of that, while intent on boiling some fire-cradled mixture. There was custom to be faced here also. Only by a certain ritual might that which she must summon be approached.

Tursla's robe fell about her feet. Now she stooped once more above the recumbent man, her fingers seeking buckles, the fastening of mail. His eyes opened and he looked up to her, puzzled.

"What—do—?"

"These—" She tugged at the mail where it lay across his shoulders, her other hand picking at the stuff of his breeches. "'Off—we must go where these cannot be worn."

He blinked. "One of the Old Powers?" he asked.

Tursla shrugged. "I know not of your Old Powers. But I know a little of what we can summon here. If—" She put her forefinger to her mouth and bit upon that as she considered a point which had only that moment occurred to her. This place would welcome her, had welcomed her, because she was what she was (and what in truth was she? one small part of her now asked. But the time for any such questioning was not now). Would he also be accepted? There was no way of proving that except to try.

"We must—" She made the decision firm—"do this thing. For I have no other way of escape for you."

She helped his fumbling hands with the fastenings, the clasps, and belting, until his body with the wide powerful shoulders, the long arms which marked him as of Torblood, was bare. Then she pointed to the rock from which she had leaped that other time.

"Do not tread upon the sand," she cautioned. "Not while it lays thus. We must leap from there—into the pool."

"If I can—" but he pulled himself along as she mounted the rock.

Out she leapt and down. Once more that water closed about her. But she moved swiftly away toward the farther side of the pool, clearing the spot where he should land. The she looked up as she trod water.

"Come!"

His body looked as white as the mist curling behind him. He had climbed onto the stone she had just quitted, and she saw his muscles tense. Then he stretched out his arms and dove, cleaving the water with a loud splash.

Tursla turned on her back and floated as she had before. He was no longer her charge for she had brought him to what safety her instinct told her was all they could hope for, and the pool had not repelled him.

Tursla, her eyes up to the sky which she could see through ragged patches of mist which was being tattered by the sea wind, began to sing—without words—the notes rising and falling like the call of some bird.

5

As before at her call that sand stirred. The girl could feel no wind, yet the grains of powdery stuff arose, began to twirl as she had seen them on that night. A pillar was born, now moving faster and faster, each turn making it more solid to the eye. Now came the rounding of a head, the modeling of the body below that.

Still Tursla sang her hymn without words as the vessel was formed to hold that which she summoned. She had half forgotten Simond. If he watched in astonishment he made no sound to disturb the voice spell she wove with the same certainty as her hands could follow a design upon her loom.

At last Xactol stood there. Seeing her waiting, Tursla came from the pool, standing erect on stone from which the forming of that other had swept the last minute grain of sand.

"Sand-sister—" The girl raised her arms, but did not quite embrace the other.

"Sister—" echoed the other, in her hissing, sand-sliding voice. "What is your need?" Now her hands came forth also and Tursla's lay palm down upon them, flesh meeting sand.

"There is this one." Tursla did not turn her head to look upon Simond in the water still. "He is hunted. They must not find him."

"This is your choice, sister?" inquired that other. "Think well, for from such a choice may come many things you could have reason to look upon as ills in the future."

"Ills alone, Xactol?" asked the girl slowly.

"Nothing is altogether ill, sister. But you must think of this—you are now of Tor. If you go forth there will be no return. And those of Tor are not well looked upon by the Outlanders."

"Of Tor," Tursla repeated. "Only part of me, Sand sister. Only part of me. Even as it is with him. I have the body of Tor but the—"

"Do not say it!" commanded Xactol, interrupting her sharply. "But even if it be so, Tor body may betray you. There is a spell set upon the Marsh boundaries. Torfolk cannot go forth—and live."

"And this one?"

"He is divided. He was drawn in by the spelling of Tor, for there was that in him which answered to such a call. But his outland blood will help him to win forth again. Do you try to go with him—" Now it was the woman of sand who left unfinished a warning.

"What will happen to me?"

"I do not know. This spelling is none of ours. The Outlanders have their own witcheries and their learning in such is very old and very deep. You would go at your own peril."

"I stay at even more, sand sister. You know what cloak of

safety Mafra dared to throw over me; and, in the way they understand that claim, it is false."

"The decision is yours. What now would you have of me?"

"Can you buy us time, sand sister? There are those who will trail us to the death."

"That is so. Their rage and fear reaches out even to this place. It is like the mists which they love." The woman withdrew her right hand from where it rested under Tursla's. Now she raised that so that her finger touched the girl's forehead between and just above her eyes.

"This I give you. Use it as you will," she said in a soft voice. "I must go—"

"Will I see you again?" Tursla asked.

"Not if this choice is yours, sister, this choice I read in your thoughts. My door between the worlds is here alone."

"Then I can't—" Tursla cried out.

"But you have already chosen, sister. In your spirit's innermost place that choice lies. Go with peace. Accept what may lie before you with the courage of your spirit. There is a meaning behind what has happened to you. If we don't see it now, all will be made clear in time. Do as you know how to do."

Her arms dropped to her sides and Tursla fell once more to her knees, and veiled her eyes with one hand. But the other she rested on one knee, palm up and slightly cupped.

Xactol began to turn, her spin grew ever faster. The fine sand which had formed her whirled out and away as the body became a pillar, and the pillar, in turn, sand falling to the rock. But in Tursla's hand there remained a small pile of the sand.

When the rest of that substance was once more spread out upon the rim of pool she arose, cupping her fingers tightly about what she held. Now she hailed Simond.

"You may come forth. We must go on."

Her head jerked around. There was a sound behind. The hunters may have been questing, at last they had the trail. Like Xactol, she could now sense the rage and fear which drove them. Not even her claim of being Filled would be a protection against what moved them now. She shivered. Never before had emotions other than her own been fed to her in this way. The alienness of this was frightening. But there was no time to hesitate, to learn fear fostered by that hate.

Simond came ashore. He walked more steadily, his head

was up, but his attention was not for her, rather on their back trail as if he, too, had picked up some emanation from their pursuers.

Tursla climbed the rock to where she had left her robe. She held it up in one hand and spoke:

"Can you tear from this a portion of cloth? What I carry—" she showed him the fist which grasped the sand-dust—"must be safe until we have need for it."

He caught the cloth from her and tore a portion from the mud-stained hem. Into this she emptied the sand, making a packet of it. Then she drew on her robe. But though he had breeches and boots on now, he fastened on only the leather undershirt, left his mail lying.

When he caught her attention he stirred the mail with his boot. "It will slow me. Where do we go?"

"To the sea." Already she was on her way.

The stay in the pool might have refreshed Simond's body, brought beginning healing to his wound, for he kept pace with her as she climbed and slipped among the rocks. She could hear the come and go of the waves, the wind sweeping mist and marsh air away from her.

They came to the shore. Simond looked north and then south, finally standing to face south. "That is the way for Estcarp. Let us go—"

If I can, she thought. *How strong is that spell laid upon the Torfolk? Does it rule body only, or body and spirit both? Can my spirit break a bond laid upon the body?* But she asked none of this aloud.

So they sped along the sand just beyond the reach of the waves. From behind came a shout, and a spear flashed over the wash of the water. A warning, Tursla guessed. The hunters wanted them not dead but captive. Perhaps Unnanna still would have her sacrifice.

Suddenly the girl gasped and cried out, stumbling back. It was as if she had run into a wall and rebounded, her body bruised from the force of that encounter. Simond was already several strides farther on. He whirled about at her cry and started back.

Tursla put out her hands. There was a surface there—invisible—but as tight as the stone side of her place in the clan house. She could feel its substance.

The wall the outlanders had set about the Tormarsh! It would seem that it was indeed a barrier she could not pierce.

"Come!" Simond was back at her side, apparently what

was the wall for her did not exist for him. He caught at her, tried to drag her on.

The force of his attempt again brought her hard against that barrier.

"No—I cannot! The spells of your people—" she gasped. "Go—they cannot follow you through this!"

"Not without you!" His face was grim as he stood beside her. "Try by sea. Can you swim?"

"Not well enough." She had splashed now and then in some of the marsh pools, but to entrust herself to the sea was another matter. Yet what choice had she? That heat of hate behind was warning enough of what might happen!

"Come—"

"Stand!" That shout was from behind. Affric— She did not even have to look around to know who led the hunters.

"Go—" Tursla tried to push her companion on, through that wall which was no wall for him.

"The sea!" he repeated.

But it would seem they were too late. Another spear expertly thrown, flashed between them, struck the unseen wall and rebounded. Tursla faced around, her hand going to the breast of her robe, closing upon what she had brought from the pool side.

Affric, yes, and Brunwol, and Gawan. Behind them a score of others, closing in, their eyes avid with a lust of hatred such as she had never met before. Consciously or unconsciously they were using that hatred as a weapon, beating at her; and the hurtful blows of it made her sway, sick and spirit wounded.

But Tursla still had strength enough to bring out the packet she had made. With one hand she tore that open as she balanced the fold of cloth upon the palm of the other. Now that the sand was uncovered, she raised it level with her lips and gathered a great breath to blow it outward. As it swirled she cried aloud. Not a word, for such spelling as this was not summoned by the words of this world. Rather she shaped a sound which seemed to roar, even as the alarm trumpet of the Torfolk had done.

There was no sighting the disappearance of the sand that her breath had dispersed. From the shore itself there uprose small curlings of the white grit. Those began to whirl, even as Xactol had formed her body. Higher they grew by the instant, drawing more and more of the shore's substance into them. But they remained pillars, not taking on any other form. Far taller they were now than any of those who stood there.

Affric and his men backed away a little, eyeing the pillars with the uncertainty of men who face a hitherto-unknown menace. Yet they did not retreat far, and Tursla knew well that they still held to their deadly purpose.

The top of the tallest pillar began to nod—toward the Tormen. Tursla caught at Simond's shoulder. The strength that moved the pillars was draining from her. That she could order them much longer she doubted.

"The sea!"

Had she cried that aloud, or had he read it in her mind? She was not sure. But Simond's arm was about her and he was striding toward the wash of the waves, bearing her with him.

As the waves struck against her, the water rising from knee to waist, Tursla strove still to keep her mind upon the columns of sand. But she did not turn her head to watch how effectively her energy wrought.

There was shouting there, not now aimed at the fugitives. Some of the voices were muffled or ceased abruptly. The water was high about her now. Simond, sparing no glance for what might be happening on the shore, gave an order:

"Turn on your back. Float! Leave it to me!"

She tried to do as he wanted. So far there had been no barrier. Now as she splashed she could see the shoreline again. There was a mist. No, not a mist—that must be a whirl of sand thick enough to half hide the figures struggling in it as if they could not win forth from its embrace, rather were caught fast held in the storm of grit.

Then she was on her back and Simond was swimming, towing her with him. No longer did he head out to sea, but rather altered course to parallel the shore. Tursla had held the sand, sent it raging as long as she could. She was drained now, not able to move to aid herself even if she had known how to swim.

That shouting grew louder. Then—

Force—force pushing her back, sending her under the water. She gasped, and the salt flood was in her mouth, drawn chokingly into her lungs. She fought for breath. The barrier! This was the barrier. She wanted to shout to Simond, tell him that all his efforts were useless. There was no escape for her.

No escape! Her body, her body was sealed into Tormarsh by the spells of the outlanders! No—hope—

Aroused to a frenzy by the danger of drowning, Tursla tried to get free of the hold upon her, to strike at Simond and make him let go before she was pushed completely under the water.

"—go! Let me go!" Her mind shrieked and water once more flooded into her mouth and nose.

Out of nowhere came a blow. She felt a flash of pain as it landed. Then, nothing at all.

Slowly she came back from that place of darkness. Water—she was drowning! Simond must let her go.

But there was no water. She lay on a surface which was steady, which did not swing as did the waves. And she could breathe. No water filled her nose, covered her head. For a long moment it was enough to know that she was indeed safe from being drawn under. But—

They must be back on the shore then. With her releasing of mind control the sand would have gone. Perhaps Affric was—

Tursla opened her eyes. Above her the sky arched—clear except for a drifting cloud or two. There was no hint of the Tormarsh mist about. She raised her head—though that small action seemed very hard—she was weak, drained.

Sand, white, marked with the ripples of waves which curled in, drained away again. And rocks. And the sea. But no Affric, no Torman standing over her. She was— Tursla sat up, bracing herself by her hands.

Her wet robe was plastered thick with sand. She could even taste the grit between her teeth. There was no one—no one at all. Yet a few moments of study showed her that this was not that tongue of beach to which the Tormarsh reached.

She inched around to face inland. To her left now, a goodly distance away, rising into the air as if a hundred—no, a thousand fires burned (for it stretched along there inland as far as she could see) the mists of the marsh arose like smoke, cloaking well what might lie on the other side.

They had passed the barrier! This was the Outland.

Tursla wavered to her knees, striving to see more of this unknown world. The sand of the beach stretched for a space. Then there was a sparse growth of tough grass; beyond that, bushes. But there was no smell of the swamp.

Where was Simond?

Her loneliness, which had been good when she feared Affric and the others, now was a source of uneasiness. Where had he gone—and why?

His desertion, for her, was frightening. Was it that she was of the Torfolk? Could it be that the Outlanders' hatred for the marsh dwellers was so great, that having saved her life, he felt he had paid any debts between them and had wished no more of her company?

Bleakly Tursla settled on that fact. Perhaps in the Outlands Koris himself hated his Tor blood and his son had been raised to find it a matter of shame. Just as a Torman might, in turn, look upon half Outland blood as something to lessen him among his fellows.

She was Tor—as much as Simond knew. And as Tor—

Tursla supported her head upon her hands and tried to think. It might well be that, having made one of those decisions she had been told to consider seriously, she had cut herself totally adrift from all people now. Xactol had warned her fairly. When she left the country of the pool she would no longer have communication with that one mind?—spirit?—entity?—who could understand what she was.

Mafra—for the first time Tursla wondered, with a little catch of breath, how had it gone with the Clan Mother who had faced Unnanna and worked some magic of her own to cover their escape; though what manner of Torfolk would dare to raise either hand or voice against Mafra? The girl wished passionately at that moment that she could reverse all that had happened to her, be once more in the clan house—as it had been on the night before she had gone to keep her meeting with the sand-sister.

To look back, Tursla shook her head, that was only a waste of effort. No man or woman might ever turn again and decide upon some other path once their feet were firm set on one of their choice. She had made her decision, now by that she must live—or perhaps die.

Bleakly she looked landward. The sea was empty and she expected no help to arise out of that. Now she was hungry. Already the sun was well down in the western sky. She had not even a knife at her belt; and who knew what manner of danger might prowl the Outland at the coming of true darkness?

But if she tried to go hence it must be on hands and knees. When she attempted to rise to her feet she found herself so weak and giddy that she tottered and fell. Hunger and thirst—both were an emptiness crying to be filled.

Filled! At least now the clan would never discover her deception. If she had been filled with something else as Mafra had averred, what *was* it?

She brought her knees up against her breast, put her arms about them, huddling in upon herself, for the wind was growing colder and had a bite to it which the winds of Tormarsh never held. Now she tried to think. What was good fortune for her now? What was ill? The latter seemed a longer list. But the good—she had escaped Affric and the rest— the anger of the Torfolk which would have been dire when they discovered she would bring forth no child to swell their dwindling numbers. She had certain knowledge which she as yet did not know how to use, that which Xactol had granted her.

But if the sand-sister was forever barred from her, when and how could she ever learn?

And where might she go for shelter? Where was there food? Water? Would the hands of all dwellers in this land be raised against her when they knew her for Tor?

She—

"Holla!"

Tursla's head came up instantly.

There was a mounted man—riding through the inland brush! His head—bare head—Simond! Somehow she wobbled to her feet, called out in return though her voice sounded very thin and weak in answer to that shout of his:

"Simond!"

Now, it was as if something tight and hurting inside her had suddenly broken apart. She wavered to her feet, staggered, one foot before the other. She was not alone! He had not left her here!

The horse was coming at a trot. She could sight a second animal following; Simond had it on lead. He came in a shower of sand sent up by the pounding feet of his mount. Then he was out of the saddle and to her, his arms around her.

Tursla could only repeat his name in a witless fashion, letting him take the weight of her worn out and aching body.

"Simond! Simond!"

"It is well. All is well." He held her steady, letting the very fact that he was there, that she was not alone, seep into her mind and bring her peace.

"I had to go," he told her. "We needed horses. There is a watchtower only a little away. I came back as soon as I could."

Now she gained a measure of control.

"Simond." She made herself look directly into his eyes, sure that he would in no way try to soothe her with any false promise. "Simond, I am of Tormarsh. I do not know how you brought me past that spell your people used as a barrier to keep us from the Outland. But I remain Tor. Will your people give me any welcome?"

His hands now cupped her face, and his eyes did not shift.

"Tor chose to stand our enemy, but in return we have never sought that enmity. Also, I am partly Tor. And Koris has made Torblood a blessing not a curse in Estcarp, as all men know. He held the Axe of Volt which would come only to him. And he intended that Estcarp not be meat for those who were worse than any winter wolf! Tor holds no stigma here."

Then he laughed, and the lightness of his smile made his whole face different.

"This is an odd thing. You know my name, but I do not know yours. Will you trust me with that much to show your belief in my good will?"

She found that her face, sticky with sea water and rough with sand, stretched an answering smile.

"I am Tursla of— No, I am no longer of any clan house. Just what I am now—or whom—that I must learn."

"It will not be hard that learning. There will be those to help," he promised her.

Tursla's smile grew wider. "That I do not doubt," she replied with conviction.

FALCON BLOOD

Tanree sucked at the torn ends of her fingers, tasted the sea salt stinging them. Her hair hung in sticky loops across her sand-abraded face, too heavy with sea water to stir in the wind.

For the moment it was enough that she had won out of the waves, was alive. Sea was life for the Sulcar, yes, but it could also be death. In spite of the trained resignation of her people, other forces within her had kept her fighting ashore.

Gulls screamed overhead, sharp, piercing cries. So frantic those cries Tanree looked up into the gray sky of the after storm. The birds were under attack. Wider dark wings spread away from a body on the breast of which a white vee of feathers set an unmistakable seal. A falcon soared, swooped, clutched in cruel talons one of the gulls, bearing its prey to the top of the cliff, where it perched still within sight.

It ate, tearing flesh with a vicious beak. Cords flailed from its feet, the sign of its service.

Falcon. The girl spat gritty sand from between her teeth, her hands resting on scraped knees barely covered by her undersmock. She had thrown aside kilt, all other clothing, when she had dived from the ship pounding against a foam-crowned reef.

The ship!

She got to her feet, stared seaward. Storm anger still drove waves high. Broken-backed upon rock fangs hung the *Kast-Boar*. Her masts were but jaggered stumps. Even as Tanree watched, the waters raised the ship once more, to slam her down on the reef. She was breaking apart fast.

Tanree shuddered, looked along the scrap of narrow beach. Who else had won to shore? The Sulcar were sea born and bred; surely she could not be the only survivor.

Wedged between two rocks so that the retreating waves could not drag him back, a man lay face down. Tanree raised her broken-nailed, scraped fingers and made the Sign of Wottin, uttering the age-old plea:

95

> "*Wind and wave,*
> *Mother Sea,*
> *Lead us home.*
> *Far the harbor,*
> *Wild thy waves—*
> *Still, by thy Power,*
> *Sulcar saved!*"

Had the man moved then? Or was it only the water washing about him which had made it seem so?

He was—This was no Sulcar crewman! His body was covered from neck to mid thigh by leather, dark breeches twisted with seaweed on his legs.

"Falconer!"

She spat again with salt-scoured lips. Though the Falconers had an old pact with her people, sailed on Sulcar ships as marines, they had always been a race apart—dour, silent men who kept to themselves. Good in battle, yes, so much one must grant them. But who really knew the thoughts in their heads, always hidden by their bird-shaped helms? Though this one appeared to have shucked all his fighting gear, to appear oddly naked.

There came a sharp scream. The falcon, full fed, now beat its way down to the body. There the bird settled on the sand just beyond the reach of the waves, squatted crying as if to arouse its master.

Tanree sighed. She knew what she must do. Trudging across the sand she started for the man. Now the falcon screamed again, its whole body expressing defiance. The girl halted, eyed the bird warily. These creatures were trained to attack in battle, to go for the eyes or the exposed face of an enemy. They were very much a part of the armament of their masters.

She spoke aloud as she might to one of her own kind: "No harm to your master, flying one." She held out sore hands in the oldest peace gesture.

Those bird eyes were small reddish coals, fast upon her. Tanree had an odd flash of feeling that this one had more understanding than other birds possessed. It ceased to scream, but the eyes continued to stare, sparks of menace, as she edged around it to stand beside the unconscious man.

Tanree was no weakling. As all her race she stood tall and strong, able to lift and carry, to haul on sail lines, or move cargo, should an extra hand be needed. Sulcarfolk lived aboard their ships and both sexes were trained alike to that service.

Now she stooped and set hands in the armpits of the mercenary, pulling him farther inland, and then rolling him over so he lay face up under the sky.

Though they had shipped a dozen Falconers on this last voyage (since the *Kast-Boar* intended to strike south into waters reputed to give sea room to the shark boats of outlaws) Tanree could not have told one of the bird fighters from another. They wore their masking helms constantly and kept to themselves, only their leader speaking when necessary to the ship people.

The face of the man was encrusted with sand, but he was breathing, as the slight rise and fall of his breast under the soaked leather testified. She brushed grit away from his nostrils, his thin-lipped mouth. There were deep frown lines between his sand-dusted brows, a mask-like sternness in his face.

Tanree sat back on her heels. What did she know about this fellow survivor? First of all, the Falconers lived by harsh and narrow laws no other race would accept. Where their original home had been no outsider knew. Generations ago something had set them wandering, and then the tie with her own people had been formed. For the Falconers had wanted passage out of the south from a land only Sulcar ships touched.

They had sought ship room for all of them, perhaps some two thousand—two-thirds of those fighting men, each with a trained hawk. But it was their custom which made them utterly strange. For, though they had women and children with them, yet there was no clan or family feeling. To Falconers women were born for only one purpose: to bear children. They were made to live in villages apart, visited once a year by men selected by their officers. Such temporary unions were the only meetings between the sexes.

First they had gone to Estcarp, learning that the ancient land was hemmed in by enemies. But there had been an unbreachable barrier to their taking service there.

For in ancient Estcarp the Witches ruled, and to them a race who so degraded their females was cursed. Thus the Falconers had made their way into the no-man's-land of the southern mountains, building there their aerie on the border between Estcarp and Karsten. They had fought shoulder to shoulder with the Borderers of Estcarp in the great war. But

when, at last, a near exhausted Estcarp had faced the overpowering might of Karsten, and the Witches concentrated all
their power (many of them dying from it) to change the
earth itself, the Falconers, warned in time, had reluctantly returned to the lowlands.

Their numbers were few by then, and the men took service
as fighters where they could. For at the end of the great war,
chaos and anarchy followed. Some men, nurtured all their
lives on fighting, became outlaws; so that, though in Estcarp
itself some measure of order prevailed, much of the rest of
the continent was beset.

Tanree thought that this Falconer, lacking helm, mail shirt,
weapons, resembled any man of the Old Race. His dark hair
looked black beneath the clinging sand, his skin was paler
than her own sun-browned flesh. He had a sharp nose, rather
like the jutting beak of his bird, and his eyes were green. For
now they had opened to stare at her. His frown grew more
forbidding.

He tried to sit up, fell back, his mouth twisting in pain.
Tanree was no reader of thoughts, but she was sure his
weakness before her was like a lash laid across his face.

Once more he attempted to lever himself up, away from
her. Tanree saw one arm lay limp. She moved closer, sure of
a broken bone.

"No! You—you female!" There was such a note of loath-
ing in his voice that anger flared in her in answer.

"As you wish—" She stood up, deliberately turned her
back on him, moving away along the narrow beach, half encircled by cliff and walls of water-torn, weed-festooned rocks.

Here was the usual storm bounty brought ashore, wood—
some new torn from the *Kast-Boar*, some the wrack of earlier
storms. She made herself concentrate on finding anything
which might be of use.

Where they might now be in relation to the lands she
knew, Tanree had no idea. They had been beaten so far
south by the storm that surely they were no longer within the
boundaries of Karsten. And the unknown, in these days, was
enough to make one wary.

There was a glint in a half ball of weed. Tanree leaped to
jerk that away just as the waves strove to carry it off. A
knife—no, longer than just a knife—by some freak driven
point deep into a hunk of splintered wood. She had to exert
some strength to pull it out. No rust spotted the ten-inch
blade yet.

Such a piece of good fortune! She sat her jaw firmly and faced around, striding back to the Falconer. He had flung his sound arm across his eyes as if to shut out the world. Beside him crouched the bird uttering small guttural cries. Tanree stood over them both, knife in hand.

"Listen," she said coldly. It was not in her to desert a helpless man no matter how he might spurn her aid. "Listen, Falconer, think of me as you will. I offer no friendship cup to you either. But the sea has spat us out, therefore this is not our hour to seek the Final Gate. We cannot throw away our lives heedlessly. That being so—" she knelt by him, reaching out also for a straight piece of drift lying near, "you will accept from me the aid of what healcraft I know. Which," she admitted frankly, "is not much."

He did not move that arm hiding his eyes. But neither did he try now to evade as she slashed open the sleeve of his tunic and the padded lining beneath to bare his arm. There was no gentleness in this—to prolong handling would only cause greater pain. He uttered no sound as she set the break (thank the Power it was a simple one) and lashed his forearm against the wood with strips slashed from his own clothing. Only when she had finished did he look to her.

"How bad?"

"A clean break," she assured him. "But—" she frowned at the cliff, "how you can climb from here one-handed—"

He struggled to sit up; she knew better than to offer support. With his good arm as a brace, he was high enough to gaze at the cliff and then the sea. He shrugged.

"No matter—"

"It matters!" Tanree flared. She could not yet see a way out of this pocket, not for them both. But she would not surrender to imprisonment by rock or wave.

She fingered the dagger-knife and turned once more to examine the cliffs. To venture back into the water would only sweep them against the reef. But the surface of the wall behind them was pitted and worn enough to offer toe and hand holds. She paced along the short beach, inspecting that surface. Sulcarfolk had good heads for heights, and the Falconers were mountaineers. It was a pity this one could not sprout wings like his comrade in arms.

Wings! She tapped her teeth with the point of the knife. An idea flitted to her mind and she pinned it fast.

Now she returned to the man quickly.

"This bird of yours—" she pointed to the red-eyed hawk at his shoulder, "what powers does it have?"

"Powers!" he repeated and for the first time showed surprise. "What do you mean?"

She was impatient. "They *have* powers; all know that. Are they not your eyes and ears, scouts for you? What else can they do beside that, and fight in battle?"

"What have you in mind?" he countered.

"There are spires of rock up there." Tanree indicated the top of the cliff. "Your bird has already been aloft. I saw him kill a gull and feast upon it while above."

"So there are rock spires and—"

"Just this, bird warrior," she dropped on her heels again. "No rope can be tougher than loops of some of this weed. If you had the aid of a rope to steady you, could you climb?"

He looked at her for an instant as if she had lost even that small store of wit his people credited to females. Then his eyes narrowed as he gazed once more, measuringly, at the cliff.

"I would not have to ask that of any of *my* clan," she told him deliberately. "Such a feat would be play as our children delight in."

The red stain of anger arose on his pale face.

"How would you get the rope up there?" He had not lashed out in fury to answer her taunt as she had half expected.

"If your bird can carry up a finer strand, loop that about one of the spires there, then a thicker rope can be drawn in its wake and that double rope looped for your ladder. I would climb and do it myself, but we must go together since you have the use of but one hand."

She thought he might refuse. But instead he turned his head and uttered a crooning sound to the bird.

"We can but try," he said a moment later.

The seaweed yielded to her knife and, though he could use but the one hand, the Falconer helped twist and hold strands to her order as she fashioned her ropes. At last she had the first thin cord, one end safe knotted to a heavier one, the other in her hands.

Again the Falconer made his bird sounds and the hawk seized upon the thin cord at near midpoint. With swift, sure beat of wings it soared up, as Tanree played out the cord swiftly hoping she had judged the length aright.

Now the bird spiraled down and the cord was suddenly

loose in Tanree's grasp. Slowly and steadily she began to pull, bring upward from the sand the heavier strand to dangle along the cliff wall.

One moment at a time, think only that, Tanree warned herself as they began their ordeal. The heavier part of the rope was twisted around her companion, made as fast as she could set it. His right arm was splinted, but his fingers were as swift to seek out holds as hers. He had kicked off his boots and slung those about his neck, leaving his toes bare.

Tanree made her way beside him, within touching distance, one glance for the cliff face, a second for the man. They were aided unexpectedly when they came upon a ledge, not to be seen from below. There they crouched together, breathing heavily. Tanree estimated they had covered two thirds of their journey but the Falconer's face was wet with sweat and trickled down, to drip from his chin.

"Let us get to it!" he broke the silence between them, inching up to his feet again, his sound arm a brace against the wall.

"Wait!"

Tanree drew away, was already climbing, "Let me get aloft now. And do you keep well hold of the rope."

He protested but she did not listen, any more than she paid attention to the pain in her fingers. But, when she pulled herself over the lip of the height, she lay for a moment, her breath coming in deep, rib-shaking sobs. She wanted to do no more than lie where she was, for it seemed that strength drained steadily from her as blood flowing from an open wound.

Instead she got to her knees and crawled to that outcrop of higher rock around which the noose of the weed rope strained and frayed. She set her teeth grimly, laid hold of the taut strand they had woven. Then she called, her voice sounding in her own ears as high as the scream of the hawk that now hovered overhead.

"Come!"

She drew upon the rope with muscles tested and trained to handle ships' cordage, felt a responding jerk. He was indeed climbing. Bit by bit the rope passed between her torn palms.

Then she saw his hand rise, grope inward over the cliff edge. Tanree made a last great effort, heaving with a reviving force she had not believed she could summon, falling backward, but still keeping a grasp on the rope.

The girl was dizzy and spent, aware only for a moment or

two that the rope was loose in her hands. Had—had he fallen? Tanree smeared the back of her fist across her eyes to clear them from a mist.

No, he lay head pointing toward her, though his feet still projected over the cliff. He must be drawn away from that, even as she had brought him earlier out of the grasp of the sea. Only now she could not summon up the strength to move.

Once more the falcon descended, to perch beside its master's head. Three times it screamed harshly. He was moving, drawing himself along on his belly away from the danger point, by himself.

Seeing that, Tanree clawed her way to her feet, leaning back against one of the rocky spires, needing its support. For it seemed that the rock under her feet was like the deck of the *Kast-Boar*, rising and falling, so she needs must summon sea legs to deal with its swing.

On crawled the Falconer. Then, he, too, used his good arm for a brace and raised himself, his head coming high enough to look around. That he was valiantly fighting to get to his feet she was sure. A second later his eyes went wide as they swept past her to rest upon something at her own back.

Tanree's hand curved about the hilt of the dagger. She pushed against the rock which had supported her, but she could not stand away from it as yet.

Then she, too, saw—

These spires and outcrops of rock were not the work of nature after all. Stones were purposefully piled upon huge stones. There were archways, farther back what looked like an intact wall—somber, without a break until, farther above her head than the cliff had earlier reached, there showed openings, thin and narrow such as a giant axe might have cleft. They had climbed into some ruin.

A thrust of ice chill struck Tanree. The world she had known had many such ancient places and most were ill-omened, perilous for travelers. This was an old, old land and there had been countless races rise to rule and disappear once more into dust. Not all of those peoples had been human, as Tanree reckoned it. The Sulcar knew many such remains, and wisely avoided them—unless fortified by some power spell set by a Wise One.

"Salzarat!"

The surprise on the Falconer's face had become something else as Tanree turned her head to stare. What was that faint expression? Awe—or fear? But that he knew this place, she had no doubt.

He made an effort, pulling himself up to his feet, though he clung for support to a jumble of blocks even as she did.

"Salzarat—" His voice was the hiss of a warning serpent, or that of a disturbed war bird.

Once more Tanree glanced from him to the ruins. Perhaps a lighting of the leaden clouds overhead was revealing. She saw—saw enough to make her gasp.

That farther wall, the one which appeared more intact, took on new contours. She could trace—

Was it illusion, or some cunning art practiced by the unknowns who had laid those stones? There was no wall; it was the head of a giant falcon, the fierce eyes marked by slitted holes above an out-thrust beak.

While the beak—

That closed on a mass which was too worn to do more than hint that it might once have been intended to represent a man.

The more Tanree studied the stone head, the plainer it grew. It was reaching out—out—ready to drop the prey it had already taken, to snap at her. . . .

"No!" Had she shouted that aloud or was the denial only in her mind? Those were stones (artfully fitted together, to be sure) but still only old, old stones. She shut her eyes, held them firmly shut, and then, after a few deep breaths, opened them again. No head, only stones.

But in those moments while she had fought to defeat illusion her companion had lurched forward. He pulled himself from one outcrop of ruin to the next and his Falcon had settled on his shoulder, though he did not appear aware of the weight of the bird. There was bemusement on his face, smoothing away his habitual frown. He was like a man ensorcelled, and Tanree drew away from him as he staggered past her, his gaze only for the wall.

Stones only, she continued to tell herself firmly. There was no reason for her to remain here. Shelter, food (she realized then that hunger did bite at her), what they needed to keep life in them could only lie in this land. Purposefully she followed the Falconer, but she carried her blade ready in her hand.

He stumbled along until he was under the overhang of that giant beak. The shadow of whatever it held fell on him. Now he halted, drew himself up as a man might face his officer on some occasion of import—or—a priest might begin a rite.

His voice rang out hollowly among the ruins, repeating words—or sounds (for some held the tones of those he had used in addressing his hawk). They came as wild beating cadence. Tanree shivered. She had a queer feeling that he might just be answered—by whom—or *what?*

Up near to the range of a falcon's cry rose his voice. Now the bird on his shoulder took wing. It screamed its own challenge, or greeting—so that man-voice and bird-voice mingled until Tanree could not distinguish one from the other.

Both fell into silence; once more the Falconer was moving on. He walked more steadily, not reaching out for any support, as if new strength had filled him. Passing under the beak he was—gone!

Tanree pressed one fist against her teeth. There was no doorway there! Her eyes could not deceive her that much. She wanted to run, anywhere, but as she looked wildly about her she perceived that the ruins funneled forward toward that one place and there only led the path.

This was a path of the Old Ones; evil lurked here. She could feel the crawl of it as if a slug passed, befouling her skin. Only—Tanree's chin came up, her jaw set stubbornly. She was Sulcar. If there were no other road, then this one she would take.

Forward she went, forcing herself to walk with confidence, though she was ever alert. Now the shadow of the beak enveloped her, and, though there was no warmth of sunlight to be shut out, still she was chilled.

Also—there *was* a door. Some trick of the stone setting and the beak shadow had concealed it from sight until one was near touching distance. With a deep breath which was more than half protest against her own action, Tanree advanced.

Through darkness within, she could see a gray of light. This wall must be thick enough to provide not just a door or gate but a tunnel way. And she could see movement between her and that light; the Falconer.

She quickened step so that she was only a little behind him when they came out in what was a mighty courtyard. Walls towered all about, but it was what was within the courtyard itself which stopped Tanree near in mid-step.

Men! Horses!

Then she saw the breakage, here a headless body, there

only the shards of a mount. They had been painted once and the color in some way had sunk far into the substance which formed them, for it remained, if faded.

The motionless company was drawn up in good order, all facing to her left. Men stood, the reins of their mounts in their hands, and on the forks of their saddles falcons perched. A regiment of fighting men awaiting orders.

Her companion skirted that array of the ancient soldiers, almost as if he had not seen them, or, if he had, they were of no matter. He headed in the direction toward which they faced.

There were two wide steps there, and beyond the cavern of another door, wide as a monster mouth ready to suck them in. Up one step he pulled, now the second. . . . He *knew* what lay beyond; this was Falconer past, not of her people. But Tanree could not remain behind. She studied the faces of the warriors as she passed by. They each held their masking helm upon one hip as if it were needful to bare their faces, as they did not generally do. So she noted that each of the company differed from his fellows in some degree, though they were all plainly of the same race. These had been modeled from life.

As she came also into the doorway, Tanree heard again the mingled call of bird and man. At least the two she followed were still unharmed, though her sense of lurking evil was strong.

What lay beyond the door was a dim twilight. She stood at the end of a great hall, stretching into shadows right and left. Nor was the chamber empty. Rather here were more statues; and some were robed and coiffed. Women! Women in an Aerie? She studied the nearest to make sure.

The weathering which had eroded that company in the courtyard had not done any damage here. Dust lay heavy on the shoulders of the life-size image to be sure, but that was all. The face was frozen into immobility. But the expression. Sly exultation, an avid . . . hunger? Those eyes staring straight ahead, did they indeed hold a spark of knowledge deep within?

Tanree pushed aside imagination. These were not alive. But their faces—she looked to another, studied a third—all held that gloating, that hunger-about-to-be-assuaged; while the male images were as blank of any emotion as if they had never been meant to suggest life at all.

The Falconer had already reached the other end of the

hall. Now he was silent, facing a dais on which were four figures. These were not in solemn array, rather frozen into a
tableau of action. Deadly action, Tanree saw as she trotted
forward, puffs of dust rising from the floor underfoot.

A man sat, or rather sprawled, in a throne-chair. His head
had fallen forward, and both hands were clenched on the hilt
of a dagger driven into him at heart level. Another and
younger man lunged, sword in his hand, aiming at the image
of a woman who cowered away, such an expression of rage
and hate intermingled on her features as made Tanree shiver.

But the fourth of that company stood a little apart, no fear
to be read on *her* countenance. Her robe was plainer than
that of the other woman, with no glint of jewels at wrist,
throat or waist. Her unbound hair fell over her shoulders,
cascading down, nearly sweeping the floor.

In spite of the twilight here that wealth of hair appeared to
gleam. Her eyes—they, too, were dark red—unhuman, knowing, exulting, cruel—alive!

Tanree found she could not turn her gaze from those eyes.

Perhaps she cried out then, or perhaps only some inner defense quailed in answer to invasion. Snake-like, slug-like, it
crawled, oozed into her mind, forging a link between them.

This was no stone image, man-wrought. Tanree swayed
against the pull of that which gnawed and plucked, seeking to
control her.

"She-devil!" The Falconer spat, the bead of moisture striking the breast of the red-haired woman. Tanree almost expected to see the other turn her attention to the man whose
face was twisted with half-insane rage. But his cry had weakened the spell laid upon her. She was now able to look away
from the compelling eyes.

The Falconer swung around. His good hand closed upon
the sword which the image of the young man held. He jerked
at that impotently. There was a curious wavering, as if the
chamber and all in it were but part of a wind-riffled painted
banner.

"Kill!"

Tanree herself wavered under that command in her mind.
Kill this one who would dare threaten *her*, Jonkara, Opener
of Gates, Commander of Shadows.

Rage took fire. Through the blaze she marched, knowing
what must be done to this man who dared to challenge. She
was the hand of Jonkara, a tool of force.

Deep within Tanree something else stirred, could not be totally battered into submission.

I am a weapon to serve. I am—

"I am *Tanree*" cried that other part of her. "This is no quarrel of mine. I am Sulcar, of the seas—of another blood and breed!"

She blinked and that insane rippling ceased for an instant of clear sight. The Falconer still struggled to gain the sword.

"Now!" Once more that wave of compulsion beat against her, heart high, as might a shore wave. "Now—slay! Blood—give me blood that I may live again. We are women. Nay, *you* shall be more than woman when this blood flows and my door is opened by it. Kill—strike behind the shoulder. Or, better still, draw your steel across his throat. He is but a man! He is the enemy—kill!"

Tanree swayed, her body might be answering to the flow of a current. Without her will her hand arose, blade ready, the distance between her and the Falconer closed. She could easily do this, blood would indeed flow. Jonkara would be free of the bonds laid upon her by the meddling of fools.

"Strike!"

Tanree saw her hand move. Then that other will within her flared for a last valiant effort.

"I am Tanree!" A feeble cry against a potent spell. "There is no power here before whom Sulcar bows!"

The Falconer whirled, looked to her. No fear in his eyes, only cold hate. The bird on his shoulder spread wings, screamed. Tanree could not be sure—was there indeed a curl of red about its feet, anchoring it to its human perch?

"She-devil!" He flung at her. Abandoning his fight for the sword, he raised his hand as if to strike Tanree across the face. Out of the air came a curl of tenuous red, to catch about his upraised wrist, so even though he fought furiously, he was held prisoner.

"Strike quickly!" The demand came with mind-bruising force.

"I do not kill!" Finger by finger Tanree forced her hand to open. The blade fell, to clang on the stone floor.

"*Fool!*" The power sent swift punishing pain into her head. Crying out, Tanree staggered. Her outflung hand fell upon that same sword the Falconer had sought to loosen. It turned, came into her hold swiftly and easily.

"Kill!"

That current of hate and power filled her. Her flesh

tingled, there was heat within her as if she blazed like an oil-dipped feast torch.

"Kill!"

She could not control the stone sword. Both of her hands closed about its cold hilt. She raised it. The man before her did not move or seek in any way to dodge the threat she offered. Only his eyes were alive now—no fear in them, only a hate as hot as what filled her.

Fight—she must fight as she had the waves of the storm-lashed sea. She was herself, Tanree—Sulcar—no tool for something evil which should long since have gone into the Middle Dark.

"Kill!"

With the greatest effort she made her body move, drawing upon that will within her which the other could not master. The sword fell.

Stone struck stone—or was that true? Once more the air rippled; life overrode ancient death for a fraction of time between two beats of the heart, two breaths. The sword had jarred against Jonkara.

"Fool—" a fading cry.

There was no sword hilt in her hands, only powder sifting between her fingers. And no sparks of life in those red eyes either. From where the stone sword had struck full on the image's shoulder cracks opened. The figure crumbled, fell. Nor did what Jonkara had been vanish alone. All those others were breaking too, becoming dust which set Tanree coughing, raising her hands to protect her eyes.

Evil had ebbed. The chamber was cold, empty of what had waited here. A hand caught her shoulder, pulling at her.

"Out!" This voice was human. "Out—Salzarat falls!"

Rubbing at her smarting eyes, Tanree allowed him to lead her. There were crashing sounds, a rumbling. She cringed as a huge block landed nearby. They fled, dodging and twisting. Until at last they were under the open sky, still coughing, tears streaming from their eyes, their faces smeared with gray grit.

Fresh wind, carrying with it the clean savor of the sea, lapped about them. Tanree crouched on a mat of dead grass through which the first green spears of spring pushed. So close to her that their shoulders touched, was the Falconer. His bird was gone.

They shared a small rise Tanree did not remember climbing. What lay below, between them and the sea cliff's edge, was a tumble of stone so shattered no one now could define wall or passage. Her companion turned his head to look directly into her face. His expression was one of wonder.

"It is all gone! The curse is gone. So she is beaten at last! But you are a woman, and Jonkara could always work her will through any woman—that was her power and our undoing. She held every woman within her grasp. Knowing that, we raised what defenses we could. For we could never trust those who might again open Jonkara's dread door. Why in truth did you not slay me? My blood would have freed her, and she would have given you a measure of her power—as always she had done."

"She was no one to command *me*!" Tanree's self-confidence returned with every breath she drew. "I am Sulcar, not one of your women. "So—this Jonkara—she was why you hate and fear women?"

"Perhaps. She ruled us so. Her curse held us until the death of Langward, who dying, as you saw, from the steel of his own Queen, somehow freed a portion of us. He had been seeking long for a key to imprison Jonkara. He succeeded in part. Those of us still free fled, so our legends say, making sure no woman would ever again hold us in bond."

He rubbed his hands across his face, streaking the dust of vanished Salzarat.

"This is an old land. I think though that none walk it now. We must remain here—unless your people come seeking you. So upon us the shadow of another curse falls."

Tanree shrugged. "I am Sulcar but there was none left to call me clan sister. I worked on the *Kast-Boar* without kintie. There will be no one to come hunting because of me." She stood up, her hands resting on her hips, and turned her back deliberately upon the sea.

"Falconer, if we be cursed, then that we live with. And, while one lives, the future may still hold much, both good and ill. We need only face squarely what comes."

There was a scream from the sky above them. The clouds parted, and through weak sunlight wheeled the falcon. Tanree threw back her head to watch it.

"This is your land, as the sea is mine. What make you of it, Falconer?"

He also got to his feet. "My name is Rivery. And your words have merit. It is a time for curses to slink back into shadows, allowing us to walk in the light, to see what lies ahead."

Shoulder to shoulder they went down from the hillock, the falcon swooping and soaring above their heads.

LEGACY FROM SORN FEN

By the western wall of Klavenport on the Sea of Autumn Mists—but you do not want a bard's beginning to my tale, Goodmen? Well enough, I have no speak-harp to twang at all the proper times. And this is not altogether a tale for lords-in-their-halls. Though the beginning did lie in Klavenport right enough.

It began with one Higbold. It was after the Invaders' War and those were times when small men, if they had their wits sharpened, could rise in the world—swiftly, if fortune favored them. Which is a bard's way of saying they knew when to use the knife point, when to swear falsely, when to put hands on what was not rightfully theirs.

Higbold had his rats running to his whistle, and then his hounds to his horn. Finally no one spoke (save behind a shielding hand, glancing now and then over his shoulder) about his beginnings. He settled in the Gate Keep of Klavenport, took command there, married a wife who was hall-born. (There were such to be given to landless and shieldless men then, their kin so harried by war, or dead in it, that they went gladly to any one who offered a roof over their heads, meat in the dish and mead in the cup before them). Higbold's lady was no more nor less than her sisters in following expediency

Save that from the harsh days before her marriage she held memories. Perhaps it was those which made her face down Higbold himself in offering charity to those begging from door to door.

Among those came Caleb. He lacked an eye and walked with a lurch which nigh spilled him sprawling every time he took a full stride. What age he was no one could say; cruel mauling puts years on a man.

It might have been that the Lady Isbel knew him from the old days, but if so neither spoke of that. He became one of the household, working mainly in the small walled garden. They say that he was one with the power of growing things, that herbs stood straight and sweet-smelling for him, flowers bloomed richly under his tending.

111

Higbold had nothing to interest him in the garden. Save that now and then he met someone there where they could stand well in the open, walls too often having ears. For Higbold's ambition did not end in the keepership of the Klavenport Gate. Ah, no, such a man's ambition never ceases to grow. But you can gain only so much by showing a doubled fist or a bared sword. After a certain point you must accomplish your means more subtly, by influencing men's minds, not enslaving their bodies. Higbold studied well.

What was said and done in the garden one night in early midsummer was never known. But Higbold had a witness he did not learn about until too late. Servants gossip as always about their masters, and there is a rumor that Caleb went to the Lady Isbel to talk privately. Then he took his small bundle of worldly goods and went forth, not only from the gate keep, but out of Klavenport as well, heading west on the highway.

Near the port there had been repairing, rebuilding, and the marks of the Invaders' War had faded from the land. But Caleb did not keep long to the highway. He was a prudent man, and knew that roads made for swift travel can lead hunters on a man's tracks.

Cross-country was hard, doubly so for his twisted body. He came to the fringes of the Fen of Sorn. Ah, I see you shake your heads and draw faces at that! Rightly do you so, Goodmen, rightly. We all know that there are parts of High Hallack which belong to the Old Ones, where men with sense in their thick skulls do not walk.

But it was there Caleb found that others had been before him. They were herdsmen who had been driving the wild hill cattle (those which ranged free during the war) to market. Something had frightened the beasts and sent them running. Now the herders, half-mad with the thought of losing all reward of their hard labor, tracked them into the fen.

However, in so doing, they came upon something else. No, I shall not try to describe what they startled out of its lair. You all know that there are secrets upon secrets in places like the fen. Enough to say that this had the appearance of a woman, enough to incite the lust of the drovers who had been kept long from the lifting of any skirt. Having cornered the creature, they were having their sport.

Caleb had not left Klavenport unarmed. In spite of his twisted body he was an expert with crossbow. Now he again proved his skill. Twice he fired and men howled like

beasts—or worse than beasts seeing what they had been doing—beasts do not so use their females.

Caleb shouted as if he were leading a group of men-at-
arms. The herders floundered away. Then he went down to
what they had left broken behind them.

No man knows what happened thereafter, for Caleb spoke
of it to no one. In time he went on alone, though his face
was white and his work-hardened hands shook.

He did not venture into the fen, but traveled, almost as
one with a set purpose, along its edge. Two nights did he
camp so. What he did and with whom he spoke, why those
came—who can tell? On the morning of the third day he
turned his back on Sorn Fen and started toward the highway.

It was odd but as he walked his lurching skip-step was not
so evident, as if, with every stride he took, his twisted body
seemed straighter. By the night of the fourth day he walked
near as well as any man who was tired and footsore. It was
then that he came to the burned-out shell of the Inn of the
Forks.

Once that had been a prosperous house. Much silver had
spun across its tables into the hands of the keeper and his
family. It was built at a spot where two roads, one angling
north, one south, met, to continue thereon into Klavenport.
But the day of its glory passed before the Battle of Falcon
Cut. For five winter seasons or more its charred timbers had
been a dismal monument to the ravages of war, offering no
cheer for the traveler.

Now Caleb stood looking at its sad state and—

Believe this or not as you will, Goodmen. But suddenly
here was no burned-out ruin. Rather stood an inn. Caleb,
showing no surprise, crossed the road to enter. Enter it as
master, for as such he was hailed by those about their
business within its courtyard.

Now there were more travelers up and down the western
roads, for this was the season of trade with Klavenport. So it
was not long before the tale of the restored inn reached the
city. There were those unable to believe such a report, who
rode out, curious, to prove it true.

They found it much as the earlier inn had been, though
those who had known it before the war claimed there were
certain differences. However, when they were challenged to
name these, they were vague. All united in the information
that Caleb was host there and that he had changed with the
coming of prosperity, for prosperous he certainly now was.

Higbold heard those reports. He did not frown, but he rubbed his forefinger back and forth under his thick lower lip—which was a habit of his when he thought deeply, considering this point and that. Then he summoned to him a flaunty, saucy piece in skirts. She had long thrown herself in his direction whenever she could. It was common knowledge that, while Higbold had indeed bedded his lady in the early days of their marriage, to make sure that none could break the tie binding them, he was no longer to be found in her chamber, taking his pleasures elsewhere. Though as yet with none under his own roof.

Now he spoke privately with Elfra, and set in her hands a slip of parchment. Then openly he berated her loudly, had her bustled roughly, thrown into the street without so much as a cloak about her shoulders. She wept and wailed, and took off along the western road.

In time she reached the Inn at the Forks. Her journey had not been an easy one so she crept into the courtyard as much a beggar in looks as any of the stinking, shuffling crowd who hung around a merchant's door in the city. Save that when she spoke to Caleb she gave him a bit of parchment with on it a message which might have been writ in my lady's hand. Caleb welcomed her and at length he made her waiting maid in the tap room. She did briskly well, such employment suiting her nature.

The days passed. Time slid from summer into autumn. At length the Ice Dragon sent his frost breath over the land. It was then that Elfra stole away with a merchant bound for Klavenport. Caleb, hearing of her going, shrugged and said that if she thought so to better her life the choice was hers.

But Elfra stayed with the merchant only long enough to reach the gate. From there she went directly to Higbold's own chamber. At first, as he listened, there was that in his face which was not good to see. But she did not take warning, sure that he looked so only because her tale was so wild. To prove the truth of her words she held her hand over the table.

About her thumb (so large it was that she could not wear it elsewhere on her woman's hand) was a ring of green stone curiously patterned with faint red lines as if veined with blood. Holding it directly in Higbold's sight, Elfra made a wish.

Below on the table there appeared a necklace of gems, such a necklace as might well be the ransom for a whole city in the days of the war. Higbold sucked in his breath, his face gone blank, his eyes half hooded by their lids.

Then his hand shot out and imprisoned her wrist in a grim grip and he had that ring. She looked into his face and began to whimper, learning too late that she was only a tool, and one which had served its purpose now, and having served its purpose—

She was gone!

But Higbold cupped the ring between his palms and smiled evilly.

Shortly thereafter at the Inn flames burst out. No man could fight their fierce heat as they ate away what the magic of the Old Ones had brought into being. Once more Caleb stood in the cold owning nothing. Nothing, that is, except his iron will.

He wasted no time in regrets or in bewailing that lack of caution which had lost him his treasure. Rather he turned and began to stride along the road. When he came to a certain place he cut away from the path of men. Though snow blew about him, and a knife-edged wind cut like a lash at his back, he headed for the fen.

Again time passed. No one rebuilt, by magic or otherwise, the Inn. Only with Higbold things happened. Those who had once been firm against him became his supporters or else suffered various kinds of chastening misfortune. His lady kept to her chamber. It was rumored that she ailed and perhaps would not live out the year.

There had never been a king of High Hallack, for the great lords held themselves all equal, one to another. None would have given support to a fellow to set him over the rest. But Higbold was not of their company, and so it might be a matter of either unite against him, or acknowledge his rulership. Still those men expected to be foremost in opposition to his rise seemed oddly hesitant to take any step to prevent it.

In the meantime there were rumors concerning a man who lived on the fringe of Sorn Fen and who was a tamer of beasts, even a seller of them. A merchant, enterprising and on the search for something unique, was enough intrigued by such tales to make a detour. He came into Klavenport from that side venture with three strange animals.

They were small, yet they had the look of the fierce snow cats of the high range. Only these were obviously tame, so tame that they quickly enchanted the merchants' wives and the ladies of the city into wanting them for pets. Twice the merchant returned to the fen fringe and bought more of the cats—well pleased each time with his bargain.

Then he needed an export permit and had to go to Higbold. So he came to the Keep bringing a "sweetener" for dealing after the custom—that being one of the cats. Higbold was not one with a liking for animals. His horses were tools to be used, and no hound ever lay in his hall or chamber. But he had the cat carried on to his lady's bower. Perhaps he thought that he would not have to consider her for long and this gift might give some coating of pretense.

Shortly after, he began to dream. Now there was certainly enough in his past to provide ill dreams for not one man but a troop. However, it was not of the past that he dreamed, but rather of the present, and perhaps a dark future. For in each of these dreams (and they were real enough to bring him starting up in bed calling for candles as he woke out of them), he had lost the ring Elfra had brought him—the ring now the core of all his schemes.

He had worn it secretly on a cord around his neck under his clothing. However, all his dreams were of it slipping from that security. So now when he slept he grasped it within his hand.

Then one morning he awoke to find it gone. Fear rode him hard until he found it among the covers on his bed. At last his night terrors drove him to putting it under his tongue as he slept. His tempers were such that those in close contact with him went in fear of their lives.

At last came the night when he dreamed again and this time the dream seemed very real. Something crouched first at the foot of his bed, and then it began a slow, slinking advance, stalking up the length of it. He could not move, but had to lie sweating, awaiting its coming.

Suddenly he roused out of that nightmare, sneezing. The ring lay where he had coughed it forth. By it crouched the strange cat, its eyes glowing so that he would swear it was no cat, but something else, more intelligent and malignant, which had poured its being into the cat's small body. It watched him with cold measurement and he was frozen, unable to put forth his hand to the ring. Then, calmly, it took up that circlet of green and red in its mouth, leaped from the bed and was gone.

Higbold cried out and grabbed. But the creature was already at the door of the chamber, streaking through as the guard came in answer to his lord's call. Higbold thrust the man aside as he raced to follow.

"The cat!" His shouts alarmed the whole keep. "Where is the cat?"

But it was the hour before daybreak when men were asleep. Those aroused by his shouting blinked and were amazed for a moment or two.

Higbold well knew that there were a hundred, no, a thousand places within that pile where such a small animal might hide, or drop to eternal loss that which it carried. That thought created frenzy in his brain, so that at first he was like one mad, racing to and fro, shouting to watch, to catch the cat.

Then came a messenger from the gate saying that the cat had been seen to leap the wall and run from the keep, and the city, out into the country. Deep in him Higbold knew a growing cold which was like the chill of death, since it heralded the end of all his plans. For if the keep provided such a wealth of hiding places, then what of the countryside?

He returned, struck silent now with the fullness of his loss, to his chamber. There he battered his bare fists against the stone of the wall, until the pain of his self-bruising broke through the torment in his mind and he could think clearly again.

Animals could be hunted. He had hounds in his kennels, though he had never wasted time in the forms of the chase in which the high-born delighted. He would hunt that cat as no beast in High Hallack had ever been hunted before. Having come to his senses, he gave orders in a tone of voice that made those about him flinch and look sideways, keeping as distant as they dared.

In the hour before dawn the hunt was up, though it was a small party riding out of the keep. Higbold had ordered with him only the master of hounds with a brace of the best trail keepers, and his squire.

The trail was so fresh and clear the hounds ran eagerly. But they did not pad along the highway, taking at once to open ground. This speedily grew more difficult for the riders, until the dogs far outstripped the men. Only their belling voices, raised now and then, told those laboring after that they still held the track. Higbold now had his fear under tight control, he did not push his horse, but there was a tenseness in the lines of his body which suggested that, if he could have grown wings, he would have soared ahead in an instant.

Wilder and rougher grew the country. The laboring squire's horse was lamed and had to drop behind. Higbold did not even spare him a glance. The sun was up and ahead was that smooth green of the fen country. In Higbold that frozen cold was nigh his heart. If the fleeing cat took into that there would be no following.

When they reached the outer fringe of that dire land the trail turned at an angle and ran along the edge, as if the creature had willfully decided not to trust to the promised safety beyond.

At length they came upon a small hut, built of the very material of this forsaken land, boulders and stones set together for its walls, a thatch of rough branches for roof. As they approached the hounds were suddenly thrown back as if they had run into an invisible wall. They yapped and leaped, and were again hurled to earth, their clamor wild.

Their master dismounted from his blowing horse and ran forward. Then he, too, met resistance. He stumbled and almost fell, putting out his hands and running them from right to left. He might have been stroking some surface.

Higbold came out of the saddle and strode forward.

"What is it?" For the first time in hours he spoke, his words grating on the ear.

"There—there is a wall, Lord—" quavered the master, and he shrank back from both the place and Higbold.

Higbold continued to tramp on. He passed the master and the slavering, whining hounds. The man, the dogs, were mad. There was no wall, there was only the hut and what he sought in it.

He set hand on the warped surface of the door and slammed it open with the full force of his frustration.

Before him was a rough table, a stool. On the stool sat Caleb. On the tabletop crouched the cat, purring under the measured stroking of the man's gentle hand. By the animal lay the ring.

Higbold strove to put out his hand, to snatch up that treasure. From the moment he sighted it, that had his full attention. The animal, the man, meant nothing to him. But now Caleb's other hand dropped loosely over the circlet. Higbold was powerless to move.

"Higbold," Caleb addressed him directly, using no polite forms or title, "you are an evil man, but one of power—too much power. In the past year you have used that very cleverly. A crown is nigh within your grasp—is that not so?"

Soft and smooth he spoke as one entirely without fear. He had no weapon, only lounged at his ease. Higbold's hatred now outweighed his fear, so that he wanted nothing so much as to smash the other's face into crimson ruin. Yet he could not stir so much as a finger.

"You have, I think," Caleb continued, "greatly enjoyed your possession of this." He raised his hand a little to show the ring.

"Mine—!" Higbold's throat hurt as he shaped that thick word.

"No." Caleb shook his head, still gently, as one might to a child who demanded what was not and never could be his. "I shall tell you a tale, Higbold. This ring was a gift, freely given to me. I was able to ease somewhat the dying of one who was not of our kind, but had been death-dealt by those like you in spirit. Had she not been taken unawares she would have had her defenses, defenses such as you now taste. But she was tricked, and then used with such cruelty as would shame any one daring to call himself one of us. Because I tried to aid, though there was little I could do, I was left this token—and my keeping it was confirmed by her people. It can only be used for a limited time, however. I intended to use it for good. That is a thought to make you smile, isn't it, Higbold?

"Then you used your lady's name to beg of me aid for one I thought badly treated. So, in my blindness, I brought about my own betrayal. I am a simple man, but there are things even the simple can do. To have Higbold for High King over this land—that is wrong—beyond one's own wishes or fears.

"So I spoke again to those of the fen, and with their aid I set a trap—to bring you hither. And you came, easily enough. Now." He lifted his hand and let the ring lie. It seemed there was a glow about it and again Higbold's eyes were drawn to it and he saw nothing else. Out of sight, beyond the gleaming green and red of the ring, a voice spoke.

"Take up the ring you wish so much, Higbold. Set it on your finger once again. Then go and claim your kingdom!"

Higbold found that now he could stretch forth his hand. His fingers closed about the ring. Hurriedly, lest it be rift from him once more, he pushed it on his finger.

He did not look again at Caleb, instead he turned and went out of the hut, as if the other man had ceased to exist. The hounds lay on their muddied bellies, whimpering a little as they licked at paws sore from their long run. Their master squatted on his heels watching for his lord's return. Their two horses stood with drooping heads, foam roping their bits.

Higbold did not move toward his mount, nor did he speak to the waiting hound master. Instead he faced west and south a little. As one who marches toward a visible and long desired goal, paying no heed to that about him, he strode toward the fen. His hound master did not move to stop him. Staring drop-jawed, he watched him go, until he was swallowed up in the mists.

Caleb came forth from the hut, the cat riding on his shoulder, and stood at ease. It was he who broke silence first.

"Return to your lady, my friend, and say to her that Higbold has gone to seek his kingdom. He shall not return."

Then he, also, went to where the mists of the fen wreathed him around and he could no longer be seen.

When the master came again to Klavenport he told the Lady Isbel what he had seen and heard. Thereafter, she seemed to gather strength (as if some poison drained or shadow lifted from her) and came forth from her chamber. She set about making arrangements to give gifts from the wealth of Higbold.

When summer reached its height she rode forth before dawn, taking only one waiting maid (one who had come with her from her father's house and was tied with long bonds of loyalty). They were seen to follow the highway for a space as the guards watched. Thereafter no man marked where they went, and they were not seen again.

Whether she went to seek her lord, or another, who knows? For the Fen of Sorn renders not to our blood its many secrets.

SWORD of UNBELIEF

1

Fury Driven

My eyes ached as I forced them to study the hard ground. From them a dull pain spread into the bony sockets that were their frames. The tough, mountain-bred mount I had saved from our desperate encounter with the wolf-ravagers stumbled. I caught at the saddle horn as vertigo struck with the sharp thrust of an unparried sword.

I could taste death, death and old blood, as I ran my tongue over lips where the salt of my own sweat plastered the dull gray dust of this land to my unwashed skin. Again I wavered. But this time my pony's stumble was greater. Strong as he was, and war trained, he had come near to the end of endurance.

Before me the Waste was a long tongue of gray rock, giving rootage only to sparse and twisted brush, so misshapen in its growing that it might well have been attacked by some creeping evil. For there *was* evil in this country, every sense of mine warned that, as I urged Fallon on at a slow walk.

That wind which whipped at my cloak was bitter, carrying the breath of the Ice Dragon. It raised fine grains of gray sand to scour my face beneath the half shading of my helm. I must find some shelter, and soon, or the fury of a Dune Moving Storm would catch me and provide a grave place which might exist for a day, a week, or centuries—depending upon the caprice of that same wind and sand.

An outcrop of angular rock stood to my left. Toward that I sent Fallon, his head hanging low as he went. In the lee of that tall fang I slipped from the saddle, keeping my feet only by a quick grasp of the rock itself. The ache in my head struck downwards through my shoulders and back.

I loosed my cloak a little and, crouching by the pony, flung it over both his head and mine. Little enough shelter against the drive of the punishing grains, but it was the best I had. However, another fear gnawed at me. This flurry would wipe out the trail I had followed these two days past. With that gone, I must depend upon myself, and in myself I had less confidence.

Had I been fully trained as those of my Talent and blood had always been—then I could have accomplished what must be done with far less effort. But, though my mother was a Witch of Estcarp, and I was learned in the powers of a Wise Woman, (and had indeed done battle using those powers in the past), yet at this moment I knew fear as an ever-present pain within me, stronger than any ache of body or fatigue of mind.

As I crouched beside Fallon, this dread arose like a flood of bile into my throat, the which I would have vomited forth if I could. Yet, it was too great a part of me to allow itself to be so sundered. Feverishly I drew upon those lesser arts I had learned, striving so to still the fast beating of my heart, the clouding of my thoughts by panic. I must think rather of him whom I sought, and of those who had taken him, for what purpose I could not imagine. For it is the way of the wolf-heads to kill; torment, yes, if they were undisturbed, but kill at the end of their play. Yet they had drawn back into this forbidden and forbidding land taking with them a prisoner, one worth no ransom. And the reason for that taking I could not guess.

I set a bridle of calmness upon my thoughts. Only so might I use that other Talent which was mine from birth. So now I set my mind-picture upon him whom I sought—Jervon, fighting man, and more, far more to me.

I could see him, yes, even as I had sighted him last by the fire of our small camp, his hands stretched out to warm themselves at the flames. If only I had not—! No, regret was only weakening. I must not think of what I had not done, but what I must now be prepared to do.

There had been blood on the snow-shifted ground when I had returned, the fire stamped into cold charred brands. Two outlaws' bodies hideously ripped—but Jervon . . . no. So they had taken him for some purpose I could not understand.

The dead wolfheads I left to the woods beasts. Fallon I

had discovered, shivering and wet with sweat, within the brush and brought him to me by the summoning power. I had waited no longer, knowing that my desire to look upon the shrine of the Old Ones, which I had turned aside to do, might well mean Jervon's death, and no pleasant death either.

Now, crouching here, I cupped one hand across my closed eyes.

"Jervon!" My mind call went out even as I had brought Fallon to me. But I failed. There arose a cloud between me and the man I would find. Yet I was as certain that behind that shadow he still lived. For when one's life is entwined with another's and death comes, the knowledge of that passing through the Last Gate is also clear—to one trained in even the simplest of the Great Mysteries.

This Waste was a grim and much hated place. Many were the remains of the Old Ones here, and men of true human blood did not enter it willingly. I am not of High Hallack, though I was born in the Dales. My parents came from storied Estcarp overseas, a land where much of the Old Knowledge has been preserved. And my mother was one of those who used that knowledge—even though she had wed, and so, by their laws, put herself apart.

What I knew I had of Aufrica out of Wark, a mistress of minor magic and a Wise Woman. Herbs I knew, both harmful and healing, and I could call upon certain lesser powers—even upon a great one, as once I had done to save him who was born at the same birth with me. But there were powers beyond powers here that I knew not. Only I must take this way and do what I could for Jervon who was more to me than Elyn, my brother, had ever been, and who had once, without any of the Talent to aid him, come with me into battle with a very ancient and strong evil, which battle we had mercifully won.

"Jervon!" I called his name aloud, but my voice was only a faint whisper. For the wind shrieked like a legion of disembodied demons around me. Fallon near jerked his head from my hold on his bridle, and I speedily set myself to calming him, setting over his beast mind a safeguard against panic.

It seemed to last for hours, that perilous sheltering by the fang rock. Then the wind died and we pulled out of sand drifted near to my knees. I took one of my precious flasks of water and wet the corner of my cloak, using that to wash out Fallon's nostrils, the sand away from his eyes. He nudged at my shoulder, stretching his head toward the water bottle in a voiceless plea for a drink. That I did not dare give him until I knew what manner of country we would cross and whether there would be any streams or tarns along the way.

Night was very near. But that strangeness of the Waste banished some of the dark. For here and there were scattered rock spires which gave off a flickering radiance, enough to travel by.

I did not mount as yet, knowing that Fallon must have a rest from carrying a rider. Though I am slender of body, I am no lightweight with mail about me, a sword and helm. So I plowed through the sand, leading Fallon. And heard him snort and blow his dislike of what I would have him do—venture farther into this desolation.

Again, I sent forth a searching thought. I could not reach Jervon. No—that muddling cloud still hung between us. But I could tell in what direction they had gone. Though the constant concentration to hold that thread made my head throb with renewed pain.

Also there were strange shadows in this place. It would seem that nothing threw across the land a clear dark definition of itself, as was normal. Rather those shadows took on shapes which made the imagination quicken with vague hints of things invisible which still could be seen in this way, monstrous forms and unnatural blendings. And, if one allowed fear the upper hand, those appeared ripely ready to detach themselves and move unfettered by any trick of light or dark.

I wondered at those I followed. War had been the harsh life of this land now for so many years it was hard to remember what peace had been like. High Hallack had been overrun by invaders whose superior arms and organization had devastated more than half the Dales before men were able to erect their defense. There had been no central overlord among us; it was not the custom of the men of High Hallack to give deference beyond the lord in whose holding they had been born and bred. So, until the Four of the north had sunk their differences and made a pact, there had been no rallying point. Men had fought separately for their own lands, and died, to lie in the earth there.

Then had come the final effort. Not only did the Dale lords unite for the first time in history to make a common cause, but they had also treated with others—out of this same Waste—the Wereriders of legend. Together what was left of High Hallack arose with all the might it could summon to smash the Hounds of Alizon, driving them back to the sea, mainly to their own deaths therein. But a land so rent produces in turn those with a natural bent toward evil, scavengers and outlaws, ready to plunder both sides if the chance offered. Now such were the bane of our exhausted and war-worn country.

These were such that I followed. It could well be that, since they were hardy enough to lair within the Waste, they might not be wholly human either. Rather be possessed by some emanation of the Dark which had long lurked here.

For the Old Ones, when they withdrew from the Daleland, had left behind them pools of energy. Some of these granted peace and well being, so that one could enter therein timorously, to come forth again renewed in spirit and body. But others were wholly of the Dark. And if he was destroyed at once the intruder was lucky. It was worse, far worse, to live as a creature of a shadow's bidding.

The ghostly light streamed on before me. I lifted my head, turned this way and that, as might a hound seeking scent. All traces of trail had been wiped away by the wind. However I was sure that I followed the right path. So we came to two stelae which fronted each other as if they might once have formed part of an ancient gate. Yet there was no wall, just these pillars, from the tip of which streamed cloudward thin ribbons of a greenish light. They had been formed by men, or some agency with intelligence, for they had the likenesses of heavy-bladed sabers. Yet on their sides I could see, half eroded by time, pits and hollows which, when the eye fastened straight upon them, took on the semblance of faces—strange faces—long and narrow, with large noses overhanging pointed chins. Also it seemed that the eyes (which were pits) turned upon me, not in interest or in warning, but as if in deep, age-old despair.

Though I felt no emanation of evil, neither did I like to pass between those sword pillars. Still it was that way my road ran. Quickly I sketched with my hand certain symbols before I stepped forward, drawing Fallon on rein-hold behind me.

These pillars stood at the entrance of a narrow gash of valley which led downward, the steep sides rising ever higher. Here the dark had full sway for there were no more of the luminous stones, so that I went with that slow caution I had learned in the years I had ridden to war.

I listened. Outside this valley I had heard the murmur of the wind, but here was a deep quiet, until my straining ears caught a sound which could only be that of running water. There was a dampness now in the air, for which I was momentarily grateful. Fallon pushed against me, eager to slake his thirst.

But where there was water in this desert land there could also well be a camp of those I pursued. So I did not hasten, and I held back the pony. He snorted and the sound echoed hollowly. I froze, listening for any answer which might mean my coming was marked. If the wolves I followed were human, certainly their sight here would be no better than mine, even more limited for they did not have—or so I hoped—the Talent to aid it.

On we went step by hesitant step. Then my boot, slipping across the ground, struck against some obstruction. I stooped, to feel about with my hands. Here was a cluster of small rocks, and beyond that, not too far, the water. I felt a path as clear as I could. As far as I could tell, a spring broke ground on my left, some way up the wall of the valley, and the water poured from that into a basin which in turn must have some outlet on the other side.

I scooped up a handful of the liquid, smelled it. There was no stench of minerals or of other deadliness. I splashed it over my face below the edge of my helm, washing away storm grit. Then I drank from my cupped hands, and squeezed aside to let Fallon have his way. The noise of his gulping was loud enough, but I no longer feared detection. Those I sought had come this way, yes. My refreshed mind assured me of that. But there was no camp hereabout.

"Jervon!" I pressed both hands over my eyes, pushing back my helm, reaching out in mind-search again. For a moment it was as if my touch found a weakness in that mist I had encountered before. I touched—He was alive, mauled yet not badly injured! But when I tried to deepen contact, that I might read through him the numbers and nature of the force which held him, there was once more a cutting off of communication, as suddenly as a sword might descend between us.

The nature of that interference I could judge. There was that ahead which was aware of me, but only when I tried to reach Jervon. For as I hunkered there, my mind barrier up, I did not sense any testing of that. In me now fear was lessened; instead another emotion woke to life. Once before I had fought against very ancient evil—with love—for the body and soul of a man. Then I had sought my brother Elyn trapped in a cursed place, though what I felt for Elyn, of my own blood and birth, was but a pale shadow to that which filled me when Jervon looked upon me. I am not one who speaks easily of what she thinks the deepest upon, but in that moment I knew how completely Jervon's fate and mine were rooted together. And I experienced fury against that which had cut the cord between us.

Recognizing that fury, I drew deep upon it, used the hot emotion to fill me with new strength. Even as fear weakened that which was my own, so could anger give it sword and shield, providing I might control that anger. There in the dark, by that unseen pool, I fashioned my invisible armor, sharpened those weapons which no one but myself could ever wield. For they were forged out of my wit and my emotion even as a smith beats a true edged sword out of clean metal.

2

The Shadow Hunter

It was folly to advance farther into the dark. I dared not risk a fall and perhaps a broken bone for me or for Fallon. Though every surge of emotion urged me on, I held to logic and reason. Here dark was so thick it was as if the ground about generated some blackness. Above hung clouds to veil even the stars.

I fumbled in my saddlebag and brought out a handspan of journey bread, hard enough perhaps to crack teeth gnawing it unwarily. This I soaked in water and fed the greatest portion to Fallon, whose lips nuzzled my hand to search out the smallest crumb. Then I used my will and forced upon his mind the order that he was not to stray, before I settled in between two rocks and drew my cloak about me as poor protection against this damp chill.

Though I had not thought to sleep, the fatigue of my body overcame the discipline of my mind and I dropped into a dark even deeper than that which enfolded me here. In that dark, presences moved and I was aware of them, only not clearly enough to draw any meaning from such fleetings.

I woke suddenly, into the gray of early dawn; I had been summoned as if someone had clearly called my name, or a battle trumpet had blown nearby. Now I could see the dim pool with the runnel of water leaping down the rocks to feed it. On the other side of that Fallon grazed on clumps of tough grass, which were not green but sickly ashen, withered by the chill of the season.

There was indeed an outlet for the pool basin, a kind of trough which ran on into the morning fog beyond. I moved stiffly, but, now that my mind was once more alert, I cast ahead for that blankness which hid Jervon and his captors.

It was there and this time I did not make the mistake of trying to pierce it, and so alert whatever I had touched the night before. At any rate, for the present, there was only one road, that walled by rises of stone on which I could not even see finger holds. Yet there were markings there—eroded and time worn as those upon the stelae guardians—too regular to be nature's work, too strange to be read by me. Save that I misliked the general outlines of some of those symbols, for with their very shape they aroused misgivings.

As I broke my fast with another small portion of water-soaked bread, I kept my eyes resolutely turned away from those shadowy scrawls. Rather did I strive to see into the mist which filled this cut in the earth. And again I listened—but there was nothing to hear save the water.

Having filled my two saddle bottles, I mounted, but I let Fallon for the moment take his own pace. The way was much cluttered with rocks, with here and there a landslip over or around which we crept with care.

The sense of new danger came slowly upon me, so intent was I on keeping contact with that peculiar blankness which I believed imprisoned Jervon. This was first like a foul smell which is but a suggestion of rottenness, but which gradually grows the stronger as one approaches the source of corruption. Fallon snorted, tossing his head, only kept to the path by my will.

Oddly enough I could not sense any of the ancient evil in this thing, though I bent my mind and my Talent to test it by all which I had learned from Aufrica and the use of my own power. It was not of any source I knew—for the taint was that of human not of the Old Ones. Yet also during our hunting of the Waste outlaws I had not met the Old Ones either.

Now my flesh roughed as if more than the chill of the fog struck at me. Fear battled for release from the iron guard I had set upon my emotions. With that fear came a disgust and anger.

I found myself riding with hand upon sword hilt. Listening—ever listening—though my ears caught nothing but the thud of Fallon's hooves, now and again the ring of an iron shoe against an edge of rock.

The fog closed about, beads of moisture dripped from my helm, shone oily wet upon my mail, dampened Fallon's heavier winter coat into points.

Then—

Movement!

Fallon threw up his head to voice a shrill squeal of fear. At the same instant that which I had sensed struck and lapped me round.

Through the rim of the fog came horror unleashed. The thing was mounted even as I, and some trick of the fog made it loom larger than it was. But that which it rode was no horse of flesh and blood—rather a rack of bones held together by a lacing of rotted and dried flesh. It was, like its mount, a thing long dead and yet given a terrible life.

Its weapon was terror, not any sword. As I stiffened and drew deeply upon my power I realized it for what it was—a thoughtform born out of ancient fear and hatred. So did it continue to feed upon such emotions, drawing into it at each feeding a greater substance.

My fear, my anger, must have both summoned and fed it. But it was real. That I could swear to, as much as if I laid hand upon that outstretched arm of bone. Fallon's wide-eyed terror was meat to it also. While it trailed behind it, like a cloak, a deep depression of the spirit.

Fallon reared, screamed. That mount of bone opened wide its jaws in answer. I struggled with the panic-mad horse under me, glad for a moment that I had this to fight, for it awoke my mind from the blast of fear the specter brought with it.

I raised my voice and shouted, as I would a battle cry, certain Words. Yet the rider did not waver, nor did the mount. I summoned my will to master my own senses. This thing needed terror and despair to live, let me clamp tight upon my own and it would have no power—

Fallon sweated so that the smell was rank in the narrow defile of that way. My will had clamped upon him also, held him steady. He no longer screamed, but from his throat issued a sound not unlike the moaning of a man stricken close to death.

It was a thing fashioned of fear, and, without fear . . . I made myself into a bulwark, once more spoke my defiance. I did not shout this time, rather I schooled my voice into obedience, even as I held Fallon.

The thing was within arm's length, the stench of it thick in my nostrils, the glare of its eyeless skull turned upon me. Then . . . it faded into the mist. Fallon still gave forth that unanimal-like moaning and great shudders ran through his body. I urged him forward, and he went one unsteady step at a time, while the fog coiled and spun around as if to entrap us.

It was enough for a moment that the horror had been vanquished. I hoped dimly that what I knew of such was the truth, that they were tied to certain places on earth where raw emotions had first given them birth.

As we paced along beside the small stream I heard sounds, not from ahead, but from behind. Faint they were at first, but growing stronger—there was the beat of hooves in such a loud tattoo that I thought some rider came at a speed far too reckless for the stony way. I heard also voices calling with the mist, though never could I make out the words, for the sounds came muffled and distorted. Still there reached me the impression of a hunt behind. A strange picture flashed into my mind of one crouched low on a wild-eyed horse, behind him, unseen, the terror which drove him.

So keen and clear was this picture that I swung around when I reached a pile of rocks against which I could set my back. I drew my sword. There was a rushing past where I crouched, my left hand tangled within Fallon's reins for he was like to bolt. But nothing material cleared the mist. Again ancient shadows had deceived me.

Though I waited tensely for whatever pursued that lone rider of the distant past, there was nothing. Nothing save the uneasy sense that here were remnants of ancient terror caught forever in the mist. Then, ashamed at my own lack of self-control, I started on again, this time leading Fallon, stroking his head and talking softly to him, urging into his mind a confidence I did not wholly feel.

The walls about us began to widen out. Also that mist was tattered and driven by a wind which whistled down the valley, buffeting us with the frost it carried. But also it brought me something else, the scent of wood smoke, of a fire which has been recently dampened out.

We came to a curve in the near wall which served as a guide through the now disappearing mist. I dropped Fallon's reins and ordered him to stand so, cautiously crept forward;

though the probe of my Talent picked up no whisper of a human mind. Still so strange was the Waste that I could believe those who harbored here might well have some defense against my power.

There had been a camp there right enough. A drowned fire still gave off a strong odor. And there were horse droppings along one side. I could see tracks crossing and recrossing each other, though the sand and gravel did not hold them clearly. But plainest of all was what had been painted on one massive rock which jutted forth from the wall. That was no work of years before; the symbols must have been freshly drawn for they were hardly weathered or scoured by sand.

One was a crudely drawn head of some animal—a wolf or hound—it could have been either. It interlaced the edge of the other, a far more complex and better executed symbol. I found myself standing before that, my forefinger almost of itself following its curves by tracing the air.

When I realized what I was doing I snatched my hand back to my side, my fingers balled into a fist. This was not of my learning, though it was a potent thing. And dangerous. . . . There was an unpleasant *otherness* about the symbol which aroused wariness. However, I believed, though I did not understand its complete meaning, I did pick up the reason for those mated drawings. For among the Dales there was an old custom that, when a lasting truce or alliance was made, the lords of both parties chose a place on the boundaries of their domains and there carved the signs of their two houses so twined in just the same fashion.

So here I had come upon a notice that the outlaws I hunted had indeed made common cause with some dweller of the Waste who was not of their blood or kind. Though I had suspected no less, having trailed them through the haunted valley, yet I could wish it otherwise.

To have some knowledge but not enough is a thing which eats upon one. If I might have read that other symbol I could be warned as to what—or who—I had to face. As I began a careful search about the deserted camp I alerted the Talent to sniff out any clue to the non-human. But the impressions my mind gathered were only of the same wolfish breed as we had hunted—desperate and dangerous enough.

Jervon had been there and he still lived. I had half steeled my mind to find him dead, for the Waste wolves did not take captives. What did they want with him? Or were they but the servants and hands of another force? The impression grew on me that the latter was so. That they had some purpose in bringing him hither could not be denied.

My years with Aufrica had taught me well that there are two kinds of what the untalented term "magic" or "witchery." It was contagious magic which I used to track Jervon, for about my throat I wore the amulet of a strange stone shaped not unlike an eye, which he had found and carried for a luck piece since he was a boy, and then had put into my keeping upon our handfasting, having in those years of war no other bride-jewel to offer.

I knew there was also sympathic magic which works according to the laws of correspondence and now I prepared to call upon that. From my healer's bag I brought forth a length of ash stick, peeled, blessed by the moon, bound with a small ring of silver wire, which is moon metal. Now I faced that symbol on the rock, pointed to it with ash rod which was no longer than my palm and fingers together.

Immediately the wand came to life in my hold, not to trace the characters, rather turning and twisting in a manner to suggest it would leap from my grasp rather than face what was so carven there. So I knew what I suspected was true, that this was a thing of the Dark from which the Light recoiled.

Now I touched the wand with the eye-stone which I drew forth from beneath my mail, rubbing the stone down one side and up the other. Then I held out my hand with the lightest hold upon the ash. Again it twisted, pointing ahead.

My battle with fear in the mist had drawn too heavily upon my inner resources; I could no longer depend upon mind search to follow those whom I sought. However, with the wand I had a sure pointer, in which I could trust. So I continued to hold it as I mounted Fallon and rode out of that camp, turning my back upon the entwined symbols of an unholy alliance.

The valley widened even farther, as if it had been but a narrow throat to open country beyond. I saw trees now, as misshapen as the brush, and monoliths, as well as tumbles of stone, which suggested ruins so old they could not be dated by my own species.

There were tracks again. But within a very short time we came to a place where those turned to the right at an abrupt swing. Only, in my hand, the wand did not alter course, but still pointed straight ahead. There was only one solution to accept: Jervon was no longer with the wolf pack which had pulled him down.

Had there been some monstrous meeting beneath those symbols and he who I sought been given to that Other whose sign was set boldly on the rock? I dismounted to search the ground with a scout's patience. At last I was rewarded with faint traces. The main body I hunted had indeed turned here, but two mounts had kept to the straight track. One of those must carry Jervon.

If he rode with only one outlaw as guard—I drew a sharp swift breath . . . This might well herald a chance for rescue with the odds much in my favor. I mounted again and urged Fallon to a faster pace than he had kept during that day's travel, watching keenly the country ahead.

3

The Frozen Flame

Here in the open the mist was tattered by the wind and one could see farther. So my eyes caught a flash of light. Yet it was plain that this did not rise from any fire but rather sparked into the sky, perhaps as a beacon.

Now the stones of the forgotten ruins drew together, formed tumbled walls, with here or there some uprise of worked rock which might have once been a stela, or even a statue. These were now so worn away by erosion that such shapes remained only vaguely unpleasant ones, hinting of ancient monstrous beings. Gods or guardians? What man now living could say?

The sun broke through, yet here it had not even the pallid light of mid-winter, rather a drained, bespoiled radiance, with nothing to warm either body or heart. And still shadows clung to the rocks, though I resolutely refused more than to glance at them. I knew the power of illusion, for much of that lies within the Talent.

Before me rose a wall, massive in its blocks, some larger than myself, even when mounted on Fallon. This time had not used so harshly. The pale sun struck points of icy fire from gray-white crystals embedded in its surface. The way I followed led to the single break in that wall, a gateway so narrow that it would seem no more than one had ever been meant to pass through at a time.

Now the wand in my hand flipped so that I barely prevented it from slipping through my fingers. Its silver-bound tip pointed to a dark stain smeared on that wall near the height of my thigh, riding as I was. Blood—and that of him whom I now sought!

I could only draw hope because the smear was so small a one. Jervon had not been overborne without a fight, that I was already sure of. He was too seasoned in war to be easily taken, and the bodies I had found at our last camp had testified to his skill in defense. Yet this was the first sign I had seen that he had been wounded. Now I glanced at the pavement under foot, expecting to sight more splotches.

The wall was the first of three such. And they varied in color, for the outer one, in spite of its clusters of crystals, was as gray as the rest of this Waste. The second, some twenty paces beyond, was dull green. Yet it was not any growing thing which had clothed it, but part of the blocks themselves.

The third was the rusty-brown-red of dried blood and in it the stones were smaller. The entrance through to it was still narrower; so that, despite my misgivings, I was forced to dismount and essay that on foot.

If there were any blood smears here to mark Jervon's passing, those were hidden by the natural coloring of the stone. Before me stood a squat building, only a fraction higher than the wall, windowless and dour, the stone of its making a lusterless, thick black, as if it had been fashioned from shadows. From the roof of this issued, straight up to defy the sullen sun, the beam of light that had shone across the land.

Now that I drew nearer I could see that beam pulsated in waves, almost like the ever-changing and moving flames of a fire. Yet I was sure it was not born from any honest burning of wood.

Windowless the place might be, but there existed a deeply recessed doorway; so deep and dark a portal I could not be sure if any barrier stood within. I paused, using my senses to test what lay about me, for to go blindly into danger would not serve either Jervon's cause or my own.

Hearing? There was no sound, not even the sigh of wind across twisted shrub and sliding sand. Smell? I could not pick up any of the faint rottenness which had alerted me to the coming of the phantom in the valley. Sight? The deep door, the pulsing flame, unmarked ground between me and that doorway. Touch . . . ?

I held up my hand, the wand lying across the palm. That moved again, wavering from side to side with a growing speed until it had switched around and the wire-wound tip pointed to me, or back of me to the wall entrance through which I had just squeezed. There was warning enough in that. What lay ahead was highly inimical to such forces as I dared call upon. And I was somehow certain if I took these last few strides, passed within that portal, I would be facing danger worse than any wolf blade or phantom hunter.

If only I knew more! Once before I had gone to battle with one of the evil Old Ones in ignorance and using only my few poor weapons. Jervon, at that hour (having far more to fear than I, for he possessed none of the safeguards of the Talent), had come with me, trusting only in the power of cold iron and his own courage.

Could I do less now? As I stood there, the fluttering wand in my hand, I thought of what Jervon was to me. First, an unwanted road companion through a hostile land, one who made me impatient for I feared that he might in some way turn me from my purpose. Then—

My life was bound to Jervon's. I could not deny that. Whatever force had brought him here, it was for no purpose except his destruction—and perhaps also mine. Yet I accepted that and walked toward the doorway.

There was no door to face me. Only, once I had stepped under the shadow of that overhang, there was a cloud of darkness so thick it seemed one might gather together folds of it in one's fingers as one could a curtain woven on a Dale loom. I raised the hand I could no longer see until I thought the wand was level with my lips. Then I breathed upon it and spoke three words.

So tiny a light, as if a candle no thicker than my own little finger, shone feebly. But as that sparked into being I drew a deep breath. There was not yet any pressure on me. In so little had I won a token victory.

That other time I had had an advantage because what dwelt anciently in such a place had been all powerful for so long that it had not seen in me a worthy opponent. Therefore it had not unleashed its full strength against me until too late. I did not know what lay ahead, nor could I hold any hope that it would be the same here.

Time is often distorted and altered in those places of the Old Ones. All human memory is filled with legends of men who consorted with Those of Power for what seemed a day or year, and returned to find that their own world had swept on far faster. Now it appeared otherwise to me.

The very darkness, which was hardly troubled by the light on which my spirit fed, was like a flood of sticky clay or quicksand catching at my feet, so that it was a physical effort to fight against it in order to advance. As yet there had been no other assault upon me. Slowly, I gained the impression that what intelligence had raised this place for its shell of protection was otherwise occupied, so intent upon that concentration that it was not yet aware of me.

Even as the pinpoint of flame I held before me, that thought strengthened my courage. Yet I dared not depend upon such concentration holding. At any moment it might be broken, by some unknown, unseen system of alarm, to turn the force of Its interest in my direction.

I fought against the sticky dark, one step, two. It seemed to me that this journey had consumed hours of time. My body ached once more with the effort I must exert in order to advance. One more stride—

Thus I passed from complete dark into light so suddenly that, for two breaths, three, I was blinded. Then, blinking, I was able to see. The space in which I stood was round, with two great chairs, by their dimensions made for bodies larger than humankind, facing each other across a dazzling pillar which formed the innermost core.

Then I saw that it was not really a pillar, but rather a rounded shaft of ceaseless rolling radiance. No heat radiated from it; only an inner flickering suggested the flames it mimicked.

My inner warning sounded an alarm. Instantly I averted my eyes. There stood the force and purpose of this place. I had come out behind the nearer chair, its back a barrier, but I could see the other. Something had fallen from its wide seat to lie like a pile of wrung out rags on the floor.

Jervon—?

But even as I took a step toward that body, for dead that man must be by the very limpness of his form, I saw more clearly the face turned toward the light, the eyes wide in horror. And a stubby beard pointed outward from the chin. One of the outlaws!

Then Jervon—?

Carefully averting my gaze from that challenging, beckoning fire, I edged around the chair before me. Yes, he whom I sought sat there. There were bonds about his arms, loops bringing together his booted ankles. His helm was gone and there was a gash on his forehead which had been only roughly bandaged so that congealed red drops lay on the cheek beneath.

He was—alive?

I reached forth my hand. The wand trembled. Yes, there still was a spark of life in him, held so by the stubbornness of his own will and courage. But his eyes were locked on the pillar of fire and I knew that the substance of the man I knew was being rift out of him into that flame,

I could do two things. Recklessly, I first tried mind-seek. No, his consciousness was too depleted to respond. If I attempted to break the binding of the flame I could overturn the result of his own courage, loose him and lose him. There was a great strength in Jervon. I had seen it in action many times over during the seasons we had ridden together as comrades and lovers (seldom can those two be made one, but so it was with us).

So—I must follow him—into the flame. Front that Power on its own ground.

If only I knew more! I beat my hands together in my impotent frustration. This was a great force, and one I had no knowledge of. I did not know if I could face it with any Talent of my own. It might be invincible in its own stronghold.

I moved slowly on to look at the dead outlaw. He had been emptied of life force, easier prey by far than Jervon. The way he had fallen made it seem he had been contemptuously thrown aside.

But I knew Jervon. And upon that knowledge I could build now. It would do me no good to take his body from this place, even if the flame power would allow that. For then he could never regain what he had already lost—what must be returned to him . . .

Returned—how?

Desperate I was, for I might lose all, his life, mine, and perhaps more than just the lives of our bodies. But I could see no other way.

Deliberately I went to that other throne, careful not to touch the wasted body as I stepped over it. I am glad I did not hesitate now, that my inner strength carried me up unflinchingly to where that dead man had sat. I settled myself within the curve of the arms, under the shadow of the high back. My wand I took in both hands, forcing it up against the power which tried to forestall me, until the point was aimed at Jervon's breast.

I did not believe that the power I would confront was of

my plane of existence at all. Rather I thought that the frozen
flames were but a small manifestation visible to our world. I
must seek it on its own ground if I were to have a chance.

The outlaw had been its creature already. Doubtless he had
lain under its spell even before he had entered here, perhaps
sent by it to find such strong meat as Jervon. And Jervon it
had not completely taken. Also it might never have tried to
absorb one learned in the Talent.

Such a hope was very thin; I could count on nothing save
my own small learning and my determination. But it was not
in me to leave this place without Jervon. We would win or
lose together.

So—the battlefield lay within the flame.

My grip on the wand was iron tight. Now I deliberately
raised my eyes, stared straight into that play of curbed fire. I
need only release my will for a very little.

4

Elsewhere and Elsewhen

I was—elsewhere. How can one summon words to describe
what is so wholly alien to all one's experience? Colors rippled
here that had no names I knew, sensations wrenched at the
inner core of my determination and Talent as if they would
pull me apart while I yet lived. Or did I live now? I was
aware of no body in this place, five senses no longer served
me, for I realized I did not "see" but rather depended upon a
different form of perception.

Only seconds, breaths long, was I given; then a compelling
force swept up the consciousness which was all that remained
of my identity and drew me forward across a fantastic and
awesome country.

For *country* it was—! Though it was subtly *wrong*, my human instinct told me. There were growing things, which did
not in the least resemble any I had ever seen, of eye-searing
yellow, threatening red. These writhed and beat upon the air
as if they fought against their rooting, would be free to do
their will, and yet were anchored by another's ordering.
Branches tip-clawed the earth or swept high into the air in
ceaseless movement.

Then I was beyond them, carried so by the force which I
had momentarily surrendered to. And I put aside my preoc-

cupation with the strangeness of this place, to fasten inwardly, nurse my Talent with all my strength.

Yet must I also conceal from that which summoned me that I had that hard core of defiance within me. For I was sure that I must not dissipate that before I fronted the Power which ruled here.

I had heard legends through Aufrica (though from whom she had gained them she never said) that when the Old Ones held the Dales they had meddled with the very stuff of life itself, and that the adepts among them had opened "gates" which led to other dominions in which the human was as unnatural as that which passed swiftly below me now. That this might be such a "gate" I have begun to believe. But its guardianship was alien.

Here was a stretch of yellow ground unbroken by any of the monstrous growths. Patterned deeply on its surface were many tracks and trails, some deep-worn as well-used roads. Yet my own feet, if I still possessed those appendages, did not seek to tread there. Rather I had the sensation of being wafted well above that broken surface.

Those tracks and ways converged, angling toward some point ahead. And, as I passed on, I began to see moving figures, ones which pressed forward step by reluctant step. Yet none was clear, but rather cloaked in ever shifting color so that one could not define their true outlines. Some were dully grey, one or two a deep black that reminded me of the dark through which I had passed to reach the chamber of the flame. Others showed as sickly green, or a sullen, blood/rust red. As I swept over them I longed to shriek aloud my pain, for it seemed that from each there came some thrust of despair and horror which was like the cut of a sword one could not guard against. Thus I realized that these were victims of this place even as I might be.

Why I winged my way rather than trode theirs I could not guess. Unless that which ruled here knew me for what I was and would have me quickly within its grasp! And it was not good to think of that. I had made my choice, and must hold firmly to my resolution.

Thicker became the figures plodding so slowly. Now I began to believe that their doom was deliberately prolonged by purpose, that their helpless suffering was meat and drink to something—

Was Jervon one of those?

I tried to delay my own passage, hover above those misty

lights which were still substantial enough to leave tracks on
the plain. But then a second thought came to me, that in allowing myself to show interest in any of those tormented
wayfarers I could in turn betray the more plainly what I was
and why I had come.

So I turned my new sense of perception from those travelers, and allowed the compulsion full rein to draw me in. I
came at last to where that yellow plain gave way abruptly to
a chasm.

The walls of that were the dull red of the final wall which
had guarded the flame building, and in shape it was round.
Down its sides the lights which tracked the plain made a
painful descent, now so thronged together that their colors
seemed to blend and mingle. Though I thought in truth no
entity was aware of its fellows, but only of its own sore fate.

Down I was drawn, past those toiling victims. Once more
into a pool of dead blackness and loss of all perception. Here
I began to exercise those safeguards I had learned, seeds of
which had been mine from birth. I was myself, me, Elys—a
woman, a seer, a fighter. And I must remain me and not allow that Other to take away my oneness with myself and my
past.

Still I raised no opposition save that belief in myself which
I kept within me. At this moment I must put even Jervon
from my conscious mind and concentrate on my own personality. Instinct told me this, and for a Wise Woman such instinct is a command.

The dark began to thin and I could see light again. But in
that sickly yellowish glow there was nothing to be marked,
save directly under me, or that part of me which had come
seeking this grim venture, a throne.

It was fashioned of the black, the dark itself, and on it
there wavered a ruddy mist in which whirled gem-like parti-
cles.

"Welcome."

It was not sound which reached me, rather a vibration
which shuddered through whatever form I now wore.

Slowly I settled down, until I fronted that towering throne
and the unstable form it contained. Very small was I, so that
this was like looking up at the face of some high Dale hill.

"Good—"

Again the word vibrated through me, bringing with it both
pain and—may the Power I serve forgive me—also a kind of

pleasure which defiled that which I held to be the innermost core of my being.

"It has been long and long since this happened—"

The glittering mist of the throne was melting, developing more of a form.

"Are there then again those to summon for the Gate?"

That *form* leaned forward on its throne. The glitter points flowed together, formed two discs which might serve the alien for eyes. Now those centered upon me.

"Where is the gift then, servant of—" The name the thing mouthed was like a flame lapping about me, so strong was the Power that carried, even though I was no follower of It.

Before I could frame an answer, its shadowy head bobbed in what might be a nod.

"So the gift comes—yet I think it not of your devising. Think you I can be so easily deceived?" And the form shook with what might be silent and horrible laughter. The contempt in which it held me and all my species was like a loathsome stench in the air of that place.

"Your kind has served me," the vibration which was speech continued. "Long and well have they served me. Nor have I ever withheld their rewards. For when I feed, *those* feed. Behold!"

It stretched forth an extension of the upper body which might well serve it for arm, and then I could perceive indeed that all it had fed upon was a part of it. But not in peace. For the torment of those it consumed and yet nourished within its own substance was that they were conscious of what had happened to them, and that consciousness lasted throughout ages without respite. While as a part of this Thing they were also forced to feed in turn, damning themselves to further torture which was endless.

Even as I watched one of those long appendages flickered even farther out and returned, grasped in it a writhing core of grayness which was one with those shapes I had watched on the plain above. This it clasped to its body so that the gray sank into its mass and another life force was sentenced to an existence of terror and despair.

Seeing that, my mind stirred. Even as that rider I had seen in the valley was a thought-form fed into life by the terror of those whose emotions strengthened it, so was this Thing a product of similar forces.

I had heard it said that men are apt to make their gods in their own images, attributing to those gods their own emotions, save that those emotions are deemed far greater than any human mind and heart can generate. Thus this Thing might once have been born—to serve a people whose god it was, who fed it for generations. So that at last it was no longer dependent upon their willingly brought sacrifices, but could indeed control mankind and so exert its own dominion.

If that were indeed the truth, then the weapon against it was . . . *unbelief.* And, in spite of the evidence of my senses, here I must bring that weapon into being.

The glittering eyes that were set so on me did not change and the despair and horror which it exuded in waves wrapped me around with all the force long generations of worship could generate within it.

"Small creature—" again it shook with that unvoiced demonic laughter. "I am, I exist—no matter from what small seed of thought I was born. Look upon me!"

Now its substance grew even thicker and it indeed formed a body. This unclothed body was godlike in its beauty—its tainted beauty—brazenly male. And the eyes shrank, to become normal-sized in a face whose features were those truly of some super being without a flaw.

Except the flaw of knowledge of what it was and from what it had come. And that knowledge I clung to. It did not show bones and rotting flesh, but that was its true state.

"Look upon me!" Once more the command rang out. "Females of your kind found me good to look upon in the old days before I grew tired of your world, and that which closed Gates swept across the land. Look—and come!"

And that vile pleasure, which had troubled me before, again assailed me. Against that I set the training of my Talent—the austerity in which we learn to master all that which is of the body. Though I felt myself waver a little forward, yet my determination held me fast.

Then those perfect lips smiled—evilly.

"You are more than I have tasted for a long time. This shall indeed be a dainty feasting." Now it raised a fine muscled arm, beckoned to me with its long fingers. "Come— you cannot withstand me. Come willingly and the reward will be very great indeed."

My thought arose in answer and I shaped the name it had given me and with that name certain words. It was a forlorn hope. As that head tossed back and it laughed openly, I knew how vain that hope was.

"Names! You think that you can lay upon me your will by *names*? Ah, but that which I gave you is but the name men—some men—called me. It is not the name by which I know myself. And without that—you have no weapon. However, this is exciting—that you dare to stand against *me*! I have fed, and I have gathered strength, and I have waited for those who closed the Gates perhaps to hunt me. But they have not come, and you, worm thing who dares to face me—you are of such as they would not trouble themselves to look upon, far less do you stand equal to them.

"Only you shall give me sport, and that will be pleasant. You have come seeking one, have you not? Others have been led by pride and kinship to do so. They were fitly rewarded as you shall see when you join them. But name me no names which have not power!"

This time I did not try to answer. But feverishly I went seeking in my memory for the smallest trace of knowledge I had. Aufrica's learning had been shared with me to the best of her ability. We had visited certain forgotten shrines in the old days and sometimes dared to summon influences, long weakened by the years, which had once been dwelling in them. Spells I knew, but before this creature such were but as the rhyming games small children play.

No—I would not allow room to that despair which insidiously nibbled at my mind! What I could do I would!

The creature on the throne laughed for the third time.

"Very well. Struggle if you wish, worm one. It amuses me. Now—look what comes—"

It pointed to the left and I dared to look. There had come, very slowly, plainly fighting the compulsion which drew it, one of those columns of light. This one was not black, not gray, nor yet red, but a yellow which was clear and bright. In that moment I knew that this was what this world would see of Jervon.

Nor did it crawl abjectly as had the one the false god had claimed in my sight, but stood erect, as it fought against the power of the thing on the throne.

"Jervon!" I dared at that moment to send forth a thought-call. And instantly and valiantly was it answered:

"Elys!"

But the thing who commanded here looked from one of us to the other and smiled its evil smile.

5

Together We Stand

"So sweet a feasting—" A tongue tip appeared between the lips of the handsome face, swept back and forth as if indeed savoring some pleasant taste. "You give me much, small ones—much!"

"But not all!" I made answer. And that yellow flame which was Jervon no longer advanced, but stood with me, as we had stood together through the years when there was a blooding of swords and a need for defense. For I knew that this was not all of Jervon, that still in his ensorceled body he held stubbornly to his identity even as I went armed behind the wall of mine.

That which sat enthroned leaned forward a little, its beautiful and vile face turned to us.

"I hunger—and I feed—so simple is it."

It stretched out one of those seeming arms to an unnatural length, gathering to its bosom another crawling blob. In my mind there was a shriek of despair.

"You see how easy it is?"

Rather did I in turn reach with the Power for Jervon. And it was indeed as if we now stood hand-linked before this thing that should never have been. All the clean strength of Jervon's manhood was at war with what abode here. And to that I joined my Power, limited as it might be. I formed symbols and perceived them glow in the air, as if written in fire.

But the Thing laughed and stretched out a hand of mist to sweep those easily away.

"Small are your gifts, female. Do you think I cannot wipe them from sight? So and so and so—" That hand of mist moved back and forth.

"Jervon," I sent my own message, "it feeds upon fear."

"Yes, Elys, and upon the souls of men also." It seemed to me that his reply was so steady it was as if I had indeed found an anchorage which I needed.

Twice more the creature fed upon those blobs which crawled about the base of its throne. But always its eyes were on us. For what it waited, save that it must have our greater fear to season its feasting, I could not guess.

But that pause gave me time to draw in all which I knew, suspected, or hoped might aid us. How does one kill a god?

With unbelief, my logic told me. But here and now unbelief
was nigh impossible to summon.

We who have been burdened with the Talent must believe,
yes. For we know well that there are presences beyond our
comprehension, both good and evil, who may be summoned
by man. Though we cannot begin to understand their true
nature, limited as we are by the instincts and emotions of our
corporal bodies. I seek certain of these intangible presences
every time I exercise the Power which is mine, small that it
is. And in Jervon also there is belief—though his presences
might not be mine. For we do not all walk the same roads,
though in the end those roads must meet at a certain Gate
which is the greatest of all, and beyond which lies what we
cannot begin to imagine with our earthbound minds and
hearts.

Only to this Thing I owed no belief. I was not one who
had bowed in the courts of its temple nor sought its evil aid
in any undertaking. Therefore—for me—it was no god!

"So do you think, female," flashed its thought back in answer. "Yet you are of a like kind to those who gave me
creation. Therefore in you lie certain matters which I can
touch."

It was as if a slimy, rotting finger sleeked across my shrinking flesh. And in its wake—yes—there was that in me ready
to respond to that nauseating touch. I have weaknesses as in-
born as my Talent, those it could summon into battle against
me. Once more it laughed.

"Elys——" The thought that was Jervon's overrang that
laughter. "Elys!"

It was no more than my name, but it broke through that
feeling of abasement that anything in me could respond to
this horror. I drew once more upon logic. No man or woman
is perfect. There is much lying within us which we must look
upon with cold, measuring eyes and hate. But if we do not
yield to that hatred, nor to what gave it birth, but stand aside
to let one balance the other, then we do what those trained in
the Way can do to fight that which is base. Yes, I had in me
the force that could quicken from this thing of the utter dark.
But it was how I met that weakness, not the weakness itself
which counted.

I was Elys, a Wise woman, even as Jervon had reminded
me by the speaking of my name. Therefore I was no tool of
that which had led me to this throne. I had come of my own

free will in order to face it, not been dragged by dark forces overcoming my spirit.

"Elys—" It was the enthroned creature that uttered my name now, and there was enticement in that naming.

But I stood fast, summoning up all which was born of my long training to armor me. And the beautiful head so far above me shifted a little. Now, though keeping me still in its gaze, it also could see Jervon. It raised its hand to beckon.

The yellow flame which was my fulfillment in this life wavered toward the throne. Yet it was not muddied as were those others which crawled about us. Nor did Jervon ask aught of me in that moment, but made the struggle his own, for I knew, without his telling, that he feared I would be depleted should I undertake his defense as well as mine.

Then I moved whatever form this world had left me, standing between Jervon and the thing which reached now with its shadow hand to grasp him.

Once more I pronounced the name men had given him in their fear and horror of this baneful worship. But I sent no symbols into the air for him to sweep aside. Rather I did send a thought picture and this was of an empty throne crumbling in long decay.

Fear I fought, and anger I reined in, making both feed and serve *me* in what I would do. This was—not!

I could not close off that perception which assured me that it was. But I held valiantly to the small weapon I had. I did not worship, I did not believe, nor did Jervon. Therefore: this thing was *NOT*!

Yet it was growing more and more solid even as I so denied it. Beckoning—BEING!

The imagination of countless generations of men had fashioned it; how could I hope to dismantle it with only a denial?

An empty throne—a non-being—!

I threw all that was me, all which I sensed I drew now from Jervon with his willing consent, into that picture. This was no god of mine, I did not feed it—it could not exist!

Torment indeed was that denial, for ever it called to a part of me, to force homage and worship. Yet that I held out against. No god of mine! There must be faith to bring a god alive, to perform deeds in his name. Without faith there was no existence.

I knew better than to summon the Powers I did kneel before. In this place all worship the enthroned thing would take to itself, whether given in its filthy name or not. No, this was

the bareness of my spirit and my belief in myself, and Jervon's belief in himself—(the which he was loosing to
me)—that mattered. I did not accept, and I refused homage
because it was—*NOT*!

The thing lost its lazy assurance, its evil smile and laughter,
even the quasi-human form it had assumed to tempt me.
There was nothing in the throne place now but a ravening
flame touched with the deep black of its evil. That swept
back and forth as might the head of a great serpent elevated
above a coiled body, waiting to strike.

Its rage was that of madness. The long years it had existed
had not prepared it for this. It was here, it could seize my
kind, absorb into it their spirits.

But could it?

Humans contain many layers of consciousness, many emotions. Any who deal with the Talent—and many who do
not—know this. The throned thing fed upon fear and those
viler parts of us. The miserable blobs it drew to it, which
were now packed tightly around me, swaying in time to me
swaying of that flame on the throne, were dominated by the
worst that had lain in the humanity they had once been, not
the best. They had been held prisoner by their fears and their
belief, until they had been summoned here to be delivered
helplessly to their master.

A master who could in turn not hold them unless they surrendered, whom they had created and could now destroy—if
they so willed it!

I threw that thought afield as I might whirl about me an
unsheathed sword. If they were all lost in the depths of their
foul belief then it would avail me nothing. But if only a few
could join us—only a few!

The thing on the throne was quick. It lapped out and
down, and took with that lapping the first row of the blob
things, swelling in power as it absorbed their energy.

"Elys—Elys—"

Only my name, but into it Jervon put all he could to
hearten and sustain me. I was aware of a brighter burst of
the clear golden flame to my left.

Again the false god pounced to feast. There was something
too hasty in its movements, as if time was no longer its servant, but might speedily be its enemy. It wanted to cram itself with life force, swell its power.

But it could not feed on unbelief. That logic I held to as
one holds to a rope which is one's only hope of aid.

An empty throne—

Now that rusted and diseased flame uttered a kind of shriek, or perhaps that was not any cry but a vibration meant to shake me, loose me from my rope of hope. It flickered out and out toward me, toward the light which was Jervon.

We did not believe, therefore we could not be its prey.

I was in the dark; my perception was totally gone. I was—in . . . No, I could not be within something which did not exist. I was *me*, Elys, and Jervon. We were no meat for a false god whose creators were long since dust, its temple forgotten.

It was as if my bare body were seared by a cold so intense that it had the same effect as fire. I was one with—no, I was not! I was Elys. And Jervon was Jervon! I would feel him through the torture of the cold, holding as I did to his own identity. We were ourselves and no servants—victims—of this thing which had no place in the world. We had no fear for it to batten on now, and those parts of us which it could awaken, those we could control.

There was an empty throne—there was nothingness. Nothing but Elys and Jervon who did not believe—

Pain, cold, pain, and still I held and now Jervon called to me and somehow I found the strength to give to him even as earlier he had loosed his for me. Together we stood, and because of that both of us were the stronger, for in our union was the best part of us both—mind and spirit.

Darkness, cold, pain—and then a sense of change, of being lost. But I would not allow fear to stir. A god who was naught could not slay.

I opened my eyes—for I saw with them now and not with that special sense I had had in that other place. Before me was a column of light, but it was wan, sinking, growing paler even in the space of a blink or two. I moved; my body was stiff, cold, my hands and feet had no feeling in them as I slid forward on the wide seat where I had awakened, looking about me for something familiar and known.

This—this was the round chamber where I had found Jervon.

Jervon!

Stumbling, weaving, I staggered to that other chair, fumbling with my dagger so that I might cut the ropes which bound his stiff body. His eyes were closed, but he had not tumbled flaccidly down as had the outlaw who had been drained. I sawed at his hide bonds with my numb and fumbling hands, twice dropping the blade so I had to grope for it in the half light. For the flaming pillar in the center gave forth but little radiance now—more like the dread glow which sometimes gathers on dead bodies.

"Jervon!" I called to him, shook him as best I could with those blockish hands. His body fell forward so his head rested on my shoulder and his weight nearly bore me tumbling backward. "Jervon!"

It seemed in that moment that I had lost. For if I alone had won out of that evil place then there was no further hope for me.

"Jervon!"

There was a breath against my cheek, expelled by a moan. I gathered him to me in a hold, which even the false god could not have broken, until his voice came, low and with a stammering catch in it:

"My dear lady, would you break my ribs for me—" and there was a thread of weak laughter in that which set me laughing too, until I near shook with the force of that reaction.

I almost could not believe our battle won. But before us, where we crouched together on the wide seat of that throne, the last glimmer of light died. There was no gateway now into elsewhere. Outside the outlaws of the Waste might be waiting, but we two had battled something greater than any malice of theirs, and for the moment we were content.

THE TOADS of GRIMMERDALE

1

The drifts of ice-crusted snow were growing both taller and wider. Hertha stopped to catch her breath, ramming the butt of the hunting spear she had been using as a staff into the one before her, the smooth shaft breaking through the crust with difficulty. She frowned at the broken hole without seeing it.

There was a long dagger at her belt, the short hafted spear in her mittened hand. Under her cloak she hugged to her the all too small bundle which she had brought with her out of Horla's Hold. The other burden which she carried lay within her, and she forced herself to face squarely the fate that had been brought upon her.

Now her lips firmed into a line, her chin went up. Suddenly she spat with a hiss of breath. Shame—why should she feel shame? Had Kuno expected her to whine and wail, perhaps crawl before him so he could "forgive" her, prove thus to his followers his greatness of spirit?

She showed her teeth as might a cornered vixen, and aimed a harder blow at the drift. There was no reason for her to feel shame, the burden in her was not of wanton seeking. Such things happened in times of war. She guessed that when matters worked so Kuno had not been backward himself in taking a woman of the enemy.

It remained that her noble brother had sent her forth from Horla's Hold because she had not allowed his kitchen hags to brew some foul potion to perhaps poison her, as well as what she bore. Had she so died he could have piously crossed hands at the Thunderer's Altar and spoken of Fate's will, and all would have ended neatly. In fact she might believe that perhaps that had been his true intention.

For a moment Hertha was startled at the grim march of her thoughts. Kuno—Kuno was her *brother!* Two years ago

150

she could not have thought so of him or any man! When yet the war had not neared the Hold. But that was long before she set out the Landendale. Before she knew the world as it was and not as she had believed it.

Hertha was glad she had been able to learn her lesson quickly. The thin-skinned maid she had once been could not have fronted Kuno, could not have taken this road—

She felt the warmth of anger, a sullen, glowing anger, as heating as if she carried a small brazier of coals under her cloak's edge. So she went on, setting her rough boots firmly to crunch across the drift edge. Nor did she turn to look back down at that stone-walled keep which had sheltered those of her blood for five generations. The sun was well westward; she must not linger on the trail. Few paths were broken now; times in number she must halt and use the spear to sound out the footing. But it was easy to keep in eye her landmarks of Mulma's Needle and the Wyvern's Wing.

Hertha was sure Kuno expected her to come creeping woefully back to accept his conditions. She smiled wryly. Kuno was so very certain of everything. And since he had beaten off the attack of a straggling band of the enemy trying to fight their way to the dubious safety of the coast, he had been insufferable.

The Dales were free in truth. But for Kuno to act as if the victories hard won there were his alone—! It had required all the might of High Hallack, together with strange allies from the Waste, to break the invaders, to hunt and harry them back to the sea from which they had come. And that had taken a score of years to do it.

Trewsdale had escaped, not because of any virtue, but by chance. Because fire and sword had not riven, there was no reason to cry upon unbroken walls as gamecocks. Kuno had harried men already three-quarters beaten.

She reached the divide, to plod steadily on. The wind had been at work here, and her path was free of snow. It was very old, that road, one of the reminders to be found all across the dale land that her own people were latecomers. Who had cut these ways for their own treading?

The well-weathered carvings at the foot of the Wyvern's Wing could be seen easily now. So eroded they were by time that none could trace their meaning. But men—or intelligent beings—had shaped them to a purpose, and that task must have been long in the doing. Hertha reached out her mittened fingers to stroke one of the now vague curves. She did not believe they had any virtue in themselves, though the field workers did. But they marked well her road.

Down slope again from this point, and now the wind's lash did not cut at her. Though again, snow drifted. Two tens of days yet to the feast of Year Turn. This was the last of the Year of the Hornet, next lay the Year of the Unicorn, which was a more fortunate sign.

With the increase of snow, Hertha once more found the footing dangerous. Bits of broken crust worked in over the tops of her boots, even though she had drawn tight their top straps, and melted soddenly against her foot sacks. She plodded on as the track entered a fringe of scrub trees.

Evergreens, the foliage was dark in the dwindling light. But they arose to roof over a road, keeping off the drifts. She came to a stream where ice had bridged from one stony bank to the other. There she turned east to gain Gunnora's Shrine.

About its walls was a tangle of winter-killed garden. It was a low building, and an archway faced her. No gate or door barred that and she walked boldly in.

Once inside the outer wall she could see windows, round as the eyes of some great feline regarding her sleepily, flanking a door by which hung a heavy bell-pull of wrought metal in the form of Gunnora's symbol of a ripened grain stalk entwined with a fruit-laden branch.

Hertha leaned her spear against the wall that her hand might be free for a summons pull. What answered was not any peal of bell, rather an odd, muted sound as if some one called in words she did not understand. That, too, she accepted, though she had not been this way before, and had only a few whispered words to send her here.

The leaves of the door parted. Though no one stood there to give her house greeting, Hertha took that for an invitation to enter. She moved into gentle warmth, a fragrance of herbs and flowers, as if she had, in that single step, passed from the sure death of midwinter into the life of spring.

With the warmth and fragrance came a lightening of heart, so that the taut lines in her face smoothed a little, and her aching shoulders and back lost some of the stiffening tension.

What light there was issued from two lamps, set on columns, one right, one left. She was in a narrow entry, its walls painted with such colors as to make her believe that she had truly entered a garden. Before her those ranks of flowers rippled and she realized that there hung a curtain, fashioned to repeat the wall design. Since there still came no greeting, she put out her hand to the folds of the curtain.

Before she could finger it, the length looped a side of itself, and she came into a large room. There was a table there with a chair drawn up to it. Before that place was set out dishes, some covered as if they held viands which were to be kept warm, a goblet of crystal filled with a green liquid.

"Eat—drink—" a voice sighed through the chamber.

Startled, Hertha looked about the room, over her shoulder. No one. And now that hunger of which she had hardly been aware awoke full force. She dropped the spear to the floor, laid her bundle beside it, let her cloak fall over both and sat down in the chair.

Though she could see no one, she spoke:

"To the giver of the feast, fair thanks. For the welcome of the gate, gratitude. To the ruler of this house, fair fortune and bright sun on the morrow—" The formal words rang a little hollow here. Hertha smiled at a sudden thought.

This was Gunnora's shrine. Would the Great Lady need the well wishing of any mortal? Yet it seemed fitting that she make the guest speech.

There was no answer, though she hoped for one. At last, a little hesitatingly, she sampled the food spread before her and found it such fare as might be on the feast table of a Dales Lord. The green drink was refreshing, yet warming, with a subtle taste of herbs. She held it in her mouth, trying to guess which gave it that flavor.

When she had finished, she found that the last and largest covered basin held warm water on the surface of which floated petals of flowers. Flowers in the dead of winter! And beside it was a towel, so she washed her hands, and leaned back in the chair, wondering what came next in Gunnora's hall.

The silence in the room seemed to grow the greater. Hertha stirred. Surely there were priestesses at the Shrine? Some one had prepared that meal, offered it to her with those two words. She had come here for a purpose, and the need for action roused in her again.

"Great Lady." Hertha arose. Since she could see no one, she would speak to the empty room. There was a door at the other end of the chamber but it was closed.

"Great Lady," she began again. She had never been deeply religious, though she kept Light Day, made the harvest sacrifices, listened respectfully to the Mount of Astron at Morn

Service. When she had been a little maid, her foster mother had given her Gunnora's amulet and later, according to custom, that had been laid on the house altar when she came to marriageable age. Of Gunnora's mysteries she knew only what she had heard repeated woman to woman when they sat apart from the men. For Gunnora was only for womankind and when one was carrying ripening seed within one, then she listened—

For the second time her words echoed. Now her feeling of impatience changed to something else—awe, perhaps, or fear? Yet Gunnora did not hold by the petty rules of men. It did not matter when you sought her if you be lawful wife or not.

As Hertha's distrust grew, the second door swung silently open—another invitation. Leaving her cloak, bundle, spear where they lay, the girl went on. Here the smell of flowers and herbs was stronger. Lazy curls of scented smoke arose from two braziers standing at the head and foot of a couch. That was set as an altar at the foot of a pillar carved with the ripened grain, the fruited branch.

"Rest—" the sighing voice bade. Hertha, the need for sleep suddenly as great as her hunger had been, moved to that waiting bed, stretched out her wearied and aching body. The curls of smoke thickened, spread over her like a coverlet. She closed her eyes.

She was in a place of half light in which she sensed others coming and going, busied about tasks. But she felt alone, lost. Then one moved to her and she saw a face she knew, though a barrier of years had half dimmed it in her mind.

"Elfreda!" Hertha believed she had not called that name aloud, only thought it. But her foster mother smiled, holding out her arms in the old, old welcome.

"Little dove, little love—" The old words were as soothing as healing salve laid on an angry wound.

Tears came for Hertha had not allowed them to flow before. She wept out sore hurt and was comforted. Then that shade who was Elfreda drew her on, past all those about their work, into a place of light in which there was Another. And that one Hertha could not look upon directly. But she heard a question asked, and to that she made truthful answer.

"No," she pressed her hands to her body, "what I carry I do not want to lose."

Then that brightness which was the Other grew. But there was another question and again Hertha answered:

"I hold two desires—that this child be mine alone, taking of no other heritage from the manner of its begetting, and of him who forced me so. And, second, I wish to bring to account the one who will not stand as its father—"

There was a long moment before the reply came. Then a spear of light shot from the center core of the radiance traced a symbol before Hertha. Though she had no training in the Mysteries, yet this was plain for her reading.

Her first prayer would be answered. The coming child would be only of her, taking naught from her ravisher. The destiny for it was auspicious. Then, though she waited, there was no second answer. The great One—was gone! Elfreda was still with her, and Hertha turned to her quickly:

"What of my need for justice?"

"Vengeance is not of the Lady." Elfreda shook her veiled head. "She is life, not death. Since you have chosen to give life, she will aid you in that. For the rest—you must walk another road. But—do not take it, my love—for out of darkness comes even greater dark."

Then Hertha lost Elfreda also and there was nothing, only the memory of what happened in that place. So she fell into deeper slumber where no dreams walked.

She awoke, how much later she never knew. She was renewed in mind and body, feeling as if some leachcraft had been at work during her rest, banishing all ills. There was no more smoke rising from the braziers; the scent of flowers was faint.

When she arose from the couch, she knelt before the pillar, bowing her head, giving thanks. Yet still in her worked her second desire, in nowise lessened by Elfreda's warning.

In the outer room there was again food and drink waiting. And she ate and drank before she went forth from Gunnora's house. There was no kin far or near she might take refuge with. Kuno had made loud her shame when he sent her forth. She had a few bits of jewelry, none of worth, sewn into her girdle, some pieces of trade money. Beyond that she had only a housewife's skills, and those not of the common sort, rather the distilling of herbs, the making of ointments, the fine sewing of a lady's teaching. She could read, write, sing a stave—none of these arts conducive to the earning of one's bread.

Yet her spirit refused to be darkened by hard facts. From her waking that sense of things about to come right held, and she thought it best that she limit the future to one day ahead at a time.

In the direction she now faced lay two holdings. Nordendale was the first. It was small and perhaps in a state of disorder. The lord of the dale and his heir had both fallen at the battle of Ruther's Pass two years gone. Who kept order there now, if there were any who ruled, she did not know. Beyond that lay Grimmerdale.

Grimmerdale! Hertha set down the goblet from which she had drained the last drop. Grimmerdale—

Just as the shrine of Gunnora was among the heights near the ancient road, so did Grimmerdale have a place of mystery. But no kind and welcoming one if rumor spoke true. Not of her race at all, but one as old as the ridge road. In fact, perhaps that road had first been cut to run there.

Hertha tried to recall all she had heard of Grimmerdale. Somewhere in the heights lay the Circle of the Toads. Men had gone there, asked for certain things. By report they had received all they asked for. What had Elfreda warned? That Gunnora did not grant death—that one must follow another path to find that. Grimmerdale might be the answer.

She looked about her, almost in challenge, half expecting to feel condemnation in the air of the room. But there was nothing.

"For the feast, my thanks," she spoke the guesting words, "for the roof, my blessing, for the future all good, as I take my road again."

She fastened her cloak, drew the hood over her head. Then with bundle in one hand and spear in the other, went out into the light of day, her face to the ridges behind which lay Grimmerdale.

On the final slope above Nordendale, she paused in the afternoon to study the small settlement below. It was inhabited, there was a curl of smoke from more than one chimney, the marks of sleds, of footprints in the snow. But the tower keep showed no such signs of life.

How far ahead still lay Grimmerdale she had no knowledge, and night came early in the winter. One of those cottages below was larger than the rest. Nordendale had once been a regular halt for herdsmen with wool from mountain sheep on their way to the market at Komm High. That market was of the past, but the inn might still abide, at least be willing to give her shelter.

She was breathing hard by the time she trudged into the slush of the road below. But she had been right, over the door of the largest cottage hung a wind-battered board, its painted device long weathered away, but still proclaiming this an inn. She made for that, passing a couple of men on the way. They stared at her as if she were a fire-drake or wyvern. Strangers must be few in Nordendale.

The smell of food, sour village ale and too many people too long in an unaired space was like a smothering fog as she came into the common room. There was a wide hearth at one end, large enough to take a good-sized log, and fire burned there, giving off a goodly heat.

A trestle table with flanking benches, and a smaller one stacked with tankards, settles by the hearth, were the only furnishings. As Hertha entered, a wench in a stained smock and kirtle, two men on a hearth settle turned and stared with the same astonishment she had seen without.

She pushed back her hood and looked back at them with that belief in herself which was her heritage.

"Good fortune to this house."

For a moment they made no answer at all, seemingly too taken back at seeing a stranger to speak. Then the maid servant came forward, wiping her hands on her already well bespattered apron.

"Good fortune—" Her eyes were busy taking in the fine material of Hertha's cloak, her air of ease. She added quickly—"Lady. How may we serve you?"

"With food—a bed—if such you have."

"Food—food we have, but it be plain, coarse feeding, lady," the girl stammered. "Let me but call mistress—"

She ran to an inner door, bolting through it as if Hertha were minded to pursue her.

She rather laid aside her spear and bundle, threw back the edges of her cloak and went to stand before the hearth, pulling with her teeth at mitten fastenings, to bare her chilled hands. The men hunched away along the settle, mummouthed and still staring.

Hertha had thought her clothing plain. She wore one of the divided riding skirts, cut shorter for scrambling up and down hills—and it was now shabby and much worn, yet very serviceable. There was an embroidered edge on her jerkin, but no wider than some farm daughter might have. And her hair was tight braided, with no band of ribbon or silver to hold it so. Yet she might be clad in some festival finery the way they looked upon her. She stood as impassive as she could under their stares.

A woman wearing the close coif of a matron, a loose shawl

about her bent shoulders, a kirtle, but little cleaner than the maid's, looped up about her wide hips and thick thighs, bustled in.

"Welcome, my lady. Thrice welcome! Up you, Henkin, Fim, let the lady to the fire!" The men pushed away in a hurry at her ordering.

"Malka says you would bide the night. This roof is honored."

"I give thanks."

"Your man—outside? We have stabling—"

Hertha shook her head, "I journey alone and on foot." At the look on the woman's face she added, "In these days we take what fortune offers, we do not always please ourselves."

"Alas, lady, that is true speaking if such ever came to ear! Sit you down!" She jerked off her shawl and used it to dust along the settle.

Later, in a bed spread with coverings fire warmed, in a room which manifestly had been shut up for some time, Hertha lay in what comfort such a place could offer and mused over what she had learned from her hostess.

As she had heard, Nordendale had fallen on dreary times. Along with their lord and his heir, most of their able-bodied men had been slain. Those who survived and drifted back lacked leadership and had done little to restore what had been a prosperous village. There were very few travelers along the road; she had been the first since winter closed in. Things were supposed to be somewhat better in the east and south and her tale of going to kinsmen there had seemed plausible to those below.

Better still she had news of Grimmerdale. There was another inn there, a larger place, with more patronage, which the mistress here spoke of wistfully. An east-west road, now seeing much travel with levies going home, ran there. But the innkeeper had a wife who could not keep serving maids, being of jealous nature.

Of the Toads she dared not ask, and no one had volunteered such information, save that the mistress here had warned against the taking farther of the Old Road, saying it was better to keep to the highway, though she admitted that was also dangerous and it was well to be ready to take to the brush at the sighting of some travelers.

As yet Hertha had no more than the faint stirrings of a plan. But she was content to wait before she shaped it more firmly.

2

The inn room was long but low, the crossbeams of its ceiling not far above the crown of a tall man's head. There were smoking oil lamps hanging on chains from those beams. But the light those gave was both murky and limited. Only at the far corner where a carven screen afforded some privacy were there tallow candles set out on a table. The odor of their burning added to the general smell of the room.

The room was crowded enough to loosen the thin-lipped mouth of Uletka Rory as her small eyes darted hither and yon, missing no detail of service or lack of service, as her two laboring slaves limped and scuttled between benches and stools. She herself waited upon the candlelit table, a mark of favor. She knew high blood when she saw it.

Not that in this case she was altogether right, in spite of her years of dealing with travelers. One of the men there, yes, was the younger son of a dale lord. But his family holding had long since vanished in the red tide of war, and no one was left in Corriedale to name him master. One had been Master of Archers for another lord, promoted hurriedly after three better men had been killed. The third, well, he was not one who talked, and neither of his present companions knew his past.

Of the three he was the middle in age. Though that, too, could not be easily guessed, since he was one of those lean, spare-framed men who once they begin to sprout beard hair can be any age from youth to middle years. Not that he went bearded now—his chin and jaws were as smooth as if he had scraped them within the hour, displaying along the jawline the seam of a scar which drew a little at one lip corner.

He wore his hair cropped closer than most, also, perhaps because of the heavy helm now planted on the table at his right hand. That was battered enough to have served through the war. The crest it had once mounted was splintered down to a meaningless knob, though the protective bowl was unbreached.

His mail shirt, under a scuffed and worn tabbard, was whole. The plain hilted sword in his belt sheath, the war bow now resting against the wall at his back, were the well kept tools of a professional. But if he was mercenary he had not been successful lately. He wore none of those fine buckles or studs which could be easily snapped off to pay for food or lodging. Only when he put out his hand to take up his tankard did the candlelight glint on something which was not dull steel or leather. For the bowguard on his wrist was true treasure, a wide band of cunningly wrought gold set with small colored stones, though the pattern of that design was so complicated that to make anything of it required close study.

He sat now sober faced, as if he were deep in thought, his eyes half veiled by heavy lids. But he was in truth listening, not so much to the half-drunken mumblings of his companions, but to words arising here and there in the common room.

Most of those gathered there were either workers on the land come in to nurse an earthen mug of home-brewed barley beer and exchange grumbles with their fellows or else drifting men-at-arms seeking employment, with their lords dead or ruined so that they had to release the men of their levies. The war was over, these were the victors. But the land they turned to was barren, largely devastated, and it would take much time and energy to win back prosperity for High Hallack.

What the invaders from overseas had not early raped, looted for shiploads sent back to their own lands, they had destroyed in a frenzy when the tide of war began to wash them away. He had been with the war bands in the smoking port, sent to mop up desperate enemies who had fallen back too late to find their companions had taken off in the last ships, leaving them to be ground between the men of the dales and the sullen sea itself.

The smoke of the port had risen from piles of supplies set burning, oil poured over them and torches applied to the spoilage. The stench of it had been near enough to kill a man. Having stripped the country bare, and this being the midwinter, the enemy had made a last defiant gesture with that great fire. It would be a long cold line of days before the coming of summer, and even then men would go pinched of belly until harvest time—if they could find enough grain to plant, if sheep still roamed the upper dales, or cattle, wild now, found forage in the edges of the Waste—to make a beginning of new flocks and herds.

There were many dales swept clean of people. The men were dead in battle, the women either fled inland if they were lucky, or else slaved for the invaders overseas—or were dead also. Perhaps those were the luckiest of all. Yes, there had been a great shaking and leveling, sorting and spilling.

He had put down the tankard. Now his other hand went to that bowguard, turning it about, though he did not look down at it, but rather stared at the screen and listened.

In such a time a man with boldness, and a plan, could begin a new life. That was what had brought him inland, kept him from taking service with Fritigen of Summersdale. Who would be Master of Archers when he could be more, much more?

The invaders had not reached this Grimmerdale, but there were other lands beyond with darker luck. He was going to find one of those—one where there was no lord left to sound the war horn. If there were a lady trying to hold a heritage, well, that might even fit well with his ambitions. Now his tongue showed for an instant on his lower lip, flicking across as if he savored in anticipation some dish which pleased him. He did not altogether believe in an over-ride of good or ill fortune. In his calculations a man mostly made his own luck by knowing what he wanted and bending all his actions toward that end. But he had a feeling that this was the time when he must move if he were ever to bring to truth the dream which had lain in him since early boyhood.

He, Trystan out of nowhere, was going to end Lord Trystan of some not inconsiderable stretch of land—with a keep for his home and a dale under his rule. And the time to move was here and now.

"Fill!" His near companion, young Urre, pounded his tankard on the tabletop so that one of the candles shook, spattering hot grease. He bellowed an oath and threw his empty pot beyond the screen to clatter across the flagstones.

The lame pot boy stooped to pick it up, casting a frightened look at Urre and a second at his scowling mistress who was already on her way with a tray of freshly filled tankards. Trystan pushed back from the table. They were following a path he had seen too many nights. Urre would drink himself sodden, sick not only with the rank stuff they called drink back here in the hills, but also with his life, wherein he could only bewail what he had lost, taking no thought of what might be gained.

Onsway would listen attentively to his mumbling, willing to play liege man as long as Urre's money lasted or he could use his kin ties to win them food and lodging at some keep. When Urre made a final sot of himself, Onsway would no longer wallow in the sty beside him. While he, himself, thought it time now to cut the thread which had brought them this far in uneasy company. Neither had anything to give, and he knew now that traveling longer with them he would not do.

But he was not minded to quit this inn soon. Its position on the highway was such that a man could pick up a wealth of information by just sitting and listening. Also—here he had already picked out two likely prospects for his own purposes. The money pouch at his belt was flat enough, he could not afford to spin a coin before the dazzled eyes of an archer or pike man and offer employment.

However, there were men like himself to be found, rootless man who wanted roots in better circumstances than they had known, men who could see the advantage of service under a rising man with opportunities for rising, too, in his wake. One did not need a large war band to overawe masterless peasants. Half a dozen well armed and experienced fighting men at his back, a dale without a lord, and he would be in!

Excitement awoke in him as it did every time his plan reached that place in his thoughts. But he had learned long since to keep a tight rein on his emotions. He was a controlled man, abstemious to a degree astounding among his fellows, though he did what he could to conceal that difference. He could loot, he could whore, he could kill—and he had—but always calculatingly.

"I'm for bed." He arose and reached for his bow. "The road this day was long—"

Urre might not have heard him at all; his attention was fixed on the tray of tankards. Onsway nodded absently; he was watching Urre as he always did. But the mistress was alert to the hint of more profit.

"Bed, good master? Three bits—and a fire on the hearth, too."

"Good enough." He nodded, and she screeched for the pot boy who came at a limping waddle, wiping his grimed hands on the black rags of an apron knotted about him.

It seemed that while the inn gave the impression of space below, on the second floor it was much more cramped. At least the room into which Trystan tramped was a narrow slit of space with a single window covered by a shutter heavily barred. There was a litter of dried rushes on the floor and a rough bed frame on which lay a pile of bedding as if tossed. The hearth fire promised did not exist. But there was a legged brazier with some glowing coals which gave off a little heat, and a stool beside a warp-sided chest which did service as a table. The pot boy set the candle down on that and was ready to scuttle away when Trystan, who had gone to the window, hailed him.

"What manner of siege have you had here, boy? This shutter has been so long barred it is rusted tight."

The boy cringed back against the edge of the door, his slack mouth hanging open. He was an ugly lout, and looked half-witted into the bargain, Trystan thought, surely there was something more than just stupidity in his face, when he looked to the window there was surely fear also.

"Thhheee tooods—" His speech was thick. He had lifted his hands breast high, was clasping them so tightly together that his knuckles stood out as bony knobs.

Trystan had heard the enemy called many things, but never toads, nor had he believed they had raided Grimmerdale.

"Toads?" He made a question of the word.

The boy turned his head away so that he looked neither to the window nor Trystan. It was very evident he planned escape. The man crossed the narrow room with an effortless and noiseless stride, caught him by the shoulder.

"What manner of toads?" He shook the boy slightly.

"Toodss—Thhheee toods—" The boy seemed to think Trystan should know of what he spoke. "They—that sit 'mong the Standing Stones—that what do men evil." His voice, while thick no longer sputtered so. "All men know the Toods o' Grimmerdale!" Then, with a twist which showed he had had long experience in escaping, he broke from Trystan's hold and was gone. The man did not pursue him.

Rather he stood frowning in the light of the single candle. Toads—and Grimmerdale—together they had a faintly familiar sound. Now he set memory to work. Toads and Grimmerdale—what did he know of either?

The dale was of importance, more so now than in the days before the war when men favored a more southern route to the port. That highway had fallen almost at once into invader hands, and they had kept it fortified and patroled. The answer then had been this secondary road, which heretofore had been used mainly by shepherds and herdsmen. Three different trails from up country united at the western mouth of Grimmerdale.

However had he not once heard of yet a fourth way, one which ran the ridges, yet was mainly shunned, a very old way, antedating the coming of his own people? Now—he

nodded as memory supplied answers. The Toads of Grimmerdale! One of the many stories about the remnants of those
other people, or things, which had already mostly faded from
this land so that the coming of man did not dislodge them, for
the land had been largely deserted before the first settlement
ship arrived.

Still there were places in plenty where certain powers and
presences were felt this day, where things could be in-
voked—by men who were crazed enough to summon them.
Had the lords of High Hallack not been driven at the last to
make such a bargain with the unknown when they signed the
solemn treaty with the Were Riders? All men knew that it
had been the aid of those strange outlanders which had broken the invaders at the last.

Some of the presences were beneficial, others neutral, the
third dangerous. Perhaps not actively so in these days. Men
were not hunted, harried or attacked by them. But they had
their own places, and the man who was rash enough to tres-
pass there did so at risk.

Among such were the Standing Stones of the Toads of
Grimmerdale. The story went that they would answer appeals, but that the manner of answer sometimes did not
please the petitioner. For years now men had avoided their
place.

But why a shuttered window? If, as according to legend the
toads (people were not sure now if they really *were* toads)
did not roam from their portion of the Dale, had they once?
Making it necessary to bolt and bar against them? And why a
second-story window in this fusty room?

Moved by a curiosity he did not wholly understand, Trystan drew his belt knife, pried at the fastenings. They were
deeply bitten with rust, and he was sure that this had not
been opened night or day for years. At last they yielded to
his efforts; he was now stubborn about it, somehow even a
little angry.

Even though he was at last able to withdraw the bar, he
had a second struggle with the warped wood, finally using
sword point to lever it. The shutters grated open, the chill of
the night entered, making him aware at once of how very
odorous and sour was the fug within.

Trystan looked out upon snow and a straggle of dark trees,
with the upslope of the dale wall beyond. There were no
other buildings set between the inn and that rise. And the
thick vegetation showing dark above the sweep of white on

the ground suggested that the land was uncultivated. The trees there were not tall, it was mainly brush alone, and he did not like it.

His war-trained instincts saw there a menace. Any enemy could creep in its cover to within a spear cast of the inn. Yet perhaps those of Grimmerdale did not have such fears and so saw no reason to grub out and burn bare.

The slope began gradually and shortly the tangled growth thinned out, as if someone had there taken the precautions Trystan thought right. Above was smooth snow, very white and unbroken in the moonlight. Then came outcrops of rock. But after he had studied those with an eye taught to take quick inventory of a countryside, he was sure they were not natural formations but had been set with a purpose.

They did not form a connected wall. There were wide spaces between as if they had served as posts for some stringing of fence. Yet for that purpose they were extra thick.

And that first row led to a series of five such lines, though more distantly they were close together. Trystan was aware of two things. One, bright as the moon was, it did not, he was sure, account for all the light among the stones. There was a radiance which seemed to rise either from them, or the ground about them. Second, no snow lay on the land from the point where the lines of rock pillar began. Above the stones also there was a misting, as if something there bewildered or hindered clear sight.

Trystan blinked, rubbed his hand across his eyes, looked again. The clouding was more pronounced when he did so, as if whatever lay there increased the longer he watched it.

That this was not of human Grimmerdale he was certain. It had all signs of being one of those strange places where old powers lingered. And that this was the refuge or stronghold of the "toads" he was now sure. That the shutter had been bolted against the weird sight he could also understand, and he rammed and pounded the warped wood back into place, though he could not reset the bar he had levered out.

Slowly he put aside mail and outer clothing, laying it across the chest. He spread out the bedding over the hide webbing. Surprisingly the rough sheets and the two woven covers were clean. They even (now that he had drawn lungfuls of fresh air to awaken his sense of smell) were fragrant with some kind of herb.

Trystan stretched out, pulled the covers about his ears, drowsy and content, willing himself to sleep.

He awoke to a clatter at the door. At first he frowned up at the cobwebbed rafters above. What had he dreamed? Deep in his mind there was a troubled feeling, a sense that a message of some importance had been lost. He shook his head against such fancies and padded to the door, opened it for the entrance of the elder serving man, a dour-faced, skeleton-thin fellow who was more cleanly of person than the pot boy. He carried a covered kettle which he put down on the chest before he spoke.

"Water for washing, master. There be grain-mush, pig cheek and ale below."

"Well enough." Trystan slid the lid off the pot. Steam curled up. He had not expected this small luxury and he took its arrival as an omen of fortune for the day.

Below, the long room was empty. The lame boy was washing off tabletops, splashing water on the floor in great scummy drollops. His mistress stood, hands on her hips, her elbows outspread like crooked wings, her sharp chin with its two haired warts outthrust as a spear to threaten the other woman before her, well cloaked against the outside winter, but with her hood thrown back to expose her face.

That face was thin with sharp features which were lacking in any claim to comeliness since the stretched skin was mottled with unsightly brown patches. But her cloak, Trystan saw, was good wool, certainly not that of a peasant wench. She carried a bundle in one hand, and in the other was a short-hafted hunting spear, its butt scarred as if it had served her more as a journey staff than a weapon.

"Well enough, wench. But here you work for the food in your mouth, the clothing on your back." The mistress shot a single glance at Trystan before she centered her attention once more on the girl.

Girl, Trystan thought she was. Though by the Favor of Likerwolf certainly her face was not that of a dewy maid, being rather enough to turn a man's thoughts more quickly to other things when he looked upon her.

"Put your gear on the shelf yonder," the mistress said. "Then to work, if you speak the truth on wanting that."

She did not watch to see her orders obeyed, but came to the table where Trystan had seated himself.

"Grain-mush, master. And a slicing of pig jowl—ale fresh drawn—"

He nodded, sitting much as he had the night before, fingering the finely wrought guard about his wrist, his eyes half closed as if he were still wearied, or else turned his thoughts on things not about him.

The mistress stumped away. But he was not aware she had returned, until someone slid a tray onto the tabletop. It was the girl. Her shrouding of cloak was gone, so that the tight bodices, the pleated skirt could be seen. And he was right, she did not wear peasant clothes. That was a skirt divided for riding, though it had now been shortened enough to show boots, scuffed and worn, straw protruding from their tops. Her figure was thin, yet shapely enough to make a man wonder at the fate which wedded it to that horror of a face. She did not need her spear for protection, all she need do was show her face to any would-be ravisher and she would be as safe as the statue of Gunnora the farmers carried through their fields at first sowing.

"Your food, master." She was deft, far more so than the mistress, as she slid the platter of crisp browned mush, the pink sliced thin meat, onto the board.

"Thanks given," Trystan found himself making civil answer as he might in some keep were one of the damsels there noticing him in courtesy.

He reached for the tankard and at that moment saw her head sway, her eyes wide open rested on his hand. He thought, with a start of surprise, that her interest was no slight one. But when he looked again, she was moving away, her eyes downcast as any proper serving wench.

"There will be more, master?" she asked in a colorless voice. But her voice also betrayed her. No girl save one hold bred would have such an accent.

There had been many upsets in the dales. What was it to him if some keep woman had been flung out of her soft nest to tramp the roads, serve in an inn for bread and a roof? With her face she could not hope to catch a man to fend for her—unless he be struck blind before their meeting.

"No," he told her. She walked away with the light and soundless step which might have equaled a forest hunter's, the grace of one who sat at high tables by right of blood.

Well, he, too, would sit at a high table come next year's end. Of that he was certain as if it had been laid upon him by some Power Master as an unbreakable geas. But it would be because of his own two hands, the cunning of his mind. As such his rise would be worth more than blood right. She had come down, he would go up. Seeing her made him just more confident of the need for moving on with his plan.

3

The road along the ridges was even harder footing after Nordendale, Hertha discovered. There were gaps where landslides had cut away sections, making the going very slow. However she kept on, certain this was the only way to approach what she sought.

As she climbed and slid, with caution, even in places had to leap recklessly with her spear as a vaulting pole, she considered what might lie ahead. In seeking Gunnora she had kept to the beliefs of her people. But if she continued to the shrine of the Toads she turned her back on what safety she knew.

Around her neck was hung a small bag of grain and dried herbs, Gunnora's talisman for home and hearth. Another such was sewn into the breast of her undersmock. And in the straw which lined each boot were other leaves with their protection for the wayfarer. Before she had set out on this journey she had marshaled all she knew of protective charms. But whether such held against alien powers, she could not tell. To each race its own magic. The Old Ones were not men and their beliefs and customs must have been far different. That being so, did she now tempt great evil?

Always when she reached that point she remembered. And memory was as sharp as any spur on a rider's heel. She had been going to the abbey in Lethendale, Kuno having suggested it. Perhaps that was why he had turned from her, feeling guilt in the matter.

Going to Lethendale, she must ever remember how that journey was, every dark part of it. For if she did not hold that in mind, then she would lose the booster of anger for her courage. A small party because Kuno was sure there was naught to fear from the fleeing invaders. But after all it was not the invaders she had had to fear.

There had come a rain of arrows out of nowhere. She could hear yet the bubbling cry of young Jannesk as he fell from the saddle with one through his throat. They had not even seen the attackers, and all the men had been shot down in moments. She had urged her mount on, only to have him entangle feet in a trip rope. She could remember only flying over his head thereafter—

She awoke in the dark, her hands tied, looking out into a clearing where a fire burned between rocks. Men sat about it tearing at chunks of half-roasted meat. *Those* had been the invaders. And she had lain cold, knowing well what they meant for her when they had satisfied one appetite and were ready—

They had come to her at last. Even with tied hands she had fought. So they had laughed and cuffed her among them, tearing at her garments and handling her shamefully, though they did not have time for the last insult and degradation of all. No, that was left for some—some *man* of her own people!

Thinking on it now made rage rise to warm her even though the sun had withdrawn from this slope and there was a chill rising wind.

For the ambushers had been attacked in turn, fell under spear and arrow out of the dark. Half conscious, she had been left lying until a harsh weight on her, hard, bruising hands brought her back to terror and pain.

She had never seen his face, but she had seen (and it was branded on her memory for all time) the bowguard encircling the wrist tightened as a bar across her throat to choke her unconscious. When she had once more stirred she was alone.

Someone had thrown a cloak over her nakedness. There was a horse nearby. There was for the rest only dead men under a falling snow. She never understood why they had not killed her and been done with it. Perhaps in that little skirmish her attacker had been overridden by his companions. But at the time she had been sorely tempted to lie where she was and let the cold put an end to her. Only the return of that temper which was her heritage roused her. Somewhere living was the man who should have been her savior and instead had rift from her what was to be given only as a free gift. To bring him down, for that she would live.

Later, when she found she carried new life, yes, she had been tempted again—to do as they urged, rid herself of that. In the end she could not. For though part of the child was of evil, yet a part was hers. Then she recalled Gunnora and the magic which could aid. So she had withstood Kuno's urging, even his brutal anger.

She held to two things with all the stubborn strength she could muster—that she would bear this child which must be hers only, and that she would have justice on the man who would never in truth be its father. The first part of her desire Gunnora had given, now she went for answer to the second.

At last night came and she found a place among the rocks where she could creep in, the stone walls giving refuge from the wind, a carpet of dried leaves to blanket her. She must have slept, for when she roused she was not sure where she was. Then she was aware of the influence which must have brought her awake. There was an uneasiness in the very air about her, a tension as if she stood on the verge of some great event.

With the spear as her staff, Hertha came farther into the open. The moon showed her unmarked snow ahead, made dark pits of her own tracks leading here. With it for a light she started on.

A wan radiance, having no light of fire, shone in the distance. It came from no torch either, she was sure. But it might well mark what she sought.

Here the Old Road was unbroken, though narrow. She prodded the snow ahead, lest there be some hidden crevice. But she hurried as if to some important meeting.

Tall shapes arose, stones set on end in rows. For the outer lines there were wide spaces between, but the inner ones were placed closer and closer together. She followed a road cut straight between these pillars.

On the crest of each rested a small cone of light, as if these were not rocks but giant candles to light her way. And the light was cold instead of warm, blue instead of orange-red as true flame. Also here the moonlight was gone, so that even though there was no roof she could see, yet it was shut away.

Three stone rows she passed, then four more, each with the stones closer together, so that the seventh brought them touching to form a wall. The road dwindled to a path which led through a gate therein.

Hertha knew that even had she wanted to retreat, now she could not. It was as if her feet were held to the path and that moved, bearing her with it.

So she came into a hexagon-shaped space within the wall. There was a low curbing of stone to fence off the centermost portion and in each angle blazed a flame at ground level. But she could go no farther, just as she could not draw away.

Within the walled area were five blocks of green stone. Those glistened in the weird light as if they were carved of polished gems. Their tops had been squared off to give seating for those who awaited her.

What she had expected Hertha was not sure. But what she saw was so alien to all she knew that she did not even feel fear, but rather wonder that such could exist in a world where men also walked. Now she could understand why these bore the name of toads, for that was the closest mankind could come in descriptive comparison.

Whether they went on two limbs or four, she could not be sure the way they hunched upon their blocks. But they were no toads in spite of their resemblance. Their bodies were bloated of paunch, the four limbs seemingly too slender beside that heaviness. Their heads sat upon narrow shoulders with no division of neck. And those heads were massive, with large golden eyes high on their hairless skulls, noses which were slits only, and wide mouths stretching above only a vestige of chin.

"Welcome, Seeker—"

The words rang in her head, not her ears. Nor could she tell which of the creatures spoke then.

Now that Hertha had reached her goal she found no words, she was too bemused by the sight of those she had sought. Yet it seemed that she did not have to explain, for the mind speech continued:

"You have come seeking our aid. What would you, daughter of men, lose that which weighs your body?"

At that Hertha found her tongue to speak.

"Not so. Though the seed in me was planted not by lawful custom, but in pain and torment of mind and body, yet will I retain it. I shall bear a child who shall be mine alone, as Gunnora has answered my prayers."

"Then what seek you here?"

"Justice! Justice upon him who took me by force and in shame!"

"Why think you, daughter of men, that you and your matters mean aught to us who were great in this land before your feeble kind came, and who will continue to abide even after man is again gone? What have we to do with you?"

"I do not know. Only I have listened to old tales, and I have come."

She had an odd sensation then. If one could sense laughter, she was feeling it. They were amused, and, knowing that, she lost some of her assurance.

Again a surge of amusement, and then a feeling as if they had withdrawn, conferred among themselves. Hertha would have fled but she could not. And she was afraid as she had not been since she faced horror on the road to Lethendale.

"Upon whom ask you justice, daughter of men? What is his name, where lies he this night?"

She answered with the truth. "I know neither. I have not even seen his face. Yet—" she forgot her fear, knew only that hate which goaded her on, "I have that which shall make him known to me. And I may find him here in Grimmerdale since many men now pass along this road, the war being ended."

Again that withdrawal. Then another question.

"Do you not know that services such as ours do not come without payment? What have you to offer us in return, daughter of men?"

Hertha was startled. She had never really thought past making her plea here. That she had been so stupid amazed her. Of course there would be payment! Instinctively she dropped her bundle, clasped her hands in guard over where the child lay.

Amusement once more.

"Nay, daughter of men. From Gunnora you have claimed that life, nor do we want it. But justice can serve us, too. We will give you the key to that which you wish, and the end will be ours. To this do you agree?"

"I do." Though she did not quite understand.

"Look you—there!" One of the beings raised a forefoot and pointed over her shoulder. Hertha turned her head. There was a small glowing spot on the surface of the stone pillar. She put out her hand and at her touch a bit of stone loosened so she held a small pebble.

"Take that, daughter of men. When you find him you seek, see it lies in his bed at the coming of night. Then your justice will fall upon him—here! And so you will not forget, nor think again and change your mind, we shall set a reminder where you will see it each time you look into your mirror."

Again the being pointed, this time at Hertha. From the forelimb curled a thin line of vapor. That curdled to form a ball which flew at her. Though she flinched and tried to duck, it broke against her face with a tingling feeling which lasted only for a second.

"You will wear that until he comes hither, daughter of men. So will you remember your bargain."

What happened then she was not sure, it was all confused. When she was clearheaded again dawn was breaking and she clawed her way out of the leaf-carpeted crevice. Was it all a dream? No, her fingers were tight about something, cramped and in pain from that hold. She looked down at a pebble of green-gray stone. So in truth she had met the Toads of Grimmerdale.

Grimmerdale itself lay spread before her, easy to see in the gathering light. The lord's castle was on the farther slope, the village and inn by the highway. And it was the inn she must reach.

Early as it was there were signs of life about the place. A man went to the stable without noticing her as she entered the courtyard. She advanced to the half-open door, determined to strike some bargain for work with the mistress, no matter how difficult the woman was reputed to be.

The great room was empty when she entered. But moments later a woman with a forbidding face stumped in. Hertha went directly to her. The woman stared at her and then grinned, maliciously.

"You've no face to make trouble, wench, one can be certain of that," she said when Hertha asked for work. "And it is true that an extra pair of hands is wanted. Not that we have a purse so fat we can toss away silver—"

As she spoke a man came down the steep inner stair, crossed to sit at a table half screened from the rest. It was almost as if his arrival turned the scales in Hertha's favor. For she was told to put aside her bundle and get to work. So it was she who took the food tray to where he sat.

He was tall, taller than Kuno, with well set, wide shoulders. And there was a sword by his side, plain hilted, in a worn scabbard. His features were sharp, his face thin, as if he might have gone on short rations too often in the past. Black hair peaked on his forehead and she could not guess his age, though she thought he might be young.

But it was when she put down her tray and he reached out for an eating knife that it seemed the world stopped for an instant. She saw the bowguard on his wrist. And her whole existence narrowed to that metal band. Some primitive instinct of safety closed about her, she was sure she had not betrayed herself.

As she turned from the table she wondered if this was by the power of the Toads, that they had brought her prey to her hand so. What had they bade her—to see that the pebble was in his bed. This was early morn, and he had just risen; what if he meant not to stay another night, but would push on? How could she then carry out their orders? Unless she followed after, somehow crept upon him at nightfall.

At any rate he seemed in no hurry to be up and off if that was his purpose. Finally, with relief, she heard him bargain with the mistress for a second night's stay. She found an excuse to go above, carrying fresh bedding for a second room to be made ready. And as she went down the narrow hall she wondered how best she could discover which room was his.

So intent was she upon this problem that she was not aware of someone behind her, until an ungentle hand fell on her shoulder and she was jerked about.

"Now here's a new one—" The voice was brash and young. Hertha looked at a man with something of the unformed boy still in his face. His thick yellow hair was uncombed, and his jaw beard stubbled, his eyes red-rimmed.

As he saw her clearly he made a grimace of distaste, shoved her from him with force, so she lost her balance and fell to the floor.

"As leave kiss a toad!" He spat. But the trail of spittle never struck her. Instead hands fell on him, slammed him against the other wall. While the man of the bowguard surveyed him steadily.

"What's to do?" The younger man struggled. "Take your hands off me, fellow!"

"Fellow, is it?" observed the other. "I am no liege man of yours, Urre. Nor are you in Roxdale now. As for the wench, she's not to blame for her face. Perhaps she should thank what ever Powers she lights a candle to that she has it. With such as you ready to lift every skirt they meet."

"Toad! He is a toad-face—" Urre worked his mouth as if he wished to spit again, then something in the other's eyes must have warned him. "Hands off me!" He twisted and the other stepped back. With an oath Urre lurched away, heading unsteadily for the stair.

Hertha got to her feet, stooped to gather up the draggle of covers she had dropped.

"Has he hurt you?"

She shook her head dumbly. It had all been so sudden, and that *he*—this one—had lifted hand in her defense dazed her. She moved away as fast as she could, but before she reached the end of the passage she looked back. He was going through a door a pace away from where the one called Urre had stopped her. So—she had learned his room. But toad face? That wet ball which had struck her last night—what had it done to her?

Hertha used her fingers to trace any alteration in her features. But to her touch she was as she had always been. A mirror—she must find a mirror! Not that the inn was likely to house such a luxury.

In the end she found one in the kitchen, in a tray which she had been set to polishing. Though her reflection was cloudy, there was no mistaking the ugly brown patches on her skin. Would they be so forever, a brand set by her trafficking with dark powers, or would they vanish with the task done? Something she had remembered from that strange voiceless conversation made her hope the latter was true.

If so, the quicker she moved to the end, the better. But she did not soon get another chance to slip aloft. The man's name was Trystan. The lame pot boy had taken an interest in him and was full of information. Trystan had been a Marshal, and Master of Archers—he was now out of employment, moving inland probably to seek a new lord. But perhaps he was thinking of raising a war band on his own, he had talked already with other veterans staying here. He did not drink much, though those others with him, Urre, who was son to a dale lord, and his liege man ordered enough to sail a ship.

Crumbs, yes, but she listened eagerly for them, determined to learn all she could of this Trystan she must enmesh in her web. She watched him, too, given occasion when she might do so without note. It gave her a queer feeling so to look upon the man who had used her and did not guess now she was near.

Had it not been for the evidence of the bowguard, she would have picked him last of those she saw beneath this roof. Urre, yes, and two or three others, willing to make free with her until they saw her face clearly. But when she had reason to pass by this Trystan he showed her small courtesies, as if her lack of comeliness meant nothing. He presented a puzzle which was disturbing.

But that did not change her plan. So, at last, when she managed close to dusk to slip up the stairway quickly, she sped down the hall to his room. There was a huddle of coverings on the bed. She could not straighten those, but she thrust the pebble deep into the bag-pillow and hurried back to the common room where men were gathering. There she obeyed a stream of orders, fetching and carrying tankards of drink, platters of food.

The fatigue of her long day of unaccustomed labor was beginning to tell. There were those among the patrons who used cruel humor to enlighten the evening. She had to be keen-witted and clear-eyed to avoid a foot slyly thrust forth to trip her, a sudden grab at her arm to dump a filled platter or tray of tankards. Twice she suffered defeat and was paid by a ringing buffet from the mistress's hand for the wasting of food.

But at length she was freed from their persecution by the mistress (not out of any feeling for her, but as a matter of saving spillage and spoilage) and set to the cleaning of plates in a noisome hole where the stench of old food and greasy slops turned her stomach and made her so ill she was afraid she could not last. Somehow she held out until finally the mistress sourly shoved her to one of the fireside settles and told her that was the best bed she could hope for. Hertha curled up, so tired she ached, while the rest of the inn people drifted off to their holes and corners—chambers were for guests alone.

The fire had been banked for the night, but the hearth was warm. Now that she had the great room to herself, though her body was tired, her mind was alert, and she rested as best she could while she waited. If all went well, surely the stone would act this night, and she determined to witness the action. Beyond that she had not planned.

Hertha waited for what seemed a long time, shifting now and then on her hard bed. Near to hand were both her cloak and the spear staff, her boots new filled with fresh straw were on her feet.

She was aware of a shadow at the head of the stairs, of steps. She watched and listened. Yes, she had been right—this was the man Trystan, and he was walking toward the door. Whirling her cloak about her, Hertha rose to follow.

4

She clung to the shadow of the inn wall for fear he might look behind. But he strode on with the sure step of a man on a mission of such importance his present surroundings had little meaning, rounding the back of the inn, tramping up the slope.

Though a moon hung overhead, there was also a veiling of cloud. Hertha dropped farther and farther behind, for the brambles of the scrub caught at her cloak, the snow weighted her skirt, and the fatigue of her long day's labor was heavy on her. Yet she felt that she must be near to Trystan when he reached his goal. Was it that she must witness the justice of the Toads? She was not sure any more, concentrating all her effort on the going.

Now she could see the stones stark above. They bore no candles on their crests this night, were only grim blots of darkness. Toward them Trystan headed on as straight a line as the growth would allow.

He reached the first line of stones, not once had he looked around. Long since Hertha abandoned caution. He was almost out of sight! She gathered up her skirts, panting heavily as she plunged and skidded to where he had disappeared.

Yes, now she could see him, though he was well ahead. But when he reached that final row, the one forming a real wall, he would have to move along it to the entrance of the Old Road. While she, already knowing the way, might gain a few precious moments by seeking the road now. And she did that, coming to better footing with her breath whistling through her lips in gasps.

She had no spear to lean on and she nursed a sharp pain in her side. But she set her teeth and wavered on, between those rows of stones, seeing the gate ahead and framed in it a dark figure. Trystan was still a little before.

There came a glow of light, the cold flames were back on pillar top. In its blue radiance her hands looked diseased and foul when she put them out to steady herself as she went.

Trystan was just within the gate of the hexagon. He had not moved, but rather stared straight ahead at whatever awaited him. His sword was belted at his side, the curve of his bow was a pointing finger behind his shoulder. He had come fully armed, yet he made no move to draw weapon now.

Hertha stumbled on. That struggle up the slope had taken much of her strength. Yet in her was the knowledge that she must be there. Before her now, just beyond her touching even if she reached forth her arm, was Trystan. His head was uncovered, the loose hood of his surcoat lay back on his shoulders. His arms dangled loosely at his sides. Hertha's gaze followed to the source of his staring concentration.

There were the green blocks. But no toad forms humped upon them. Rather lights played there, weaving in and out in a flickering dance of shades of blue, from a wan blight which might have emanated from some decaying bit on a forest floor, to a brilliant sapphire.

Hertha felt the pull of those weaving patterns, until she

forced herself (literally forced her heavy hands to cover her eyes) not to look upon the play of color. When she did so there was a sensation of release. But it was plain her companion was fast caught.

Cupping her hands to shut out all she could of the lights, she watched Trystan. He made no move to step across the low curbing and approach the blocks. He might have been turned into stone himself, rapt in a spell which had made of him ageless rock. He did not blink an eye, nor could she even detect the rise and fall of his chest in breathing.

Was this their judgment then, the making of a man into a motionless statue? Somehow Hertha was sure that whatever use the Toads intended to make of the man they had entrapped through her aid it was more than this. Down inside her something stirred. Angrily she fought against that awakening of an unbidden thought, or was it merely emotion? She drew memory to her, lashed herself with all shameful, degrading detail. This had he done to her, and this, and this! By his act she was homeless, landless, a nothing, wearing even a toad face. Whatever came now to him, he richly deserved it. She would wait and watch, and then she would go hence, and in time as Gunnora had promised, she would bear a son or daughter who had none of this father—none!

Still watching him, her hands veiling against the play of the ensorceling light, Hertha saw his lax fingers move, clench into a fist. And then she witnessed the great effort of that gesture, and she knew that he was in battle, silent though he stood. That he fought with all his strength against what held him fast.

That part of her which had stirred and awakened grew stronger. She battled it. He deserved nothing but what would come to him here; he deserved nothing from her but the justice she had asked from the Toads.

His hand-fist arose, so slowly that it might have been chained to some great weight. When Hertha looked from it to his face, she saw the agony that was causing him. She set her shoulders to the rock wall; had she but a rope she would have bound herself there, that no weakness might betray her plan.

Strange light before him and something else, formless as yet but with a cold menace greater than any fear born of battle heat. For this terror was rooted not in any ordinary danger, but grew from a horror belonging by rights far back in the beginnings of his race. How he had come here, whether this be a dream or not. Trystan was not sure. And he had no time to waste on confused memory.

What energy he possessed must be used to front that which was keeping him captive. It strove to fill him with its own life, and that he would not allow, not while he could summon will to withstand it.

Somehow he thought that if he broke the hold upon his body, he could also shatter its would-be mastery of his mind and will. Could he act against its desires, he might regain control. So he set full concentration on his hand—his fingers. It was as if his flesh were nerveless, numb—But he formed a fist. Then he brought up his arm, so slowly that, had he allowed himself to waver, he might have despaired. He knew that he must not relax his intense drive of will centered in that simple move. Weapons—what good would his bow, his sword, be against what dwelt here? He sensed dimly that this menace could well laugh at weapons forged and carried by those of his kind.

Weapons—sword—steel—there was something hovering just at the fringe of memory. Then for an instant he saw a small, sharp mind picture. Steel! That man from the Waste side dale who had set his sword as a barrier at the head of his sleeping roll, his dagger, plunged point deep in the soil at his feet the night they had left him on the edge of very ancient ruins with their mounts. Between cold iron a man lay safe, he said. Some scoffed at his superstition, others had nodded agreement. Iron—cold iron—which certain old Powers feared.

He had a sword at his belt now, a long dagger at his hip—iron—talismen? But the struggle for possession of his fist, his arm, was so hard he feared he would never have a chance to put the old belief to the proof.

What did they want of him, those who abode here? For he was aware that there was more than one will bent on him. Why had they brought him? Trystan shied away from questions. He must concentrate on his hand—his arm!

With agonizing slowness he brought his hand to his belt, forced his fingers to touch the hilt of his sword.

That was no lord's proud weapon with a silvered, jeweled hilt, but a serviceable blade nicked and scratched by long use. So that the hilt itself was metal, wound with thick wire to make a good grip which would not turn in a sweating hand. His fingertips touched that and—his hand was free!

He tightened hold instantly, drew the blade with a practiced sweep, and held it up between him and that riot of blending and weaving blue lights. Relief came, but it was only minor, he knew after a moment or two of swelling hope. What coiled here could not be so easily defeated. Always that other will weighted and plucked at his hand. The sword blade swung back and forth, he was unable to hold it steady. Soon he might not be able to continue to hold it at all!

Trystan tried to retreat even a single step. But his feet were as if set in a bog, entrapped against any move. He had only his failing hand and the sword, growing heavier every second. Now he was not holding it erect as if on guard, but doubled back as if aimed at his own body!

Out of the blue lights arose a tendril of wan, phosphorescent stuff which looped into the air and remained there, its tip pointed in his direction. Another weaved up to join it, swell its substance. A third came, a fourth was growing—

The tip, which had been narrow as a finger, was now thickening. From that smaller tips rounded and swelled into being. Suddenly Trystan was looking at a thing of active evil, a grotesque copy of a human hand, four fingers, a thumb too long and thin.

When it was fully formed it began to lower toward him. Trystan, with all his strength, brought up the sword, held its point as steady as he could against that reaching hand.

Again he knew a fleeting triumph. For at the threat of the sword, the hand's advance was stayed. Then it moved right, left, as if to strike as a foeman's point past his guard. But he was able by some miracle of last reserves to counter each attack.

Hertha watched the strange duel wide-eyed. The face of her enemy was wet; great trickles of sweat ran from his forehead to drip from his chin. His mouth was a tight snarl, lips flattened against his teeth. Yet he held that sword and the emanation of the Toads could not pass it.

"You!"

The word rang in her head with a cold arrogance which hurt.

"Take from him the sword!"

An order she must obey if she was to witness her triumph. Her triumph? Hertha crouched against the rock watching that weird battle—sword point swinging with such painful slowness, but ever just reaching the right point in time so that the blue hand did not close. The man was moving so slowly, why could the Toads not beat him by a swift dart past his guard? Unless their formation of the hand, their use of it, was as great an effort for them as his defense seemed to be for him.

"The sword!" That demand in her mind hurt.

Hertha did not stir. "I cannot!" Did she cry that aloud, whisper it. Or only think it? She was not sure. Nor why she could not carry through to the end that which had brought her here—that she did not understand either.

Dark—and her hands were bound. There were men struggling. One went down with an arrow through him. Then cries of triumph. Someone came to her through shadows. She could see only mail—a sword—

Then she was pinned down by a heavy hand. She heard laughter, evil laughter which scorched her, though her body shivered as the last of her clothing was ripped away. Once more—

NO! She would not remember it all! She would not! They could not make her—but they did. Then she was back in the here and now. And she saw Trystan fighting his stumbling, hopeless battle, knew him again for what he was.

"The sword—take from him the sword!"

Hertha lurched to her feet. The sword—she must get the sword. Then he, tooo would learn what it meant to be helpless and shamed and—and what? Dead? Did the Toads intend to kill him?

"Will you kill him?" she asked them. She had never foreseen the reckoning to be like this.

"The sword!"

They did not answer, merely spurred her to their will. Death? No, she was certain they did not mean his death. At least not death such as her kind knew it. And—but—

"The sword!"

In her mind that order was a painful lash, meant to send her unthinking to their service. But it acted otherwise, alerting her to a new sense of peril. She had evoked that which had no common meeting with her kind. Now she realized she had loosed that which not even the most powerful man or woman she knew might meddle with. Trystan could deserve the worst she was able to pull upon him. But that must be the worst by men's standards—not this!

Her left hand went to the bag of Gunnora's herbs where it rested between her swelling breasts. Her right groped on the ground, closed about a stone. Since she touched the herb bag that voice was no longer a pain in her head. It faded like a far-off calling. She readied the stone—

Trystan watched that swinging hand. His sword arm ached up into his shoulder. He was sure every moment he would lose control. Hertha bent, tore at the lacing of her bodice so that herb bag swung free. Fiercely she rubbed it back and forth on the stone. What so pitiful an effort might do—

She threw the rock through the murky air, struck against that blue hand. It changed direction, made a dart past him. Knowing that this might be his one chance, Trystan brought down the sword with all the force he could muster on the tentacle which supported the hand.

The blade passed through as if what he saw had no substance, had been woven of his own fears. There was a burst of pallid light. Then the lumpish hand which supported it was gone.

In the same moment he discovered he could move and staggered back. Then a hand fell upon his arm, jerking him in the same direction. He flailed out wildly at what could only be an enemy's hold, broke it. There was a cry and he turned his head.

A dark huddle lay at the foot of the door frame stone. Trystan advanced the sword point, ready, as strength flowed once more into him, to meet this new attack. The bundle moved; a white hand clutched at the pillar, pulled.

His bemused mind cleared. This was a woman! Not only that, but what had passed him through the air had been flung not at him, but at the hand. She had been a friend and not an enemy in that moment.

Now from behind he heard a new sound like the hiss of a disturbed serpent. Or there might be more than one snake voicing hate. He gained the side of the woman, with the standing rocks at his back, looked once more at the center space.

That tentacle which had vanished at the sword stroke might be gone, but there were others rising. This time those did not unite to form hands, but rather each produced something like unto a serpent head. They arose in such numbers that no one man could hope to front them all. Though he must try.

Once more he felt a light weight upon his shoulder, he glanced to the side. The woman was standing, one hand tight to her breast, the other resting on his upper arm now. Her hood overshadowed her face so he could not see that. But he could hear the murmur of her voice even through the hissing of the pseudo-serpents. Though he could not understand the words, there was a rhythmic flow as if she chanted a battle song for his encouragement.

One of the serpent lengths swung at them; he used the sword. At its touch the thing vanished. But one out of dozens, what was that? Again his arm grew heavy, he found movement difficult.

Trystan tried to shake off the woman's hold, not daring to take hand from his sword to repell her.

"Loose me!" he demanded, twisting his body.

She did not obey, or answer. He heard only that murmur of sound. There was a pleading note in it, a frantic pleading. He could feel her urgency, as if she begged of someone aid for them both.

Then from here her fingers dug into his shoulder muscles, there spread downward along his arm, across his back and chest, a warmth, a loosing—not of her hold, but of the bonds laid on him here. And within the center space the snake heads darted with greater vigor. Now and then two met in midair, and when they did they instantly united, becoming larger.

These darted forth, striking at the two by the gate, while Trystan cut and parried. They moved with greater speed so he was hard put to keep them off. They showed no poison fangs, nor did they even seem to have teeth within their open jaws. Yet he sensed that if those mouths closed upon him or the woman they would be utterly done.

He half turned to beat off one which had come at him from an angle. His foot slipped and he went to one knee, the sword half out of his grasp. As he grabbed it tighter he heard a cry. Still crouched, he slewed around.

The serpent head at which he had struck had only been a ruse. His lunge at it carried him away from the woman. Two other heads had captured her. To his horror he saw that one had fastened across her head, engulfing most of it on contact. The other had snapped its length of body about her waist. Gagged by the one on her head she was quiet; nor did she struggle as the pallid lengths pulled her back to the snakes' lair. Two more reached out to fasten upon her, no longer heeding Trystan, intent on their capture.

He cried out hoarsely, was on his feet again, striking savagely at those dragging her. Then he was startled by a voice which seemed to speak within his head.

"Draw back, son of men, lest we remember our broken bargain. This is no longer your affair."

"Loose her!" Trystan cut at the tentacle about her waist. It burst into light, but another was already taking its place.

"She delivered you to us, would you save her?"

"Loose her!" He did not stop to weigh the right or wrong of what had been said, he only knew that he could not see the woman drawn to that which waited, that he might not do and remain a man. He thrust again.

The serpents' coils were moving faster, drawing back into the hexagon. Trystan could not even be sure she still lived, not with that dreadful thing upon her head. She hung limp, not fighting.

"She is ours! Go you—lest we take more for feasting."

Trystan wasted no breath in argument, he leaped to the left, mounting the curb of the hexagon. There he slashed into the coils which pulled at the woman. His arms were weak, he could hardly raise the sword, even two-handed, and bring it down. Yet still he fought stubbornly to cut her free. And little by little he thought that he was winning.

Now he noted that where the coils tightened about her they did not touch her hand where it still rested clasping something between her breasts. So he strove the more to cut the coils below, severing the last as her head and shoulders were pulled over the edge of the curb.

Then it seemed that, tug though they would, the tentacles could not drag her wholly in. As they fought to do so Trystan had his last small grant of time. He now hewed those which imprisoned her head and shoulders. He saw those rising for new holds. But, as she so lay, to do their will they must come across her breast to attack, and that they apparently could not do.

Wearily he raised the blade and brought it down again, each time sure he could not do so again. At last there was a moment when she was free of them all. He flung out his left hand, clasped hers where it lay between her breasts, heaved her back and away.

There was a sharp hissing from the serpent things. They writhed and twisted. But more and more they sank to the ground, rolled there feebly. He got the woman on his shoulder, tottered back, still facing the enemy, readied as best he could be for another attack.

5

It would seem that the enemy was spent, at least the snakes did not strike outward again. Watching them warily, Trystan retreated, dared to stop and rest with the woman. He leaned above her to touch her cheek. To his fingers the flesh was cold, faintly clammy. Dead? Had the air been choked from her?

He burrowed beneath the edges of her hood, sought the pulse in her throat. He could find none, so he tried to lay his hand directly above her heart. In doing so he had to break her grip on what lay between her breasts. When he touched a small bag there, a throbbing, a warmth spread up his hand, so he jerked hastily away before he realized this was not a danger but a source of energy and life.

Her heart still beat. Best get her well away while those things in the hexagon were quiescent. For he feared their defeat was only momentary.

Trystan dared to sheath his sword, leaving both arms free to carry the woman. For all the bulk of her cloak and clothing, she was slender, less than the weight he had expected.

Now his retreat was that of a coastal sea crab, keeping part attention on the stew pot of blue light at his back, as well as on the footing ahead. He drew a full breath again only when he had put two rings of the standing stones between him and the evil those guarded.

Nor was he unaware that there was still something dragging on him, trying to force him to face about. That he battled with a firm will and his sense of self preservation, his teeth set, a grimace of effort stiffening mouth and jaw.

One by one he pushed past the standing stones. As he went, the way grew darker, the weird light fading. He was beginning to fear that he could no longer trust his own sight. Twice he found himself off the road, making a detour around a pillar which seemed to sprout before him, heading so back the way he had come.

Thus he fought both the compulsion to return and the tricks of vision, learning to fasten his attention on some point only a few steps ahead and wait until he had passed that before he set another goal.

He came at last, the woman resting over his shoulder, into the clean night, the last of the stones behind him. Now he was weak, so weary that he might have made a twenty-four-hour march and fought a brisk skirmish at the end of it. He slipped to his knees, lowered his burden to the surface of the old road, where, in the open, the wind had scoured the snow away.

There was no moon, the cloud cover was heavy. The woman was now only a dark bulk. Trystan squatted on his heels, his hands dangling loose between his knees, and tried to think coherently.

Of how he had come up here he had no memory at all. He had gone to bed in the normal manner at the inn, first waking to danger when he faced the crawling light in the hexagon. That he had also there fought a danger of the old time he had no doubt at all. But what had drawn him there?

He remembered the forcing open of the inn window to look up the slope. Had that simple curiosity of his been the trigger for this adventure? That those of the inn could live unconcerned so close to such a peril—he could hardly believe. Or because they had lived here so long, were the descendants of men rooted in Grimmerdale, had they developed an immunity to dark forces?

What had the thing or things in the hexagon said? That she who lay here had delivered him to them. If so—why? Trystan hunched forward on his knees, twitched aside the hood edge, stooping very close to look at her, though it was hard to distinguish more than just the general outline of her features in this limited light.

Suddenly her body arched away from him. She screamed with such terror as startled him as she pushed against the road under her, her whole attitude one of such agony of fear as held him motionless. Somehow she got to her feet. She had only screamed that once, now he saw her arms move under the hindering folds of her cloak. The moon broke in a thin sliver from under the curtain of the cloud, glinted on what she held in her hand.

Steel swung in an arc for him. Trystan grappled with her before that blade bit into his flesh. She was like a wild thing, twisting, thrusting, kicking, even biting as she fought him. At length he handled her as harshly as he would a man, striking his fist against the side of her chin so her body went limply once more to the road.

There was nothing to do but take her back to the inn. Had her experience in that nest of standing stones turned her brain to see enemies all about her? Resigned, he ripped a strip from the hem of her cloak, tied her hands together.

Then he got her up so she lay on his back, breathing shallowly, inert. So carrying her he slipped and slid, pushed with difficulty through the scrub to the valley below and the inn.

What the hour might be he did not know, but there was a night lantern burning above the door and that swung open beneath his push. He staggered over to the fireplace, dropped his burden by the hearth and reached for wood to build up the blaze, wanting nothing now so much as to be warm again.

Hertha's head hurt. The pain seemed to be in the side of her face. She opened her eyes. There was a dim light, but not that wan blue. No, this was flame glow. Someone hunched at the hearth setting wood lengths with expert skill to rebuild a fire. Already there was warmth which her body welcomed. She tried to sit up. Only to discover that her wrists were clumsily bound together. Then she tensed, chilled by fear, watching intently he who nursed the fire.

His head was turned from her; she could not see his face, but she had no doubts that it was Trystan. And her last memory—him looming above her, hands outstretched—to take her again as he had that other time! Revulsion sickened her so she swallowed hurriedly lest she spew openly on the floor. Cautiously she looked around. This was the large room of the inn; he must have carried her back. That he might take pleasure in a better place than the icy cold of the old road? But if he tried that she could scream, fight—surely someone would come—

He looked to her now, watching her so intently that she felt he read easily every one of her confused thoughts.

"I shall kill you," she said distinctly.

"As you tried to do?" He asked that not as if it greatly mattered, but as if he merely wondered.

"Next time I shall not turn aside!"

He laughed. And with that laughter for an instant he seemed another man, one younger, less hardened by time and deeds. "You did not turn aside this time, mistress, I had a hand in the matter." Then that half smile which had come with the laughter faded, and he regarded her with narrowed eyes, his mouth tight set lip to lip.

Hertha refused to allow him to daunt her and glared back. Then he said:

"Or are you speaking of something else, mistress? Something which happened before you drew steel on me? Was that—that *thing* right? Did I march to its lair by your doing?"

Somehow she must have given away the truth by some fraction of change he read in her face. He leaned forward and gripped her by the shoulders, dragging her closer to him in spite of her struggles, holding her so they were squarely eye to eye.

"Why? By the Sword Hand of Karther the Fair, why? What did I ever do to you, girl, to make you want to push me into that maw? Or would any man have sufficed to feed those pets? Are they your pets, or your masters? Above all, how comes humankind to deal with *them*? And if you so deal, why did you break their spell to aid me? Why, and why, and why?"

He shook her, first gently, and then, with each question, more harshly, so that her head bobbed on her shoulders and she was weak in his hands. Then he seemed to realize that she could not answer him, so he held her tight as if he must read the truth in her eyes as well as hear it from her lips.

"I have no kinsman willing to call you to a sword reckoning," she told him wearily. "Therefore I must deal as best I can. I sought those who might have justice—"

"Justice! Then I was not just a random choice for some purpose of theirs! Yet, I swear by the Nine Words of Min, I have never looked upon your face before. Did I in some battle slay close kin—father, brother, lover? But how may that be? Those I fought were the invaders. They had no women save those they rift from the Dales. And would any Dales-woman extract vengeance for one who was her master-by-force? Or is it that, girl? Did they take you and then you found a lord to your liking among them, forgetting your own blood?"

If she could have, Hertha would have spat full in his face for that insult. He must have read her anger quickly.

"So that is not it. Then why? I am no ruffler who goes about picking quarrels with comrades. Nor have I ever taken any woman who came not to me willingly—"

"No?" She found speech at last, in a wrath-hot rush of words. "So you take no woman unwillingly, brave hero? What of three months since on the road to Lethendale? Is it too usual a course of action with you that it can be so lightly put out of mind?"

Angry and fearful though she was, she could see in his expression genuine surprise.

"Lethendale?" he repeated. "Three months since? Girl, I have never been that far north. As to three months ago—I was Marshal of Forces for Lord Ingrim before he fell at the siege of the port."

He spoke so earnestly that she could almost have believed him, had not that bowguard on his wrist proved him false.

"You lie! Yes, you may not know my face. It was in darkness you took me, having overrun the invaders who had first made me captive. My brother's men were all slain. For me they had other plans. But when aid came—then still I was for the taking—as you proved, Marshal!" She made of that a name to be hissed.

"I tell you, I was at the port!" He had released her and she backed against the settle, leaving a good space between them.

"You would swear before a Truth Stone it was me? You know my face, then?"

"I would swear, yes. As for your face—I do not need that. It was in the dark you had your will of me. But there is one proof I carry ever in my mind since that time."

He raised his hand, rubbing fingers along the old scar on his chin, the fire gleaming on the bowguard. That did not match the plainness of his clothing, how could anyone forget seeing it?

"That proof being?"

"You wear it on your wrist, in plain sight. Just as I saw it then, ravisher—your bowguard!"

He held his wrist out, studying the band, "Bowguard! So that is your proof, that made you somehow send me to the Toads." He was half smiling again, but this time cruelly and with no amusement. "You did send me there, did you not?" He reached forward and, before she could dodge, pulled the hood fully from her head, stared at her.

"What have you done with the toad face, girl? Was that some trick of paint, or some magicking you laid on yourself? Much you must have wanted me so to despoil your own seeming to carry through your plan."

She raised her bound hands, touched her cheeks with cold fingers. This time there was no mirror, but if he said the loathesome spotting was gone, then it must be so.

"They did it—" she said, only half comprehending. She had pictured this meeting many times, imagined him saying this or that. He must be very hardened in such matters to hold to this pose of half amused interest.

"They? You mean the Toads? But now tell me why, having

so neatly put me in their power, you were willing to risk your life in my behalf? That I cannot understand. For it seems to me to traffic with such as abide up that hill is a fearsome thing and one which only the desperate would do. Such desperation is not lightly turned aside—so—why did you save me, girl?"

She answered with the truth. "I do not know. Perhaps because the hurt being mine, the payment should also be mine—that, a little, I think. But even more—" she paused so long he prodded her.

"But even more, girl?"

"I could not in the end leave even such a man as you to *them!*"

"Very well, that I can accept. Hate and fear and despair can drive us all to bargains we repent of later. You made one and then found you were too human to carry it through. Then later on the road you chose to try with honest steel and your own hand—"

"You—you would have taken me—again!" Hertha forced out the words. But the heat in her cheeks came not from the fire but from the old shame eating her.

"So that's what you thought? Perhaps, given the memories you carry, it was natural enough." Trystan nodded. "But now it is your turn to listen to me, girl. Item first—I have never been to Lethendale, three months ago, three years ago—never! Second: this which you have come to judge me on," he held the wrist closer, using the fingers of his other hand to tap upon it, "I did not have three months ago. When the invaders were close pent in the port during the last siege, we had many levies from the outlands come to join us. They had mopped up such raiding bands as had been caught out of there when we moved in to besiege.

"A siege is mainly a time of idleness, and idle men amuse themselves in various ways. We had only to see that the enemy did not break out along the shores while we waited for the coasting ships from Handelsburg and Vennesport to arrive to carry them from the sea. There were many games of chance played during that waiting. And, though I am supposed by most to be a cautious man, little given to such amusements, I was willing to risk a throw now and then.

"This I so won. He who staked it was like Urre, son to some dead lord, with naught but ruins and a lost home to return to if and when the war ended. Two days later he was killed in one of the sorties the invaders now and then made.

He had begged me to hold this so that when luck ran again in his way he might buy it back, for it was one of the treasures of his family. In the fighting I discovered it was not only decorative, but useful. Since he could not redeem it, being dead, I kept it—to my disfavor it would seem. As for the boy—I do not even know his name—for they called him by some nickname. He was befuddled with drink half the time, being one of the walking dead—"

"Walking dead?" His story carried conviction, not only his words but his tone, and the straight way he told it.

"That is what I call them. High Hallack has them in many—some are youngsters such as Urre, the owner of this." Again he smoothed the guard. "Others are old enough to be their fathers. The dales have been swept with fire and sword. Those which were not invaded have been bled of their men, of their crops—to feed both armies. This is a land which can now go two ways. I can sink into nothingness from exhaustion, or there can rise new leaders to restore and with courage build again."

It seemed to Hertha that he no longer spoke to her but rather voiced his own thoughts. As for her, there was a kind of emptiness within, as if something she carried had been rift from her. That thought sent her bound hands protectively to her belly.

The child within her—who had been its father? One of the lost ones, some boy who had had all taken from him and so became a dead man with no hope in the future, one without any curb upon his appetites. Doubtless he had lived for the day only, taken ruthlessly all offered during that short day. Thinking so, she sensed that queer light feeling. She had not lost the child, this child which Gunnora promised would be hers alone. What she had lost was the driving need for justice which had brought her to Grimmerdale—to traffic with the Toads.

Hertha shuddered, cold to her bones in spite of her cloak, of the fire. What had she done in her blindness, her hate and horror? Almost she had delivered an innocent man to that she dared not now think upon. What had saved her from that at the very last, to throw that stone rubbed with Gunnora's talisman? Some part of her refusing to allow such a foul crime?

And what could she ever say to this man who had now turned his head from her, was looking into the flames as if therein he could read message runes? She half raised her bound hands, he looked about with a real smile from which she shrank as she might from a blow, remembering how it might have been with him at this moment.

"There is no need for you to go bound. Or do you still thirst for my blood?" He caught her hands, pulled at the cloth tying them.

"No," Hertha answered in a low voice. "I believe you. He whom I sought is now dead."

"Do you regret that death came not at your hand?"

She stared down at her fingers resting again against her middle, wondering dully what would become of her now. Would she remain a tavern wench, should she crawl back to Kuno? No! At that her head went up again, pride returned.

"I asked, are you sorry you did not take your knife to my gamester?"

"No."

"But still there are dark thoughts troubling you—"

"Those are none of your concern." She would have risen, but he put out a hand to hold her where she was.

"There is an old custom. If a man draws a maid from dire danger, he has certain rights—"

For a moment she did not understand, when she did her bruised pride strengthened her to meet his eyes.

"You speak of maids—I am not such."

His indrawn breath made a small sound, but one loud in the silence between them. "So that was the why! You are no farm or tavern wench are you? So you could not accept what he had done to you. But have you no kinsman to ride for your honor?"

She laughed raggedly. "Marshal, my kinsman had but one wish, that I submit to ancient practices among women so that he would not be shamed before his kind. Having done so I would have been allowed to dwell by sufferance in my own home, being reminded not more than perhaps thrice daily of his great goodness."

"And this you would not do. But with your great hate against him who fathered what you carry—"

"No!" Her hands went to that talisman of Gunnora's. "I have been to the shrine of Gunnora. She has promised me my desire, the child I bear will be mine wholly, taking nothing from *him!*"

"And did she also send you to the Toads?"

Hertha shook her head. "Gunnora guards life. I knew of the Toads from old tales. I went to them in my blindness and they gave me that which I placed in your bed to draw you to them. Also they changed my face in some manner. But—that is no longer so?"

"No. Had I not known your cloak, I should not have known you. But this thing in my bed—Stay you here and wait. Only promise me this, should I return as one under orders, bar the door in my face and keep me here at all cost!"

"I promise."

He went with the light-footed tread of one who had learned to walk softly in strange places because life might well depend upon it. Now that she was alone her mind returned to the matter of what could come to her with the morn. Who would give her refuge—save perhaps the Wise Women of Lethendale. It might be that this Marshal would escort her there. Though what did he owe her, except such danger as she did not want to think on. Although her thoughts twisted and turned she saw no answer except Lethendale. Perhaps Kuno would some day—no! She would make no plan leading in that path!

Trystan was back holding two sticks such as were used to kindle brazier flames. Gripped between their ends was the pebble she had brought from the Toads' hold. As he reached the fire he hurled that bit of rock into the heart of the blaze.

He might have poured oil upon the flames so fierce was the answer as the pebble fell among the logs. Both shrank back.

"That trap is now set at naught," he observed. "I would not have any other fall into it."

She stiffened, guessing what he thought of her for the setting of the same trap.

"To say I am sorry is only mouthing words, but—"

"To one with such a burden, lady, I can return that I understand. When one is driven by a lash one takes any way to free oneself. And in the end you did not suffer that I be taken."

"Having first thrust you well into the trap! Also—you should have let them take me then as they wished. It would only have been fitting."

"Have done!" He brought his fist down on the seat of the settle beside which he knelt, "Let us make an end to what is past. It is gone. To cling to this wrong or that, keep it festering in mind and heart, is to cripple one. Now, lady," she detected a new formality in his voice, "where do you go, if not to your brother's house? It is not in your mind to return there, I gather."

She fumbled with the talisman. "In that you are right. There is but one place left—the Wise Women of Lethendale. I can beg shelter from them." She wondered if he would offer the escort she had no right to ask, but his next question surprised her.

"Lady, when you came hither, you came by the Old Road over ridge, did you not,"

"That is so. To me it seemed less dangerous than the open highway. It has, by legend, those who sometimes use it, but I deemed those less dangerous than my own kind."

"If you came from that direction you must have passed through Nordendale—what manner of holding is it?"

She had no idea why he wished such knowledge, but she told him of what she had seen of that leaderless dale, the handful of people there deep sunk in a lethargy in which they clung to the ruins of what had once been thriving life. He listened eagerly to what she told him.

"You have a seeing eye, lady, and have marked more than most, given such a short time to observe. Now listen to me, for this may be a matter of concern to both of us in the future. It is in my mind that Nordendale needs a lord, one to give the people heart, rebuild what man and time have wasted. I have come north seeking a chance to be not just my own man, but to have a holding. I am not like Urre who was born to a hall and drinks and wenches now to forget what ill tricks fortune plays.

"Who my father was—" he shrugged, "I never heard my mother say. That he was of no common blood, that I knew, though in later years she drudged in a merchant's house before the coming of the invaders for bread to our mouths and clothing for our backs. When I was yet a boy I knew that the only way I might rise was through this—" He touched the hilt of his sword. "The merchant guild welcomes no nameless man, but for a sword and a bow there is always a ready market. So I set about learning the skills of war as thoroughly as any man might. Then came the invasion and I went from lord to lord, becoming at last Marshal of Archers. Yet always before me hung the thought that in such a time of upheaval, with the old families being killed out, this was my chance.

"Now there are masterless men in plenty, too restless after years of killing to settle back behind any plough. Some will turn outlaw readily, but with a half dozen of such at my back, I can take a dale which lies vacant of rule, such as this

Nordendale. The people there need a leader, I am depriving none of lawful inheritance, but will keep the peace and defend it against outlaws—for there will be many such now. There are men here, passing through Grimmerdale, willing to be hired for such a purpose. Enough so I can pick and choose at will."

He paused and she read in his face that this indeed was the great moving wish of his life. When he did not continue she asked a question:

"I can see how a determined man can do this thing. But how does it concern me in any way?"

He looked to her straightly. She did not understand the full meaning of what she saw in his eyes.

"I think we are greatly alike, lady. So much so that we could walk the same road, to the profit of both. No, I do not ask an answer now. Tomorrow—" he got to his feet, stretching, "no, today. I will speak to those men I have marked. If they are willing to take liege oath to me, we will ride to Lethendale, where you may shelter as you wish for a space. It is not far—"

"By horse," she answered in relief, "perhaps two days west."

"Good enough. Then having left you there, I will go to Nordendale—and straightway that will cease to be masterless. Allow me, say, three score days, and I will come riding again to Lethendale. Then you will give me your answer as to whether our roads join or no."

"You forget," her hands pressed upon her belly, "I am no maid, nor widow, and yet I carry—"

"Have you not Gunnora's promise upon that subject? The child will be wholly yours. One welcome holds for you both."

She studied his face, determined to make sure if he meant that. What she read there—she caught her breath, her hands rising to her breast, pressing hard upon the talisman.

"Come as you promise to Lethendale," she said in a low voice. "You will be welcome and have your answer in good seeming."

CHANGELING

Lithendale, though no fortress for defense, rather an abiding place for the Dames who gave refuge to all, still held something of grim darkness in this early spring. Snow lay in ragged, mid-edged patches upon the ground, and the court-yards showed a gloss of damp upon worn stones. A chill wind moaned and cried at every window to the west, plucked at steamy panes with fingers just too weak to wrench a way within.

Hertha's forehead pressed against one of those thick panes. She leaned over the wide sill as if she could gain relief from the pains which rent her fiercely. The life she bore within her body might be a warrior, one who ruthlessly would tear her in twain, so eager was it ready to battle all the world.

She was not alone. There was the woman who now and then came to walk beside her and steady her. To Hertha that other was a faceless puppet, someone from a dream, or rather a dark night's sending which had no end. In one hand the girl clasped, so tightly that even its time-smoothed ridges drove deep into her flesh, her one talisman, Gunnora's amulet. Hertha did not pray—not now. Would any petition to one of the Old Ones be heard arising from this abbey dedicated to another power?

Setting her teeth, Hertha lurched away from the window, took one step, then two, before, once more, grinding pain sent her staggering. She was on the bed, her body arching. Dank sweat plastered her hair to her forehead.

"Gunnora!" Had she screamed aloud or had the name only rung in her mind? A last thrust of pain was a spear within her, twisting agony. Then—

The peace, end of all pain. She drifted.

In the dark which enfolded her she heard a throaty, gurgling laughter, a laughter which was evil, a threat. In that same dark she saw—

There was a circle of stones and to these clung—no, they did not cling—only the deformity of their bloated bodies made it seem so. Rather they sat, their monstrous heads all

196

turned, their bulbous eyes watching her with malicious joy and triumph. Hertha remembered. Now she cried out, not any petition to a Power of the Old Ones, rather with a fear she thought safely gone, buried in time.

She wanted to run, even to raise her hands as a barrier between those eyes and hers. Though the girl knew that even if she so veiled her own sight, she could not escape. The Toads of Grimmerdale! She had recklessly, wrongly sought them once, cheated them, fought them, and now they were here!

"My lady."

The words were faint, far off, had nothing to do with present horror and fear. Still it would seem that somehow they acted as a charm against the Toad things, for those faded. Hertha, shivering, spent, opened her eyes.

Inghela, the stout Dame, wise in herb lore and nursing, stood in the light of two lamps. That wan day Hertha had watched so endlessly through the distorted thick glass of the window must have ended. Dame Inghela's grasp held the girl's limp wrist. There was an intent searching in her eyes, so dark and clear under the line of her folded linen headdress.

Hertha summoned strength. Her mouth was parched, dry, as if she had fed on ashes.

"The child?" In her own hearing her voice was very thin and hoarse.

"You have a daughter, my lady."

A daughter! For one moment of pure joy Hertha's heart moved with a quicker beat. She willed her arms to rise, even though it felt that each was braceleted with lead. Gunnora's promise—a child who would have nothing in it of the ravisher who had forced its birth. Hertha's own, her own!

"Give me," her voice was still weak, yet life, and now will, were fast returning to her, "give me my daughter!"

The Dame did not move. There was no bundle of warm wrappings in her arms. It seemed to the girl that the woman's measuring glance was stronger, an emotion in it which Hertha could not read.

She tried to raise herself higher on the bed.

"Is the child dead?" She believed that she had managed to ask that without betraying the surge of emotion which tore her as sharply as had the pains earlier.

"No." Now Dame Inghela did move. Hertha watched as the Dame stooped to lift from a box-like bed a bundle that gave a sudden, ear-piercing squall, struggled against the confinement of the blanket about it.

Not dead—then what? There was ill fortune in the way the Dame had met her question, Hertha was sure. She held out her arms, willing them not to tremble, setting herself to bear any evil.

The baby must be far from death. Its battling against the swaddling was vigorous. Hertha grasped the bundle, resolutely turned back the coverings to look upon what Gunnora had promised, a child to be wholly and only hers.

She looked down upon a small wrinkled, reddened body of the newborn, and she knew! Revulsion, for only a moment, burned in her as if she might still vomit forth the evil which must have lain dormant in her since this new life had been conceived.

Evidence of her sin, her dealing with the powers of evil, ancient and strong evil, only that lay now on this one, not on her. She stared down into the ill formed face. The child stared back, its croaking cries still. Those bulbous eyes seeming to thrust into hers as if already the small creature knew that fate had marked it. There was the faint hint of brownish patches already staining its skin. The Toads—yes—their mark!

Hertha cradled the child with fierce protectiveness, looked defiantly over its head at the Dame.

Inghela's hands moved in the signs of ritual against the Powers of Darkness, even as her lips shaped words which were whispered too low for Hertha to catch. One of her hands caught at the loop of prayer rings at her belt and fingers began to separate one from the other.

"Changeling!" The maidservant, whom Hertha had hardly been aware of during her hours of labor, crept from behind her mistress into the circle of lamplight.

That word aroused Hertha to greater awareness.

"This is," she said slowly, distinctly, in that moment taking unto herself all which might have misformed the child, all the burden of sin she had drawn to her in her madness and her hate, "this is my daughter, Elfanor, whom I proclaim is truly of my body, my fair child, and who rests within the name of my clan."

Elfanor? Hertha wondered at that name, how had it come to her? It was one which she had never heard before. Yet it seemed to her the proper one. As for the other formal words of her acknowledgment of the child, they were empty. She had no clan, no family name, no lord to raise the child in the central hall of a keep before all those of his holding.

She was utterly alone, the more so now because of what had been laid upon this child. Hearing the click of the prayer rings Inghela fingered, Hertha knew that already her daughter had been judged, and she had been, too.

That same stubborn pride which had made her withstand the demands of a family line she could no longer lay claim to, to court a certain revenge which had now recoiled upon her in this vile fashion, that was her shield, and, perhaps, still her weapon.

"My daughter," she repeated firmly, daring the Dame, the maidservant staring avidly at what she held, to raise any protest.

"Changeling—" Once more that dread word held a cursed sound.

Dame Inghela turned swiftly, her authority plain to read on her round face as she looked at the maid and issued a swift stream of orders. The girl fled, busied herself hastily in gathering stained linen, pouring slops into a waiting bucket. Then she scuttled from the chamber. Inghela had once more taken her place by the bedside. Her steady gaze met Hertha's defiant stare.

"The child—" she began slowly.

Hertha's chin raised a fraction. She would never reveal now to this, or any other living soul, the sorrow and the torment within her.

"Is cursed. Is that what you would say, Dame? If so, the curse is mine and mine must be the answer."

Dame Inghela showed no sign of affront at what might almost be considered blasphemy when uttered in this place. Those who followed the Flame were taught, and taught, that sin left its mark upon the sinner. In so much could Hertha's words be considered confession.

"Evil seeds itself when it is watered and cherished by the will," she said slowly. Yet the gaze which held Hertha's so levelly did not condemn.

"You know my story," Hertha replied harshly. Since she had taken Elfanor into her arms the child lay quiet, the large, bulging eyes were half closed, as if, young as the babe was, she heard and understood. "Yes, I sought evil to draw upon my enemy, him who had defiled me. I sought an evil of the Old Ones openly, willingly, because all which filled me then was hate. Still the full evil did not come to fruit. He whom I sent to the Toads I fought for. He lives."

"Yet he was not the right man, as you have also said," Dame Inghela reminded her.

"That I did not know until after. I had already fought for him. Thus, this——" Her arms tightened about the small body. "I do not know any of the ancient wisdom, the sorcery of how any power could have reached within my body and changed new life I carried into this. Elfanor is mine, upon me let the burden fall. And——" it might be ill for her to speak so within this place, still that headlong need for defense, for the right to nurse some small hope within her now, led her to do so——"perhaps what one power had done to set awry, another can aid."

Once more Dame Inghela swung her hoop of rings. "Your speech is not good. Here we follow the true teachings. You have already had proof of what comes when one appeals to that which is no belief of ours!"

"True." Hertha repressed a shiver arising from cold within her, not in answer to that rebuke. At the same time she reckoned—they can put no walls about my thoughts. There are powers and powers.

She loosed one hand, her fingers found what lay upon her breast, the amulet of Gunnora. Again she recalled how she had sought out that shrine, heavy with her child, seeking what succor she could. Of how in dream—or perhaps more than dream—she had been made welcome and one of her boons granted. For she was certain at this moment that Elfanor had indeed no part of her father within her, that she was wholly Hertha's own.

As days passed Hertha never spoke again of what she might do. She was well aware that her child was the subject of many whispers, that such congratulations upon her safe delivery as were offered gave lip service only to custom.

Sudden warm winds came out of the south. The earth dried after the last of the snow's burden soaked into it. Spring was coming early. Hertha kept to her chamber much of the time, her thoughts busier than her hands, though she nursed her daughter and cared for her entirely, refusing any help from those who she knew looked upon the baby as cursed.

At the fourth week she asked for formal audience with the Abbess, her plans made.

Carrying the child, she made her courtesy of ceremony in the inner parlor, thinking fleetingly how different matters were since she had been previously received here. Then she had come wrapped in what she knew now was a false contentment, having laid upon another for a short space, the ordering of her life. At this moment she caught at that straying memory fiercely, pushed it away. She had been a fool, and must now pay for her folly, perhaps all her days.

"They say, Lady Hertha, that you desire to go forth from Lithendale." The Abbess was not a tall woman. Still the high-backed chair of age-darkened wood, all carven with Flame symbols, enthroned her. Hertha's first suspicion dulled. Perhaps she was a poor judge of the motives and thoughts of others, but here she read no malice, no accusation, only true concern.

"I must," she replied, sitting on the very edge of the stool to which the Abbess had waved her, Elfanor close against her. The baby never cried when Hertha held her so. In fact she would lie still, open eyes upon her mother's face. Hertha had to keep herself from ever searching those too-large eyes for some hint of the marsh fires she had seen once in eyes so like them. "Your reverence, I—and mine—have no place within these walls."

"Has that been said to you?" The Abbess's demand came, quick and sharp.

"Such does not have to be said. No, none has given me any unwelcome word. But it is the truth. Through me a shadow of evil has come into a place which should be at peace and holy."

"Peace we may strive for. Holiness is not of our fashioning," the Abbess returned. "If you leave here where do you go? My Lord of Nordendale—"

Hertha made a swift gesture. "Your Reverence, he was good to me when he had every right to draw steel across my throat. I brought him into such peril as perhaps none of our kind has seldom faced. You know my story, how I prayed for vengeance to creatures whose very nature is of black foulness, and later drew him into their net."

"Then fought for him again," the Abbess said slowly. "Did you not believe when you so fought that he was still the one who shamed you?"

"Yes. But what did that matter? If I had turned my own dagger point upon him for a clean death, that was my right, was it not?" Her old shame and hate clung for a moment to memory. "But no man, no matter what his sin, should be given to old evil."

"He did not hold your act against you. No, rather he did

in a measure honor you for trying to uphold your battle
against shame. This Trystan spoke with me before he rode
forth, and, since then, have you not had twice messengers
from him confirming that he has accomplished his desires in
part, that he has taken command of the leaderless people of
Nordendale, that he has brought peace and more than a
small measure of hope to others, that he wishes you to come
in all honor as his lady. He is a strong man, hard in some
ways, but also, in his core, as good as the steel he carries.
What of him? Do you go to him?"

"To him least of all, Your Reverence. He is but new come
into his lordship. Strong and valiant a man though he may
be, let him bring a bride with a 'changeling' already at her
breast, and trouble shall rise about him, as water rises about
a rock fallen into a swift flowing river which in time shall
roll it over and over, doing with it as the water wills. No, I
do not go to Nordendale. Also I beg this humbly of Your
Reverence, that you not send any message to Lord Trystan.
If he or his messenger rides hither again you will say that I
have gone to my own people."

"You have no people, so you have said," the Abbess returned sharply. "Falsehood shall not be uttered here either in
a good or bad cause."

"My Lady Abbess, I have by my own action set myself
apart from those once my kind. In truth I go to what perhaps
is my own place."

"The Waste? That means your death. To seek death
willingly is also a sin."

Hertha shook her head. "No, had I wished to travel that
path I would have taken it easily months ago. I do not go out
to die, but to seek an answer. If that seeking leads me into
strange places, then that I shall face."

"*Their* ways have never been ours. You imperil more than
your body in such a search."

"Lady, I imperiled myself so months ago. Now I have a
battle before me. Do you believe—" the girl's face flushed,
her eyes were bright, afire as those of a hunting falcon ready
for the death swoop, "that I shall not fight for this little one,
who is wholly mine? There are places of evil from the days
when our people did not know this land, but there are also
places of peace and good. Is it not true of a healer that often
a small part of a dangerous herb may be given to counteract
the illness that same herb or its like seeded in the body? If it
takes me a lifetime of searching, I will seek healing."

For a long moment the Abbess made no answer. She studied Hertha's face, as if by the very force of her will she could see through flesh and bone to the thoughts of the mind within that skull.

"This is your choice," she said slowly. "We do not use strange powers, but sometimes the Flame grants *us* also a measure of foreseeing, even as a wise woman will look into her scrying cup. I cannot tell why, but I believe that if anything can be done to lift this curse, guidance will be given you."

"And if the Lord Trystan comes?" Hertha had drawn a deep breath. She had never expected such a response from a woman so deeply wedded to rituals which denied any dependence upon other and older arts.

"He will be told the truth. That you bore one for whose future you must strive, and that you have gone so to battle, we know not where. Whether such a man will accept these statements, I do not know. That is a matter for him to decide. I cannot give your search a blessing, but insofar as one vowed to our beliefs can well-wish another, so do I you, Lady Hertha. You have courage, and your will is like a sword blade, worn somewhat by this world's battles, still sunbright and keen of edge.

"You have the mount which the Lord Trystan left for you; that I advise you to accept, even though your pride may prickle. We shall also give you one of the baggage ponies, for of those we have many, brought here by refugees, some of whom did not survive and whose goods were left for kinsmen who never came. Supplies you shall have, with what traveler's gear you wish to select from our storehouse.

"And—" once more she hesitated. "I have given you well-wishing. I cannot add to that any blessed charm, for where you go such could be a hindrance rather than an aid. Nor will I ask in which direction you travel, though I will say do not ride the open road, as this is a land in chaos and there are many masterless men to prey on travelers."

"Lady Abbess, you have given me far more than I dared dream." Hertha arose to her feet. "Perhaps your greatest gift is that you have not said to me, 'Go not, this is a useless thing!' "

There was the faintest shadow of a smile about the Abbess's lips.

"And if I said so, and wrung my hands, and called upon authority—which I do not have since you are no daughter of this roof—would you have listened? No, I believe that you have thought much and that you believe this is your life burden. So be it. We all choose our own roads, some with less cause than you."

Hertha stood very straight. This woman had that in her which might have made them friends had the circumstances been otherwise. For a single moment Hertha wondered what it would have been like to be welcomed as a "daughter" into such a house of peace. But that was a very fleeting thought. She repeated the old guesting farewell of the traveler:

"For the feasting, for the roof, I give thanks and blessing. For the future all good to this place, as I take the road again."

The Abbess bowed her head slightly. "Go in peace, Lady Hertha. As you seek so may you find." Though she said she refused the flame blessing, still her hand raised and moved in some air-drawn sign between them.

Then Hertha and Elfanor went out of the place of peace. The Abbess had indeed been generous. The horse Hertha rode, astride, garments culled from the supply left by the refugees providing her with the wide, skirt-like breeches of a noblewoman's hunting garb, was that on which Trystan had brought her here. It was not a showy beast, and it was rather small, having much of the blood, she was sure, of the tough, wild mountain breed. But such were sought by travelers for hardiness.

Trailed behind by a leading rope was an even smaller pony, well-filled packs slung one on either side of his back. Belted at Hertha's waist was a long bladed sword-dagger which she had found among the stored gear. She also had strapped to her saddle a short boar spear, its wicked head needle sharp. Elfanor rode in a cradle-like basket against Hertha's back, leaving the girl's arms free for the managing for her two beasts.

She went out in the early morning, for it was her wish to get along the known road when it would be the least traveled, on into the hills, even as the Abbess had advised. The land was indeed filled with masterless men and outlaws. Many of the lords had died in the war, leaving their holdings to the weak and the easily preyed upon. It was such men as Trystan who might in the end bring order out of this present darkness. She thought of that, and then pushed it out of mind. That she could have stood beside him and perhaps given him aid, that was like a smoke fancy, quickly blown away by the grim truth of her burden.

Before the sun was well up she was off the road to pick a crisscross path among some stones which looked as if they were the chance product of a landslip, but which, she knew from her diligent questioning at the abbey, were instead a barrier or half-closed gate to disguise the beginning of another and much older way.

It was true those Old Ones who had once held the Dales, had a liking for roads which climbed along the crests of the hills rather than curled at more ease through the valleys. Such a way had, months before, taken her to Gunnora's shrine and later to the place of the Toads. What she sought now was a return to the shrine. Gunnora alone might grant her some direction. For the Great Lady was a lover of children, one who smiled upon those who bore them, and was well known to listen to any petition for a baby in need. Whether she would aid one who was cursed—No, Hertha told herself firmly, this sin was hers and not that of the child. Any payment which must be made was to be laid where it belonged. She would take the scaly spotted skin, the eyes, all visited on Elfanor. It was her hope that Gunnora might lead her by some dream of enlightenment to learn to do just that thing.

She rode at a slow amble, stopping at times to slide from her padded saddle and nurse Elfanor. The child had not cried. Her silence was one of the strange things about her. Also Hertha noted that, at times, those rounded eyes looked out upon the world with a measurement which certainly was not of the human kind. Nor should so young a baby focus so keenly on what lay about it.

Though the ancient road kept to the heights, those who had fashioned it had arranged that travelers could not easily be revealed. Brush and trees, both thick-growing, walled it on the valley side, here and there giving way to a screen of upstanding broken rocks, all blending with the countryside so that this safeguard was not, in itself, a sign that a highway lay so concealed.

Hertha and the child sheltered that night in what might even have been a contrived campsite, for here were rocks upsprouting, several leaning at an angle so that their tips touched to form a rude imitation of roof.

There was even a basin or pit there, blackened surely by ancient fires, into which she packed sticks and the dried moss she had had the forethought to cull from branches of the brush, setting a pocket of flames, over which she crouched, nursing the baby against her. To that fire she added a scant handful of dried leaves from a packet Dame Inghela had given her. The smoke puffing up as those were consumed brought a fresh, clean scent. But it was not for that that Hertha had added her material so sparingly. Such a combination of herbs had the ability to keep at bay dark dreams. The scent cleared the head, as those learned in plant lore knew. Hertha needed this.

To travel this old road deliberately put her again under the influence which ancient powers could still exert. Whatever small safeguards she could raise against evil, those she must use.

The beasts drew closer to the fire also, feeding on the grain she took from her journey bags. She dared not turn them loose to graze at will. But there was water nearby, a spring feeding a rill from which the horse and pony had drunk noisily, where she herself rinsed out her two bottles of water, refilling them both, slaking her own thirst after the dryness of a journeycake.

Sleep came fitfully, for she had set herself a kind of inner warning which did arouse her now and then through the night to feed the fire, while ever close to her hand was the hilt of the long knife, the shaft of the boar spear.

Her body ached in spite of the way she had tried to ease her travel. Near dawn, though she lay back once more in the cup of rock, she did not sleep, rather went over in her mind the direction in which she must head at the coming of true day.

The hill road ran on, now dipping a little into some valley, now climbing above. Hertha passed rock walls on which had been graven so deeply strange symbols that even long passing of time had not altogether erased them.

On the fourth day her road branched, one part turning south. She had seen no one, though once or twice, when the trail drew closer to the valley way, she had heard sounds of others. Each sound had frozen her into waiting with a fast-beating heart.

At the splitting of the trails Hertha took the northernmost, and began to look about her for some landmark. If she was right, this was the same way she had followed months ago to Gunnora's shrine. So she should catch sight of some rock spur, some stretch of country she could remember.

There was no good camping place on this fork. The wind swept down, holding no spring softness. She swung the cradle about from her back, steadying it across her saddle, bending a little over it so that the folds of her cloak could give protection to the baby.

Shadows formed by early evening drifted down the slope. Still she rode on, for there was no promising place to alight. Then, when Hertha had nearly given up hope, she saw the building she sought. There was a glow from the door on which was hung a strip of metal fashioned into Gunnora's own sign, a ripe grain sheath with a binding of fruit-laden vine.

Her mount, which had been plodding with down-drooping head, now whinnied. Its call was answered by the pony from behind. Hertha herself raised her voice, which in her own hearing sounded hoarse from cold and lack of use:

"Good fortune to this house and the dwellers therein!"

The door split open, each half sliding back into the wall; golden light streamed out. Nor did her mount give her time to slip clumsily from her saddle, rather the horse paced on and stood, blowing, in what was an outer chamber, not a real courtyard. Still both beasts seemed quiet and content as if they had indeed come to their proper place.

Hertha, stiff and sore, feeling as if she had been riding forever, dismounted.

"Enter into peace."

The voice came from the air. She remembered how it had also done so upon her visit to the shrine. She looked doubtfully at the horse and the pony. Their loads must be shed. They had served her well and should be eased.

"Enter." A second door opened for her. "The good beasts will be tended, as will all who come in peace."

Already the warmth, the feeling of being burdenless, filled her. She did not linger, but walked forward. At that second doorway she slipped the long knife from her belt sheath and left it lying, for steel was not worn in Gunnora's hall.

The second room was as she had remembered it—a table set with food, all ready to refresh the traveler. In her basket nest Elfanor stirred, gave a small mewling cry. Her large eyes stared up into her mother's face, and never had Hertha been so sure that within the small misshapen body there was a mind which saw, which knew, which was older than the flesh and bone that contained it.

She half expected a protest from the child, or perhaps

from whatever presence abode in this chamber. Could one bring a cursed being into the light which was its opposite? Save for that one cry Elfanor did not make another sound, nor was there any answer. Hertha dropped into the chair, held the baby close to her with her left arm, stretched out her right hand to pick up a goblet from which arose faint steam, the scent of wine mulled with herbs which was a traveler's welcome on a night of cold and long wayfaring.

She drank. She spooned into her mouth the richness of a stew, food which satisfied, filled the body and eased the mind as no mouthful had done since her first visit to the shrine.

Satisfied, she sat back in her chair at last and spoke as much to the leaping flame of the two lamps on the table as to the room.

"To the giver of the feast, fair thanks from the heart. For the welcome of the gate, gratitude. To She who rules here—" Hertha hesitated. She could no longer find the proper words. For the first time the idea arose, hard and harsh, of what she had done. Ino a place of peace and light she had brought sin and evil—her own sin and evil!

On the far side of the table a second door swung open. There was dimmer light beyond. Now, filling the room, came the sweet scent of flowers at the height of their summer blooming, a kind of voiceless murmur as one might hear in the flowing of a merry stream, the hum of contented bees about their harvest, the faintest breath of wind stirring blossom-laden branches.

It would seem that the Presence here did not judge as she knew she should be judged. In her heart there was a small spring of real hope. Her travel-stained divided skirt dragging at her boots, she went forward, not slowly, reluctantly, but as one who has a purpose and knows that it must be carried out.

Smoke tendrils ringed about her, the scent grew stronger. It seemed to Hertha as if that smoke took on tangible substance, forming many arms to draw her on. Half-amused by the herb scent, she stumbled a little as she came up against a couch. There she lay down wearily. Her eyes closed.

There was a light, golden as the ker-apples of autumn, rich in its seeming as the metal men prized. It arose as a pillar stretching from the floor or ground so far into the upper regions of this other place that Hertha, no matter how far back she turned her head, could not see its crown. She saw now that it was not solid, even though her sight could not pierce it. Rather it pulsed in rhythm, as if it were tuned to the beating of a heart.

Beautiful as that column was, there was something awesome, near threatening about it. Hertha had knelt unconsciously. She wanted to reach out her hands to that light, to pray for pardon; only her hands, her arms, were locked about what she carried. She turned her eyes from the light to that burden.

The child had human form, true human form, yet it was dark, sullenly dark. Still, in its small breast, the light of the pillar awoke an answer, a spark as clear and glowing golden.

"Lady—" Hertha did not believe she spoke aloud. In this place the words came straight from the heart, from innermost thought, and that part of any who came here which was the whole truth. "I have sinned against the life which is of the good. Let not punishment fall upon the child, but rather on me. For the innocent should not suffer for the guilty."

The light flashed brightly to scald her eyes. Tears ran. Or were those tears she had not shed since first the evil that all her kind could do had caught her in a foul net?

Hertha waited for an answer. When nothing came, fear awoke. She had to hold to all her strength and courage to keep her eyes upon that searing light. She shivered, for it seemed to her that a cold wrapped around her, cutting her off not only from the mercy of the light, but from the life of her own kind as well.

She cried out. If this was death, then—

"Not the child!" Her words were not as a plea, rather a demand. Then she was more frightened, for one did not demand from the Powers, one wooed and prayed.

The light vanished as if a blink of her tormented eyes had sent it into extinction. She saw something else—

There spread now before her a place of rocks standing in a pattern, a wheel pattern. That stretched as if she were suspended in the air above. Though it had looked different from the ground, as she had seen it twice before, she knew what she envisioned now—the place of the Toads.

Devilish greenish lights glowed upon the sitting rocks at its heart. Hertha half expected those to reach for her, fearing that any protection she might once have had against those Dark Ones had been withdrawn.

However, they did not appear to be aware of her, if indeed the Toads were present. Now she moved, as one might who wore wings and used them in slow even beats. She traveled above that maze of rock ways outward to its circumference. Something else appeared. At the ends of several of the ways which led into the web of the Toads there stood straight and fast in the middle (as if they were closed doors to bar entrance) stones which shown faintly blue. Three such roads were so closed, three were open. Into Hertha's mind swept knowledge, as if this were something she had always known and which had been asleep in her mind, to be now awakened.

So had the Toads of Grimmerdale once been confined and kept from troubling the dreams of men, kept from drawing to them such foolhardy or evil people as she had been when she had first sought them out. So must they be confined again. Hertha drew a deep breath. If this was the task set her, then she was ready for it.

There came to her then a warning. Because she had once attempted to use the Toads to achieve her end, she was now vulnerable to them. To come so close to their own place was a risk of death worse than any failure or hurt of body. The choice was hers alone. Would it save Elfanor? Of even that she could not be sure, only hope, but hope was strong, it could carry one far, be meat and drink, rest and surcease. Now Hertha held to it with the full force of her will.

Once more the girl faced the winds of the heights. There had been food again waiting her when she had awakened. In the outer court she had discovered the animals, fed, saddled and burdened, ready. The sun already touched the upstanding peaks of the hills as she set out, turning once more eastward, picking a way to avoid the closer settled dales.

As she went Hertha searched for landmarks she had seen but once. Above all she must avoid any meeting with a far-roving hunter or herder out of Nordendale. The fact that the dalesmen avoided the places of the Old Ones, shunned their roads, was her only advantage.

The track which had been a clear guide to Gunnora's shrine became dimmer on its twisting way east. Beyond the reaches of Nordendale she should cut south once again for the circle of the Toads, perhaps over land where there was no trace at all of any road.

She dared not quicken pace. This track was treacherous with a winter slippage of stones and rock. With Elfanor in her carrying cradle upon her back, Hertha had to dismount now and again to lead her horse, testing the stability of the trail with the haft of the spear. Her mount had not so far refused to advance and that she took as a good sign, accepting that the animal's sense, so much keener than her own in many ways, would give any warning of trouble.

After a full day's travel she slept but fitfully, Elfanor in her arms beneath the huddle of her cloak, their rest a nest of last year's leaves and grass which Hertha scooped into place among a tangle of storm-downed trees. The second day had no sun, instead a thick mist which was half drizzle dampened her dank clothing against her.

Nordendale she passed—with a feeling of relief. She had allowed herself a short period of viewing what lay below, marking the changes which had come to that half-deserted, once masterless holding since last she had come this way. There were people in the garden patches, a movement of sheep along one hillside. But her eyes had sought at once the tower of the keep. No banner cracked in the crisp wind. Which meant the lord was not in residence. Where? Hertha bit down on her mittened hand. There could well be one place to which Trystan was now bound—Lithendale! If he had gone seeking her—She shook her head as if her jumble of thoughts could be so reduced to order. No, there was only one thing which mattered, that stone wheel above Grimmerdale!

There was little forage for the horse and pony here. They pulled toward the green now coating hillside meadows. She had to use all her skill and determination to keep them moving. At noon she bribed them with broken bits of journey cake which they mouthed eagerly, licking up the last of the crumbs from the rocks where she had dropped the pieces.

The drizzle never became true rain, only a gray misery which wrapped her around. One of those lesser irritations which could eat away at one's determination. Her garments clung to her, and she shivered continually as she rode. Tonight—if she did not halt too long at an eating or rest break—tonight she should be within such distance of Grimmerdale that the next morn she could face her task.

She had this much in her favor, Hertha decided. The Powers of the Dark Ones were fed by the night, by any absence of light. If she could get to her task by the day she would have that small advantage. Providing she could finish before dusk deepened again.

Twilight came early. Again she camped at a place from which she could see the lantern above the door of that inn where once she had served and waited with what patience she could muster, for the one man whom her singleminded purpose had sent her to deliver to vengeance. She longed for a hot drink, for shelter even as squalid as that inn had been, the sound of voices of her own kind. Instead she crouched alone, her two beasts uneasy beside her, sucking at a stick of dried meat, and nursing her child. In the last of the light she saw that once more that knowing, measuring look was back in Elfanor's eyes. Something which was not of proper mankind looked out at her, slyly, maliciously, with anticipation.

Hertha refused to believe that this was more than her imagination. She cradled the baby in her arms, after giving her the breast, rocking back and forth, crooning in a whisper one of the old, old songs she remembered her own old nurse had used to hold at bay the dark and all which might glide within thick shadows.

That night she did not sleep. It was as if the driving purpose which had brought her here fostered within her a frenetic energy, so that she had to use all her power and determination not to leave the half shelter she had found, to go straightway to the place where *they* waited.

So strong did that pull become that she knelt upon the ground, fighting with all the strength of her being the desire to move, to go—

That night might have lasted for a year, a century, more than her own lifetime, or so it seemed when the first grayish finger-claws of dawn came clutching over the hills. Hertha got stiffly to her feet. She was numb with cold, cramped in every muscle by the battle she had fought. Still lay the task ahead.

Now placing the baby's cradle on the ground, the girl opened the bag which Dame Inghela had given her. There were packets of leaves so dried and crushed that their condition was dry powder, others, withered to be sure, but still clinging to the branches from which they had sprung.

Hertha made her choices, lifting each pinch she used close to her nose to make sure that she dealt with the right one. Five such pinches she worked into a thick grease contained in a small pot, then three more, and lastly one, which was the strongest and most pungent of them all, making her sneeze, even gag when she smelled it closely.

The salve which had absorbed all these she rubbed in wide circles about her eyes. It beaded in her brows, making her squint a little from its strength of emanation. Again she used more as an ointment. Taking off her damp cap, she thrust her braids of hair back impatiently that she might anoint her ears. Last of all what was left she spread across the palms of her hands. Having so prepared herself, and fasting as required, she picked up the basket cradle and took Elfanor to the nearest shelter, a bush very thick with budding branches which overhung the ground. Slipping the cradle back under that rough canopy, Hertha set on end about the open side of the hiding place those branches of twigged herbs, forcing them into the earth, bolstering them erect with small stones.

The horse and pony had followed her. Now she recklessly crumbled all she had left of her journey cakes, leaving the bits in two piles at which they eagerly nuzzled. Getting to her feet, Hertha started forward, refusing to let herself look back. All she could do to protect Elfanor she had. She dared not let any apprehension steal into her mind, she must remember only what she had come to do.

The circle of the outer stones which was the rim of the Toad's wheel were clear enough. She held her hands together so that the greased palms were as one. Using them both then she pointed her fingertips forward, the smell of the herbs very strong.

Hertha edged along, making the circuit of the wheel's outer wall. Nor would she allow herself to glance down any of the avenues formed between the spokes of upstanding stones, but kept her gaze on the ground. She found the first of the "stopper stones" at the third such aisle.

Hertha faltered. The thing was a rough hunk of rock, not even worked as were the pillar stones, and it was as tall as her knees, so well embedded in the ground that perhaps it might be even larger. She wet her chapped lips with the tip of her tongue and considered its size, her own strength. Could she move such?

She might only find one of the missing ones and try. The girl dropped her cloak to the ground, its sodden folds hindered her shoulders and arms. Already she had sighted what she wanted. This was one! All points and angles, its blue surface standing out vividly in this place. Hertha reached it quickly, set her palms to it and pushed, to find the boulder set in the ground as securely as any forest tree.

So—but it could be moved! Having been in place once, it must be put so again. Now she exerted more strength, strove to rock it back and forth, her hands chafed by the roughness of its surface. The stone moved!

So small a triumph, but enough to encourage her. Panting, fighting, rubbing her hands near raw in spite of their protective covering (for in this place she knew that she dare not use the mittens which dangled from her wrists), she edged the rock on, brought it into place at last midpoint of one unguarded aisle, and leaned against it, panting for a space.

There was something building about her, a kind of soundless laughter, of jeering at one who dared so much surely to fail. Hertha straightened. Her lips were one firm line, her chin set. One! Now for the next—

She found a second stone, but this was half buried in rubble. She had to pull and dig to free it before she could once more try to move the rock on. It was stubborn, leaving its bed with such reluctance that once or twice she despaired of ever getting it out. Her hands left bloody prints upon its surface when she dragged it at last to the doorway it must lock. Two—

Hunger gnawed at her. She swayed dizzily now and again as she went to search for the last. Surely she could find and set that. Her wide divided skirt dragged at her legs. She felt as one wading through a vast quagmire of sucking mud, having to fight for each forward step.

There was no stone! There must be! She could not have been misled in her vision in the shrine. Those of the Power who turned to the light played no such cruel tricks. They could refuse help, but they did not deliberately deceive. Somewhere near the stone must lie. Hertha turned slowly, examining the ground. There were tumbled stones, yes, plenty of them, both large and small, but none of a blue sheen.

Could it be wholly buried in some pile as the second was half concealed? She could sight no heap in that clutter of rocks which was large enough to hide totally what she sought. Once more she made the dragging round of the outer circumference of the wheel. As she went, so did that sly laughter seem to grow within her mind, buffet her like the wind of a rising storm. She was certain that the Toads knew what she attempted, that they watched her in amusement, somehow certain that her efforts would fail. But those would not!

The circling of her search grew wider, farther away from the edge of the wheel. Now she sought out Elfanor and nursed the whimpering baby, not realizing her own fatigue until her legs seemed to fold under her and the bleeding hands with which she clasped the child to her shook with tremors she could not control.

Her hunger was gone, leaving only a dull pain in her body as she hunched forward, impatient but waiting that the child might be satisfied. The horse and the pony stood on either side of the tangled bush. They had again licked up all the food she had left but they had not strayed.

Suddenly the mount which had carried her threw up its head and nickered before Hertha could stop it. A neigh answered. She stiffened where she crouched, taking the baby from her breast and placing it quickly in the basket behind her. Elfanor opened her mouth and gave forth a furious yell.

Somehow Hertha got to her feet, stood there wavering, one hand making fast her clothing, the other resting ready on the hilt of her dagger. Though the drizzle of rain no longer fell, the clouds still hung overhead. Not dark nor close enough however to hide the fact that there was a rider coming.

There were outlaws enough in this war-torn land who had the desperate courage, or perhaps even the inclination, to follow the Old Roads. She remembered, too, nightmare tales of *things* which prowled, or were said to run the ridges. Surely no one would come here unless he was bent on some form of mischief, so evil was the reputation of this place.

The newcomer fronted the rise, and she saw he wore war mail, a snouted helm which hid much of his face. A shield swung by his saddle horn, and its device had been new painted. That was the only bit of color about him, for the horse he rode was of the same dull gray as his half armor, as dusky of mane as his surcoat.

Once she might have known him by the shield device, but the lords of the dales lay in many unknown graves up and down the lands, and new men had risen, choosing their own markings. Hertha could not put name to who would bear what he carried. The painting was crude as if someone hardly versed in such work had made an effort to picture something only imperfectly described. There was a strange cloudy representation of what might be some kind of monstrous head, cutting across it, straight and far better pictured, the blade of a drawn sword, as if that weapon barred the monster behind from some prey. Cold iron—

The thought ran in her head as if he who rode so shouted it aloud. Cold iron, which was indeed the bane of some of the Old Ones, a counter to their magic in itself.

Some outlaw, more foolhardy and reckless than most of their breed? Or a wanderer who did not know the danger he unwittingly courted in such a place? With that snouted helm so overshadowing his face she could not see him any clearer than if he wore a mask. But the voice which hailed her! Hertha drew a deep breath of protest—yes, *that* she knew!

His mount, a war charger of good breed, paced slowly onward, the reins lying easy on its neck as if the rider had no reason to control it to his will. She wanted to run, but there was no refuge, no place to go where he could not follow—even into the den of the Toads where once they did venture together.

"My lady—" His hail seemed to hang in the air between them as if she refused to let her ears hear it. His horse stood quiet as he swung down with the practiced ease of a fighting man, leaving that shield still hung in place. Now he came toward her, his booted feet making a small crunching sound on the gravel. Somehow Hertha found her voice, was able to raise hand and ward him off with the only gesture she could make.

"No!"

If he heard her he did not listen. Now she could see his sunbrowned jaw, his firm-lipped mouth below the half mask of the helm. He paused and dragged his mail-enclosed gauntlets from his hands, thrust them into his belt and then dealt expertly with the fastening snaps of the helm, pulled it off to free his head with its frosted hair blowing free in the breeze. His eyes were slightly narrowed as he regarded her with such a speculative look that Hertha longed to be away from here, safe hid from all the thoughts which his coming had awakened in her, nothing must defeat her purpose here. So, hardening her resolve, it was her turn to take a step forward, both hands up, grimed, broken of nail, raw of finger, between them, in that warding off gesture.

"My Lord Trystan—why?"

Somehow she could not find more words, though thoughts plagued her.

"I went to Lithendale; you were gone." He spoke simply, as one might to a troubled child. "They told me that you sought help in a strange and perilous place. So I came."

Hertha ran her tongue across her lips, tasted a little of the bitter coating she had laid upon her face.

"This—it is my task—" She tried to lash herself into saving anger. Always, save once, she had defended her independence, carried her own burden without any help.

"I do not know witcheries," he said gravely. "Perhaps it is true that yours may be the only hands," he glanced at her misused fingers then, "which can accomplish this. Then again, my lady, it may also be that two can do better and quicker than one what must be done."

Before Hertha could retreat he was at her side in one swift stride, trying to catch her hands. But she jerked away.

"Do not!" she cried. "They have protection."

"Protection!" One eyebrow arched upward in an odd slant which she remembered of old. "It would seem by the looks of those that you have had little of that this day. Tell me," now his voice had the ring of that which had been raised many times to command men, "what do you do here and why?"

"Why?" She must disgust him and quickly, get rid of one who had no part of this and who must not be drawn into her troubles. With a flap of her earth-stained clothing she turned and stooped to catch up the basket. Settling that against her hip, she pulled free the covers about Elfanor's face. Even under these clouds the light was without pity, showing the clear marks of the curse. While the baby's eyes were open, staring outward with that evil, knowing look. "See you?" she demanded fiercely, studying him intently, watching for the first sign of revulsion.

However he had himself well schooled, that she must admit. He did not display the disgust she was certain she would see.

"They told me—a changeling—" His voice was slow, even, again as if he were afraid to alarm. "But you think, lady, that you have found an answer here?"

"Perhaps, only perhaps." She felt odd, having prepared herself to counter the shrinking she had expected from him. What kind of a man was he who faced the results of dark evil without a change of eye or expression?

"Perhaps is sometimes all one can ask for." Again he made one of those swift, sure moves and she found the basket whirled out of her torn hands, held firm and secure in his, as he looked down at the child. "What is it that you think must be done?" he asked briskly.

She wanted to take the basket from him, to draw tight the coverings which made Elfanor safe from prying eyes as well as this cold. But her tired body made her clumsy as she stumbled, half fell forward, so that now he held the cradle upon one hip and his other arm was about her, both drawing her close and supporting her.

"Come." He countered her small attempt to pull away, led her to a pile of stones and there seated himself, the cradle resting across his knees, she herself beside him, unable to summon any strength to pull free from his hold.

She shivered, her hands lying uselessly on her knees. Then, to her great disgust, she felt tears on her cheeks. So much of her wanted to yield, to let someone else take command. Only—she need only look down at Elfanor, who as usual lay quiet, only stared up into the face of the man who held her with those unblinking eyes, the sly fires well alive deep in their depths.

Hertha summoned up all the strength she could muster, and broke free from his grip, somehow got to her feet.

"The rocks—the last one—" She must keep to her task!

"Which rock?" He did not try to hold her back, only stood himself and then placed the cradle carefully on the ground.

Hertha had already lurched away, afraid now that he would attempt to hold her again. If he did, she might yield to that traitor part of her which his coming here had awakened in a way which bewildered and weakened her resolve.

"The blue one, the last— I have searched, and searched. Two I found. The third—I cannot." She stumbled on, her torn hands outstretched as if to implore the ground itself to produce the stone she must have. "The rocks," she spoke more to herself than to him, trying to return to her singleminded hunt, shut out all which was not atuned to that, "one must be placed at each of the entrances, as a sealing. That is the task laid upon me now."

She was only half aware then he had passed her, to go to the nearest of the spoked lanes and look down at the earth-encrusted boulder she had worked so hard to set in place.

"This kind?" Trystan did not wait for her to answer. Instead, having studied the stone, he too swung out in search among the tumble of rocks which lay spread out along the crest of the ridge.

Hertha dragged her way on, stopping now and then to pull at a pile of smaller stones, hoping each time to see hidden beneath them the blue she sought. She had been near three-quarters of the way around the wheel now and there was no sign of the last one. Did it exist at all?

"Ha!"

She turned. So quickly that she lost her balance and fell painfully to her knees. For a moment she did not see him at all and then his head appeared nearly at ground level and she remembered a notch of gully which ran there.

"I think that it is down here!"

Somehow Hertha got across the ground between them. Trystan was stooped, hurling small rocks away from him with vigor. As Hertha came to the lip of that cut she could see it too, buried, only a small bit showing above the soil now that he cleared it from the rock fall. Blue like the others. But how could she raise it?

Having thrown aside the rocks, Trystan drew his sword and stabbed the earth, throwing chunks of winter-hardened clay aside, yet working more slowly and with care for the safety of his tool which was not to be foolishly blunted.

Hertha wiped the back of her hand across her forehead, smearing the herb grease on her face. She stared down at where Trystan worked with a dull despair. He might free the stone, yes, but how could she get it out of that tight lodging, then drag or roll it to the final resting place? Strength seemed to have melted out of her body.

"There it is, my lady!" He stepped away, thrusting his sword once more into its scabbard, looking down at the boulder he had uncovered with an expression of satisfaction.

From somewhere Hertha summoned croaking words. "Up—how does one get it up?"

That she could lift that piece of rock she had to acknowledge was beyond her powers. Yet the task was hers alone, she was sure of that, as she had been since the first of this ordeal.

"There is the rope which kept your pony's sacks in place." He stood, pinching his lips as he looked down at the rock. "With the aid of the horses it can be pulled out."

Hertha blinked. What he said made sense. She had been so bemused by her own fatigue that such a move had not occurred to her. It gave her a spurt of energy and she was on her feet once more, heading to where she had piled the pony's gear. There was the rope, sure enough, a strong one. Whether its strength was enough to carry through Trystan's suggestion she could not be sure until it was tried. Looping the coil over her arm and shoulder, she brought it back and tossed the end to him.

He caught it neatly out of midair as it fell, then knelt to work a length around the rock, taking advantage of any projecting angle to make the stone more secure. Finally he looked up to her.

"Bring your horse, mine, and we shall see if this will serve."

Her own placid mount caused no trouble, plodding easily enough to the gully. But his beast pulled back on the reins he had left dangling to the ground, the traditional "earth tie" of a fighting man, rolling its eyes and snorting. Hertha pulled steadily on the reins and was glad that there was no battle— the horse followed her at last, one reluctant step after another.

Trystan clambered out of the cut, was already making one end of the rope into a loop about the horn of her saddle. The other he still gripped in his hand as he mounted up, giving the now foreshortened piece of cordage a second twist about his own horn.

At his signal not only the horse he bestrode, but her own moved and she saw the rope become as taut as a bowstring, snapping hard against the edge of the gully. She feared to hear the crack of a snapping rope. Still that did not come. Trystan's horse went slowly on, step by step, her own following while the rope remained taut. The rock, indeed, freed from its earth setting, was drawn up the side of the gully as it gouged and scraped against the wall along which it swung.

The boulder arose at last over the edge, plopped near Hertha's feet. She hurried it, worrying at the knotted rope, she would have nothing left to draw upon. Trystan was beside her, his hands pushing her aside as they competently freed the stone.

"Now where? Where is this road which must be so guarded?"

She shook her head. "I must do it! Mine the sin, mine the payment!" She tried to edge past him, to set her hands to the stone's earth-grimed side. It must be done—she *must* do it!

"No." His voice seemed to come from very far away, as if her head were so full of the need for keeping her mind on action that she could not catch the words quickly. "If it needs your touch, well enough. But remember, I, too, faced the Toads once in a time."

"Because then I tricked you." Hertha was not aware again that she was crying until she tasted the salt of her own tears. "All was of my doing. Let me go. It must be placed before sundown—it must be!"

He did not answer her. Instead he bent and braced both hands to the boulder, releasing his strength, sending it rolling in a wobbling fashion across the ground. Hertha hurried after it with a cry of dismay. She reached it first, set her own energy, what remained of it, to the pushing, and felt that it gave only inches.

He was once more beside her. "Together we once fought here, my lady. So shall we fight again. I have not sought you out to lose you again in any battle which means all this one does. Heave if you will and must, but with my help also. Surely whatever power sent you here cannot deny you my aid, not now!"

Hertha could not raise breath to answer him. She labored at the stone, and it was moving more easily, rocking from side to side. If she was not fulfilling the task laid upon her, *she* would suffer. But she could not accomplish it all alone, of that she was sure.

The stone moved so slowly. Above was the darkening of clouds which were of no storm's signal but that of coming night. Night was when the Dark Ones arose to power, if they could not get the stone in place before the last of daylight reached them! Hertha's breath came in shallow gusts of panting. Before them to the left was the last of the open ways. Trystan changed position, coming about behind her so as to exert pressure from the other side.

It seemed to Hertha that the very ground denied them aid, that certain shadows crept out from the pillar bases to cover the rough portions and hide obstacles from them as they labored.

"On now, my lady, just a short way—" He, too, was panting. Then he bent even closer to the ground, going down on one knee as he set his shoulder firmly against the side of the rock.

"Stand away!" he ordered her.

She saw the strain of his body, his flushed face. For a long moment it would seem that the rock had caught past their moving. Then—

Slowly, and with a wavering from side to side (which Hertha watched with anguished anxiety, her bleeding hands pressed to her mouth) it went forward, came to a stop in the center of the way.

There was a sudden sweep of wind, sword-sharp with cold, whirling out her clothing, raising dust to blind her eyes. Somewhere from within that gritty haze came hands, arms, a body which steadied her. Was it the wailing of the wind which carried that strange chorus of grunting cries? Or did she imagine it only?

She could barely keep her feet. A moment later he caught

her up, carried her out of the whirlwind of noise and grit, back toward the bush which still sheltered Elfanor.

The wind died, she heard another sound, the vigorous crying of a baby. Trystan set her down and Hertha staggered to the cradle. It was not dark yet, the twilight was still holding off a little. She caught the basket up into her arms as she fell to her knees. Holding it tight against her with one arm, she clawed at the covering blanket. Elfanor was screaming steadily.

Hertha stared down. Her eyes were tearing, perhaps the grit of the wind storm had irritated them. She blinked and blinked furiously, fighting against that distortion of her sight. Then she could see clearly.

Her daughter's face was red with effort, her eyes screwed shut as she howled, flailing at the air with the fists she had managed to loose from her swaddling.

A red face, but—

Hertha's fear melted away. This was no changeling! She had won! The curse was gone. The eyes in the baby's face opened. They were dark, but there was no alien knowledge in them, just as that anger-reddened skin held no scaled patch of brown.

"Free! She is free!" Hertha crooned, rocking the baby, cradle and all, against her as she swayed back and forth. Firm hands clasped her shoulders. Dimly she realized that a new strength had come, that she was no longer alone.

"You freed her." His voice was clear to her.

She turned her head to look at him, all her gratitude swelling up within her like an inner fire.

"With you only could I have done it."

"Did you think I would not help?" He looked stern, harsh and hard, in the failing light. But that was not Trystan in truth, that she was sure of. For the first time in days, months, even years which she could remember, Hertha let her stiff independence seep away, allowed herself the precious safety of his hold.

"With you only," she repeated softly. She knew from the light suddenly aglow in his eyes, the softening of his lips that he heard. "Many are Gunnora's gifts—many and good."

"May her name be praised," he said then, though Gunnora was the holder of women's Power and no man worshiped at her shrine. "She has given us both much in this hour. My lady, it grows dark, shall we go?"

Hertha looked at Elfanor. Whatever rage had possessed her

at the sundering of the dark power was gone. The baby blinked sleepily.

"Yes," Hertha cried. "Let us go—home!"

The delight in his face was such at her words that she believed she had nothing else to wish for.

ANDRE NORTON

in DAW BOOKS editions